Sometimes l[...]
are not [...]

☆

CAROL ROGERS
Her desperate actions, born of a mother's grief, lead to a new courtroom drama—with her as defendant.

BILL ROGERS
At the end of his and Carol's long, hard journey, he takes comfort from the fact that they'd made the journey together.

FRANK JORDAN
The disturbed loner vents his repressed anguish on the innocent and helpless.

BESS JORDAN
The killer's mother, she saw her own heartfelt need to see justice done have astonishing repercussions on the outcome of Carol Rogers' trial.

ELLEN HAYES
As Carol's lawyer, she stakes her entire career on an act of compassion and defiance almost as reckless as that of her client.

★

"Richard Speight makes us guess. And guess again. And, in fact, guess again."

—John Seigenthaler,
Editorial Director, *USA Today*

"The reader is kept twisting in anguish, just as Carol and her family are, as the case unfolds. We find author Richard Speight guilty of writing a damned good book."

—Syracuse Post Standard

DESPERATE JUSTICE

A NOVEL BY
RICHARD SPEIGHT

WARNER BOOKS

A Warner Communications Company

WARNER BOOKS EDITION

Copyright © 1987 by Richard Speight

Cover design by Stanislaw Fernandes

Warner Books, Inc.
666 Fifth Avenue
New York, N.Y. 10103

 A Warner Communications Company

Printed in the United States of America

This book was originally published in hardcover by Warner Books.
First Printed in Paperback: January, 1989

10 9 8 7 6 5 4 3 2 1

For Barbara . . .
who first made it possible,
and then made it better

Desperate Justice

‖ONE‖

The First
Monday
in November

‖1‖

Wendy Rogers's last day on earth began, as had so many others, with the ringing of her alarm clock at precisely six-thirty in the morning.

Wendy pulled her pillow out from under her head and wrapped it tightly around her ears. "Go away," she groaned, as if the clock would listen and obey. The steady buzzing didn't stop, of course, but the downy mass of pillow at least blocked out enough of the abrasive noise to make it tolerable.

As Wendy squeezed her eyes shut and reached back for a few extra moments of sleep, the door to her room burst open.

"For Pete's sake, turn that thing off, creep!" The freshly scrubbed head and bare shoulders of her older brother Jeffrey leaned through the open doorway. He had just stepped out of the shower down the hall. His hair was still wet.

"Get out of here, jerk," Wendy growled. "You're dripping on my floor!" She sent her pillow flying across the room toward the door just as Jeffrey slammed it. The pillow flopped to the floor. She heard her brother's laughter as she reached over and pressed the little button on her alarm clock, bringing the irritating buzz to an abrupt halt.

Wendy sat up and rubbed her eyes. They felt sticky, as

they had been glued shut and freshly pried open. Getting up had never been one of her favorite things.

She swung her legs over the side of the bed and nestled her bare feet into the softness of the pink shag carpet. In the mirror across the room she could see a tousle-haired, bleary-eyed twelve-year-old face staring back at her. She could even see the creases where her face had pressed against the pillow. She stuck out her tongue at the image, screwing her features into a grotesque face.

Ugh, she thought, relaxing her expression, I'm ugly enough without doing that! She turned from the mirror and shuffled across the fluffy pink surface, letting the uneven nap gently scratch the bottoms of her feet. She headed down the hall toward the bathroom.

"Ugly" was a word seldom used in the same sentence with the name Wendy Rogers. She was the image of her mother, Carol Rogers, having the same green eyes and auburn hair, which now cascaded down around her shoulders in a mass of waves and curls. Even her braces had a certain charm; they were just the right touch, a fitting reminder of her youth and vulnerability. Even at the awkward age of twelve, Wendy was well on her way to real beauty. Tall for her age, she was slender and fine-boned, with just the slightest promise of feminine curves.

"Breakfast is ready." Wendy heard her mother's voice coming from the bottom of the open stairwell.

"Okay, Mom," Wendy shouted back. "I'm just about ready. I'll be right down!" That wasn't entirely true, but it was what she always said when her mother started calling her to breakfast. She was able to buy a little time that way; her mother never seemed to catch on.

Downstairs, Carol Rogers walked back into the kitchen. Her husband, Bill, was already at the table, ready to devour a stack of delicious golden pancakes, busily piling on dollops of fresh whipped butter, watching the thick syrup slowly ripple down the sides of the stack. Jeffrey bounced in a moment later and pulled up a chair.

Carol believed that a good breakfast was the key to a good day. This was the first day of varsity basketball practice for Jeffrey; it was especially important that he start his day off right.

She was glad that Jeffrey was excited about playing basketball. It was his favorite sport. He had looked forward to this day since the end of last season.

"What time will practice end today, Jeff?" Carol asked, just as Wendy came into the kitchen. "I'm counting on you to pick Wendy up after school. But if you're late, she can wait at school for a little while, can't you, Wendy?" Carol turned to her daughter.

"Shouldn't be more than an hour, Mom," Jeff replied. "The first day is usually pretty short."

"An hour? Good grief!" Wendy scooted her own chair up to the table. "The last time he was late, it was a lot longer than that!"

"An hour? Good grief!" mocked Jeffrey in a high-pitched voice.

"Jeff, that's enough," Bill said, pointing a finger at the boy.

"Look, Wendy," Carol said, barely masking her own irritation, "can't you just stay in the library and study for a while? I've got to get dinner ready on time. I have an important meeting tonight. It won't hurt you to wait a few minutes."

"O-kay," Wendy intoned, dragging out each syllable to emphasize her reluctance.

In truth she didn't really mind. She probably wouldn't go to the library, and she certainly wouldn't study. Instead she would visit with her friends. It would be fun. She would make it fun.

"That's better," Bill said, turning back to his pancakes.

"C'mon, slowpoke, it's time to go!" Jeffrey announced, pushing his chair away from the table.

"Gimme a minute!" Wendy barked back.

Wendy stuffed down one last bite and licked the sweet syrup from her fork. She ran back upstairs to brush her teeth and gather up her books. In a moment Jeffrey's horn blared out an impatient command. "What a jerk," she muttered. She bounded back down the stairs two at a time. "Bye, Mom," she shouted over her shoulder as she bolted out of the front door and ran toward the car.

"Bye, Wendy. Have a nice day," Carol called back. She arrived at the front hall in time to see Wendy head out the door.

Carol Rogers shaded her eyes and peered out into the morning sunlight. Wendy jumped into the front seat of Jeffrey's old and shut the door as he pulled away from the curb. Wendy rolled down the window and flashed a bright, braces-laden smile. "Tin grins are in," Carol thought, remembering the motto on the T-shirt Bill had brought home to Wendy the day her braces were put on.

Carol walked slowly back to the kitchen, smiling and enjoying for a moment the melancholy feeling that swept over her whenever she thought about her children. She was so proud of them and loved them so much, yet it hurt to watch them grow older and begin to pull away. "You're being silly again," she said to herself. She looked at Bill. He was still eating his pancakes.

Jeffrey and Wendy drove along without talking, immersed in the raucous music that poured from the car stereo, enveloping them in pounding, rhythmic waves. Wendy enjoyed the morning rides mostly because of the music. She loved to sing along to the current hit songs as they covered the distance between home and school.

When Jeffrey pulled up to the broad concrete walkway that led to Belleview Middle School, Wendy clambered out and hurried on inside, blending instantly into a mass of fresh-scrubbed, vibrant young people.

The weathered brick school building had seen thousands of children come and go. Most had left Belleview with fond memories. Belleview Middle School was the center of community activity, a warm, caring place with decent, respectable kids from decent, respectable families. Discipline had never been much of a problem at Belleview.

Wendy liked everything about the school. She was a good student and popular with her classmates. She even enjoyed some of the classes, but she'd never admit such a thing to her friends. This day, like most others, passed quickly.

Wendy's last class was American History. She was immersed in a chapter about the pre–Civil War South when the three o'clock bell rang, the final bell of the day. She marked her spot, went to her locker to gather up her books and belongings, then strolled through the large central hall at a leisurely pace. Like an identical hall downstairs, it ran the length of the building from front to back. She followed the crowd down the stairs and out the front There was no need to hurry; Jeffrey wouldn't be here for at least an hour. She pushed her stack of books and papers off to one side of the concrete walkway, up under a small hedge where they would be out of the way, and wandered off to chat with friends.

One by one the big yellow busses pulled away from their parking places along the side street that bordered the school property. One by one a stream of sedans and station wagons pulled up to the curb, paused for a moment, then quickly departed. Wendy soon found herself sitting alone on the steps as the afternoon sun began its final descent toward the horizon.

A cool breeze had come up. She shivered a bit and buttoned up her jacket, gathering her skirt around her knees. She took out her history book and soon became engrossed in a time long ago, a time of Southern belles, hoop skirts, and charming, heroic men. She gasped audibly when a hand suddenly touched her arm.

"Wendy?" It was her English teacher, Mrs. Stewart.

"Wow, you scared me!" Wendy said, her heart pounding. "I must have been daydreaming."

"I'm sorry, dear," Mrs. Stewart said. "I didn't mean to frighten you. I was about to leave, and I saw you from the window upstairs. Is everything okay? Do you need a ride or anything?"

"No, ma'am," said Wendy. "My brother is coming for me. He should be here any minute." Wendy glanced at her watch. It was four-thirty. "He shouldn't be long now."

"Are you sure? I'll be glad to take you home," Mrs. Stewart continued. "It's going to get dark soon."

Wendy hesitated. She was tempted. Clouds were moving in; it was getting cooler. But if she left and Jeffrey had to look all over for her, he would be hopping mad.

"I'll be all right. Thank you anyway," she finally answered.

"Okay, see you tomorrow, honey." Mrs. Stewart headed back to the school building. She pulled open one of the big front doors and went into the hallway, letting the door ease shut behind her.

Dusk was approaching fast. The tall trees lining the street cast long shadows that stretched out across the trampled grass and crept closer and closer to the front of the old school. It woul be dark very soon.

"I wish Jeff would come on," Wendy thought as she

her jacket tight. "What a bummer." She frowned and thought about going inside, but the darkened building didn't look inviting. Besides, she needed to be where Jeffrey would be able to see her. She flipped open her book and tried to escape back into her reading.

Gradually, though, an alarming reality began creeping in on her, competing for her attention. It wasn't possible to pinpoint any one particular moment when the feeling first hit her. But it was real, and when it finally emerged from her subconscious and took command of her thoughts, a chill played up and down her spine, grabbing her attention like a tap on the shoulder or the sound of her name.

Wendy wasn't alone. She knew intuitively that she was being watched.

She turned quickly and stared up at the glass panels in the large doors looming behind her. She saw only blackness. No one was there.

"I must be imagining things," she told herself, seeking comfort in her own words. Her imagination had run away with her. "This is ridiculous!" she said out loud. "Get a grip on yourself, Rogers!"

She closed the book and tossed it on the step, then stood up and extended her arms upward to stretch out some of the stiffness. After carrying the book to the place where she had stacked her belongings, she ambled down the cracked walkway toward the street. She stood on the curb and looked up and down, her eyes adjusting to the increasing darkness. She looked at her watch in the glare of a passing headlight. It was 5:05 P.M. Jeffrey was more than an hour late.

She headed back toward the old brick building. For the first time, she noticed a light on at the far end of the downstairs hall, somewhere near the cafeteria or the school office. It was a welcome sight. She climbed the concrete stairs and pulled on one of the big doors. It was locked. She pulled on the other. She was in luck; it hadn't closed tightly enough behind Mrs. Stewart to latch. She gave it a shove and stepped inside the deserted building.

The long hall looked foreboding, not at all the busy, bustling, ᵇooming place it had been when she last left it. It was dark and empty. Wendy's heart was pounding as she moved slowly along.

Wham! A sudden noise bounced off of the tile floors and metal lockers, and for a moment Wendy stopped dead in her tracks. She let out a small gasp, then quickly laughed, realizing that it was just the heavy door slamming shut.

She paused a moment to catch her breath, then continued down the dark hallway toward the light. It wasn't coming from the office. It was on the wrong side of the hall. It had to be the cafeteria. It might not be anything at all, really; maybe just a light that they leave on all night or something like that. Anyway, she was almost there. She began to walk faster.

All of a sudden Wendy froze in place. Was that the creaking of a board in the distance? She listened carefully, but heard nothing. She glanced back over her shoulder into the shadows, but saw nothing. By now her heart was racing out of control.

She hurried down the hall to the glass door that led to the cafeteria and peered inside. A lone ceiling light glared in the back of the large room. Nothing else: no people, no telephone, no help.

Suddenly every nerve in her body jumped to full attention.

Wendy was immobilized. She wanted to scream but couldn't. In the near-darkness, not ten feet behind her, was a man. She saw him clearly, reflected in the glass of the cafeteria door. He was walking toward her, saying nothing, just smiling a mocking, smirking smile.

"Please . . . please."

Nothing else would come out. Her heart hammered in her chest; tears welled up in her eyes. There was nowhere to go. She fumbled with the handle of the door. It wouldn't turn. She looked up toward the ceiling in desperation, jerking at the handle. The glass rattled as if it might break.

"I've got to go . . ." she stammered, half crying. The handle suddenly moved. The door sprung open.

At that instant Wendy's head snapped back violently as the man's rough hand covered her mouth. His fingers pressed against her cheek, hurting her, muffling her cries. His other arm lifted her off the ground. She kicked violently, slamming her feet his legs, scratching and clawing at his hands, trying to fingers loose. Her mind raced, but she could only react. She felt him turn her around and press his back against the partially open door, forcing it to open the rest of the way. Then he pulled her inside the cafeteria, kicked the door shut, and threw her facedown on the tile floor, slamming her head against the hard surface.

The man jerked her arms behind her and began tying her hands. She screamed a full-throated, blood-curdling scream. The man laughed, grasped a handful of her hair, jerked back her head, and stuffed something in her mouth. Then he turned her over on her back and looked at her as if he were examining his catch. She stared back, her wide eyes darting from side to side, desperate with fear, searching in vain for an avenue of escape. There was none.

The man had the crazed look of a wild beast as his eyes crawled up and down her body. He leaned back and rubbed his jaw. She tensed her muscles and tried to wriggle free, but he was straddling her legs, clamping them tightly together with his own powerful thighs. His hands gripped her throat, then slid down the front of her blouse, pausing for a moment at her tiny breasts. He jerked up her skirt, pulling it above her waist, ran his hands along her thighs, then up under the thin cotton of her underpants. Wendy squeezed her eyes shut and clenched her teeth. She turned her face to one side. She wanted to vomit, but was afraid she might choke to death. Her head throbbed.

Suddenly the man was on his feet, pulling her up, turning her around, jerking her elbows together behind her back, pulling her shoulders together painfully. Then he pushed her along in front of him toward the back of the room.

Wendy stumbled and fell. The man slapped her across the face, a powerful blow. Her cheeks stung and a ringing sensation filled her ears. He stood her up and pushed her through the double swinging doors, into the darkened kitchen, toward the back door.

As they neared the door, Wendy lunged both legs out in a final, powerful, desperate kick. One foot struck a tray of dishes stacked on a counter near the door, sending shards of glass flying across the room. The jagged glass pierced her skin; blood spurted from the cuts in her leg.

"_____!" the man called out as he surveyed the hopeless mess.

A blast of cool air struck Wendy as the man carried her outside. The door slammed shut behind them. The man let her feet drop to the rough gravel surface, jamming her elbows behind her. Wendy winced with pain. She half-stumbled, half-slid, across the gravel as he pushed her toward a battered old white car, the only car remaining in the school parking lot.

2

Jeffrey Rogers drove down the wide boulevard in silence, his eyes fixed on the road, his jaw clamped tightly shut. The glow from the instrument panel bathed his solemn face in an eerie green light.

He looked at his watch. It was 5:14 P.M. "Mom is going to be furious," he thought. There wasn't anything he could do about it. She'd just have to understand. But he knew she wouldn't.

Basketball practice had started late. There was no way he was going to ask the coach to excuse him early. No way. Making this team was too important. It was his first varsity practice, his first shot at the "big time." He wanted the coach to know he was dedicated. He had stayed to the very end. "I had to," he muttered. "What choice did I have?"

He glanced down at the luminous needle on the speedometer. It had crept past fifty again, almost as if it had a will of its own.

"Slow down, slow down," he told himself, pressing firmly on the brake pedal with his left foot. The car responded. Forty, thirty-five, thirty. Thirty miles an hour felt like a crawl. There ʳs no traffic in sight. Thirty-five didn't seem too risky under ᶜircumstances. He eased up on the brake and pressed gently ᵃccelerator, keeping his eyes peeled.

ᵉed is a ticket. That would really fix me up," he thought

as he cruised along. A ticket would be a disaster in the first half of his sixteenth year, even before the ink was dry on his license. "They'd ground me for sure," he muttered under his breath. He had just recently convinced his parents to let him have a car, and as part of the deal, he had agreed to drive Wendy to school. He was a responsible young man, really.

Jeffrey was tall for his age, with a mop of unruly brown hair capping a freckled face that promised handsomeness, but delivered an awkward charm. He was a hard worker, too. His grades weren't great, but they reflected solid effort. He had to earn what he got. His parents recognized that early on and didn't make unreasonable demands. They were all rewarded with the natural results of such effort: not great grades, but good ones.

It was on the athletic field that Jeffrey really excelled, especially the basketball court. Somehow when the ball was tossed up, the shy, gangly youth became a resolute, determined leader. Not flashy, but dependable, always in the right place at the right time. Once again, he made up in hard work what he lacked in raw skill.

In junior high he had led his team to the finals of the district tournament and had been picked for the all-star team. Best of all, the varsity coach had invited him to try out for the team the next year. The varsity coach! A personal invitation! Yes, it had been a very good year.

After a summer of hard work, yet another dream had come true. On his sixteenth birthday he and his dad had gone shopping for a car.

"Be responsible," his father had said as he handed Jeffrey the keys. "It's up to you, son. The ball's in your court now." Jeffrey knew he was serious.

"All you have to do is show us that you can be responsible, and we'll give you more freedom," his mother had said as she watched him climb behind the wheel for the first time and rub his hand along the sparkling clean dashboard. "The two go hand in hand. It's that simple."

Those words haunted Jeffrey as he pushed a little harder on the gas pedal. Be responsible. Great! They're gonna jump over me, he thought, wallowing in self-pity over the tongue-lashing he knew he had coming.

Ahead on the right, behind the endless row of trees

shadowy bulk of the old school building, barely visible against the dark gray sky. The windows were dark. A bare bulb lit up the front walk. He didn't see anyone waiting.

Jeffrey pulled up to a four-way stop, a familiar corner where he had stood every morning and every afternoon for years, a proud member of the Safety Patrol, escorting the younger children across the street. Now the corner was dark and empty. No admiring children, no Patrol Mother, no activity at all. Nothing.

An old white car had pulled up on his right, reaching the intersection at the same time he did. Jeffrey yielded, as he was supposed to do, waiting patiently for the other car to roll on by. Nothing happened. He continued to wait, determined not to screw up. He had made it this far without incident. No matter what, he would wait.

"C'mon, dummy," he said out loud, glaring toward the other driver.

Finally the white car lumbered on through the twin paths of Jeffrey's headlights. Its trunk lid was bent and gaping open, its exhaust pipe dangling precariously close to the ground, barely held in place by baling wire. A rusty, pitted muffler bounced crazily as the car hit a slight bump. The car was a mess. Jeffrey couldn't help but smile.

Jeffrey never saw the other driver's face, so quickly was it in and out of his line of vision. He never saw the pock-marked skin, or the oily hair, or the wild look in the eyes, or the strangely excited expression. Only the car. As soon as it passed, Jeffrey pressed on the gas and moved forward, pulling up to the curb in front of the main entrance to the school. He stopped the car and got out, then walked up the walkway, toward the darkened building.

"Wendy," he called out. There was no answer.

"*Wendy!*" he called out again, even louder. Still no answer. His eyes darted from side to side, searching the shadows for some sign of his sister.

"Damn," he muttered. "Where in the world can she be?" He paced back and forth along the walkway, slamming his fist into 's hands, then mounted the steps, pulling first on one door and on the other. Neither yielded to his insistence. He leaned the glass and cupped his hands around his eyes to shade his face from the bright bulb that dangled overhead. The hallway inside was dark and deserted. At the far end of the hall he could see a light coming from the cafeteria. He rattled the doors and beat on the wooden framework. No one responded.

He jumped down from the concrete porch and ran around the side of the building, calling out Wendy's name as he ran. The side doors were also locked. He circled the old building, trying every door, with the same results. Finally he found himself back at the front steps. He stood on the little porch, cupped his hands around his mouth, and yelled as loud as he possibly could.

"*Wendy! Wendy!*"

His throat hurt. He tried again.

"*Wendy!*"

Still no answer. Angry and disgusted, he stuffed his hands in his jacket pockets and jumped back down the stairs, and headed toward his car. "Boy, am I in for it," he mumbled. At the bottom of the steps he stopped dead in his tracks.

"Oh no," he whispered.

He leaned forward to get a better view, and stared dumbly at the pile of books and papers partially obscured by the shadow of the hedge that bordered the walkway.

He had almost missed the familiar objects even though he had passed within inches of them several times. They were hidden from view, shielded from the harsh glare of the bare bulb. But on that last trip down the stairway, his eyes were drawn to the shadowy forms by a kind of instinctive curiosity. Intuitively he had perceived a break in the symmetry of the scene, the presence of something that shouldn't be there, something out of place. His eyes quickly adjusted to the changing patterns of light and dark. The truth came into sharp focus, riveting him to the spot where he now stood.

He was looking at his sister's schoolbooks.

Jeffrey knew in his gut something was wrong even before his mind confirmed it.

Something was suddenly frighteningly out of place in his orderly existence.

His anger disappeared instantly, replaced by bone-chill panic. Wendy might have found another way home, she have called their mom, she might have gone off with else, she might have done a lot of things. But she hadn't; she never would have left her schoolbooks. Not this way. No way around it, something was wrong. That much he knew.

For a moment he stood in that spot, sorting the possibilities with lightning speed born of anxiety. Then he knelt down and began gathering up Wendy's belongings, piling them into a more orderly stack as if she might suddenly appear and thank him for his help. His hands were shaking. He clenched his fists as if he could make his nervousness go away by sheer force of will. Finally he forced himself to stop, to gather his wits and think more clearly.

Across the street from the school, a row of brick homes was nestled behind well-established shrubs and tidy front lawns. A porch light beckoned him to the closest one. He put down the books and ran toward that light. When he reached the other side of the street he slowed his pace to a walk, giving himself a little extra time to think. He didn't want his panic to show.

He mounted the porch stairs two at a time, but knocked on the door in a deliberate, patient way. In a moment the door cracked open. An eye peered at him from behind the safety chain, which was still in place.

Jeffrey explained his situation. The warm, welcome aroma of mealtime spilled through the crack and filled his nostrils. The man unchained the door, led Jeffrey through a neat living room, past a dining room and into a small kitchen where a gray-haired woman was attending to last-minute preparations for an evening meal. Jeffrey stared dumbly at the telephone, then lifted the receiver and fumbled through the task of dialing. Huddled against the wall in a vain attempt to gain privacy, he waited impatiently for the mechanical ringing signal to stop.

On Hillside Drive, slightly more than a mile from the place where Jeffrey now stood, Carol Rogers glanced out the window above her sink. She had spent much of the last hour making arrangements for her meeting later that night. Time had slipped by before she had realized it. She stared into the darkness and her lip; her brow was furrowed, her eyes open wide. She barely make out the outline of trees against the dark gray tossed the towel she was holding back onto the counter and walked through the breakfast area into the comfortable, well-appointed living room.

"I wish the kids would come on home," she said to Bill as she walked past his chair. "It sure is getting dark early these days."

"Don't worry, honey," he said without looking up. "They'll be along."

Carol went over to the big picture window, in search of a second opinion. It was just as dark in the front yard as it had been in the back. She stood with her arms folded across her apron, seeing nothing but her own reflection. She had an uncomfortable feeling, the same uneasiness she always felt when things weren't happening exactly as they should.

"What time are they due in?" Bill asked.

"I think Jeff's basketball practice was supposed to be over more than an hour ago, but I'm not sure. This is the first practice. Maybe they just took longer," Carol answered. "Anyway, if I had realized how dark it would be before they got home . . ."

The telephone interrupted her sentence.

Carol hurried back to the kitchen. She picked up the phone on the fourth ring. It was Jeffrey.

"Mom, is Wendy home?" Jeffrey asked.

Carol could feel the controlled excitement in his voice. Her own heartbeat increased immediately.

"No, Jeff, she isn't here," she answered. "She's supposed to be with you. Where are you, anyway?"

There was an interminable pause at the other end of the line.

"Mom, I'm worried," Jeffrey finally responded, his voice cracking. "Wendy wasn't at school. I was late. It was dark when I got there, and she wasn't there. I'm at a house across the street from the school. What should I do?"

Carol tightened her grip on the receiver. Her heart beat even faster. She made herself speak calmly, hoping to ease Jeffrey's distress.

"She might have gotten a ride with a friend, Jeff," Carol said. "Have you looked around carefully? Is the building still open? Maybe she's still in there. Did you look?" Of course he had looked. She knew that. But there had to be some explanation.

"Mom," Jeffrey said, lowering his voice to a near-whis "She's not there. I looked everywhere. She's just not t found her books under the bushes in front of the school. Mom, I'm worried!" His voice cracked again as he spoke. Carol listened intently as she stared out into the darkness. His voice didn't sound real. Was this happening, or was she imagining things?

"I'll be right there, Jeff. You go back over to the school and wait for me. Okay?"

Jeffrey wanted to get out of this house. He didn't feel free to talk. He knew that his words had been artificial, stilted. He had carefully chosen them to communicate his concern to his mother while letting these strangers know as little as possible. Finally he hung up the phone and breathed a sigh of relief. But he didn't feel any better.

He thanked the old couple, and declined their hesitant offer of help. The woman went back to her meal preparations. Jeffrey and the old man retraced their steps through the warm house, back out into the evening chill. After one last offer of assistance, the old man shut the door. Jeffrey heard the click of the deadbolt, followed by the scraping of the chain. Then the porch light went out, leaving him in total darkness.

Jeffrey stood at the top of the porch stairs, adjusting his eyes to the darkness. Then he bolted down the steps and across the empty street to his car. He opened the driver's door and started to get in, but hesitated. The books! He had forgotten Wendy's books! Leaving the car door open, he ran up the school walkway, quickly gathered his sister's belongings, then returned to the car at a run.

More than anything else he wanted to go home. He wanted to get there as quickly as possible. He wanted to cry, or to scream—anything to relieve this tension. But he sat where he was and waited for his mother to arrive. Tears began to blur his vision. He wiped his eyes clumsily with the sleeve of his jacket and waited in the cool stillness of the autumn night. Finally he saw his mother's car. He frantically waved her over.

Back on Hillside Drive, Bill Rogers had been on the phone since Carol had left to meet Jeffrey. He was calling Wendy's classmates, that gave him something to do, and kept him from surrendering to the terrible panic that was growing inside him. finished the last call with no results. Everyone expressed concern, but no one knew anything. Nothing at all. With each fruitless call he felt that much worse.

In a few moments Carol and Jeffrey drove up outside. Bill hid his hands inside of his trousers pockets and dug his fingernails into his palms as he watched them walk up the front walkway. Wendy wasn't with them. "We've got to call the police," Carol said as she pulled open the front door. "Something has happened. I just know it." Jeffrey didn't say anything. He walked on past and headed up the stairs. Bill started to reach out for Carol, but let her walk on by him instead.

"Let's not call them, Carol," he said. "Let's not blow this all out of proportion. I'm sure there's an explanation. There's just got to be. Maybe we should stay off the phone for a while. Maybe she's been trying to call us. Maybe she's worried 'cause she can't reach us. Let's not tie up the line."

"Okay, okay, you're probably right," Carol said. Bill followed her into the kitchen and stood awkwardly by her side. She leaned her head against his shoulder and closed her eyes, and then she began to cry. Finally he put his arm around her.

"It's probably something so silly, so stupid, and here I am jumping off the deep end," Carol said, forcing a smile. "In a few minutes I'll bet we'll all be laughing about how dumb we've acted."

"I hope so," Bill whispered. "I really do."

In his heart, Bill really didn't believe it was going to happen that way. He was every bit as scared as Carol was. He was very much afraid that it would be a long, long time before he and Carol would laugh again.

‖3‖

Bill Rogers called the police department at precisely 7:52 P.M., according to official records. He reported the absence of his daughter in a deliberate, matter-of-fact manner. Though he was churning on the inside, he was trying his best to remain outwardly calm. Carol was standing right beside him; he didn't want to make her feel any worse than she already did.

A patrol car responded within fifteen minutes. Two young officers presented themselves at the Rogers' front door and offered their assistance. The officers quickly realized that they had walked into something more than a routine call. Assistance was requested from the Youth Aid Division, and from Missing Persons.

Hundreds of children run away daily. Most return quickly. This was not the first such call that these officers had ever received. As the hours dragged by, more police were called in and the tension in the air increased dramatically.

During the early evening hours, Carol, Bill, and Jeffrey were interviewed at length. One officer was assigned the task of contacting Wendy's friends in hopes that someone might shed light on her whereabouts. The process was tedious, time-consuming, and fruitless. A recent picture was located and distributed to other officers patrolling the area, together with a description of the clothes Wendy had been wearing. Again, nothing turned up.

Concerned neighbors came by, some out of curiosity, others to offer assistance and support. The police set up a "command center" in the Rogers' den. The press called repeatedly. Television reporters, followed by their ubiquitous mini-cameras, prowled up and down the quiet street in search of a story, only to disappear en masse after the late-news deadline had passed. A steady stream of official and unofficial visitors trudged in and out of the Rogers' attractive Cape Cod home, filling it with noise and hectic activity.

Things were rapidly getting out of control. Carol and Bill were numb with fatigue and tense from the uncertainty of the day's events, but most of all they were burdened with a constant, depressing sense of dread and a feeling of unrealness. This wasn't happening. It couldn't be. Yet it was, and to them. They survived on coffee as the evening wore on.

At ten-fifteen that evening, the telephone rang in a modest apartment several miles away from Hillside Drive, in one of the newer sections of town. Assistant District Attorney General Tom Sanderson was watching the evening news, leaning back in his favorite chair, with his feet propped up and a bag of chips in his lap. A plastic container of sour cream dip perched precariously on the arm of the chair. The beer can in his hand was empty.

Tom Sanderson had been struggling with a weighty decision—whether or not he should get another beer. It was a tough decision. He was worn out, and all he really wanted to do was sit there. The jangling telephone was an unwelcome intrusion.

The ringing stopped briefly, then began again, and again. The caller was determined.

"All right, all right," Sanderson barked, pulling himself up from the depths of the soft, cushiony chair. "I'm coming," he muttered, glaring at the cluttered desk across the room where the phone awaited his arrival.

"Hello," he said. "This is Tom Sanderson."

He recognized the serious and insistent voice on the other right off. As he listened patiently, his fatigue dissolved an adrenalin began to flow.

"It sounds bad," Sanderson responded. "There's no point in waiting any longer for her to turn up. At the very least we have an abduction. At the worst, well, who knows. Whatever it is, we'd better get this investigation organized before things get out of hand and get screwed up. I'll meet you at the school in fifteen minutes. Make that twenty. Call the lab and have them meet us there. Keep everyone out of that kitchen. Seal the school off. Don't let anyone touch anything until someone from the lab gets there, especially the broken glass. Get a police photographer, too."

While he talked, Sanderson was jotting down notes on the pad that rested by his phone. His reactions were automatic, and correct.

"By the way, where is this school?"

He wrote down the address.

"Okay, I'll be there. One more thing. Call Al Mallory and have him meet me there."

Sanderson listened again, then reacted angrily.

"I don't give a damn! I know we haven't found a body yet, but there sure as hell might be one if we don't act quickly. He's the best there is, and we need him. You just tell him to come. He'll know what to do."

Sanderson slammed down the phone. He glanced over at the waiting chair. It sat there, bathed in the flickering glow of the television, calling him to return to its comfort. He sighed deeply, turned off the T.V., then put the half-eaten bowl of dip back into the refrigerator.

"Well, here we go again," he thought as he headed into his bedroom to change clothes.

By midnight, the Rogers' home was a beehive of unwanted activity. People were everywhere. Most of them were strangers. After a while, Carol and Bill had simply quit worrying about who they were, and what they were doing there.

When the officer on duty at the front door ushered two more men into the kitchen and started to introduce them, Carol and Bill regarded this latest intrusion more with resignation than with curiosity.

"Mr. and Mrs. Rogers," the officer said, "this is Assistant

District Attorney Tom Sanderson and Homicide Detective Al Mallory. They need to talk with you for a moment."

Carol's heart sank. She stared blankly at the two men. All she had heard was the word homicide; everything else was a blur. She felt as though someone had slammed a fist into her gut.

Bill rose and extended his hand, an empty, meaningless courtesy that seemed awkward and out of place under the circumstances. He motioned toward two empty chairs. The two men sat down. Detective Mallory spoke first.

"Mr. Rogers," he said, directing his gaze toward Bill, "I want to bring you up to date on what's going on. I think we have some idea of what might have happened."

Carol lowered her head and rested her face in the upturned palms of her hands, bracing her elbows against the surface of the table. Bill stared dumbly into Mallory's eyes. The veteran homicide detective's grim expression and serious tone had dispelled any glimmer of hope.

"Have you found her?" Bill asked. "Do you know where she might be?" He already knew the response.

"No," said Mallory, "we haven't found your daughter, Mr. Rogers. I'm afraid we have no real news at this point. I wish I could tell you something different, but I can't."

Carol began to turn her head slowly back and forth in her hands. She didn't want to hear any more, but she didn't have any choice.

"Mr. Rogers," Tom Sanderson interjected, "please understand that we are doing all we can. Al Mallory is the best detective on our force. He is going to head the investigation from this point on. Our office has offered him its complete cooperation. No effort will be spared. You can be sure of that."

"I know that, really I do," Bill Rogers began. "And I appreciate your help. It's just that . . ." He looked over at his son, Jeffrey, who had just come into the room. Jeffrey leaned against the doorjamb and looked first at his father, then at his mother.

Carol raised her head and stared at Tom Sanderson. Her eyes were bloodshot and puffy. She was struggling against the urge to scream, to cry out for help, to unleash the rising surge of anger within her.

"What have you found out?" she asked, interrupting he

band. "Tell us what you know. We have a right to know." Her
voice was cold, almost rude.

Tom Sanderson stared back at the distraught woman. He
didn't know how to handle her. Mallory bailed him out.

"Mrs. Rogers, when the call first came into headquarters,
Youth Aid sent some men out to the school to look around. They
searched the grounds thoroughly. They didn't find anything.
Another team of officers canvassed all of the homes that border
the school grounds. Again, nothing turned up. Nobody saw
anything and nobody heard anything."

"You're not here because you found nothing," Carol said,
interrupting once more. Mallory squirmed uncomfortably and
glanced sideways at Sanderson. Her impatience was obvious.

"Please forgive my wife, officer," Bill Rogers said. "She's very
upset. We both are." Carol glared at her husband.

"We understand that, Mr. Rogers," Sanderson said. "No apology is necessary, I assure you. We're here to help. We certainly
don't want to make things any worse."

Carol looked at Mallory. His steel-gray eyes reflected a gentle-
ness and sensitivity that she hadn't seen before. She felt bad.
She had aimed her anger in the wrong direction. After an uncomfortable pause, Mallory continued to speak.

"Anyway, nothing turned up at the school, at least not on the
outside. But all of the activity, the police cars and all, attracted
a lot of attention. Apparently word got around to the principal.
He came over to investigate. He was very cooperative. He opened
up the school and let our officers look around the inside."

"What did they find?" Carol asked.

"Well, it's too early to say what it means, but I'm afraid they
found signs of a disturbance."

"What do you mean?" Bill asked, his anxiety mounting with
each word that the officer uttered. Jeffrey stood transfixed and
continued to take it all in.

Mallory took a deep breath. "The cafeteria door was unlocked.
It wasn't supposed to be. Several of the tables and chairs were
out of place. They weren't stacked up like they ought to have
been. They were sort of, well, disarranged."

"What else?" Carol asked.

"Back in the kitchen there was broken glass all over the floor.
of clean glasses had been knocked over. The tray itself

was still on the counter by the back door, but the broken glass was spread out over the counter and all over the floor."

Tom Sanderson shifted impatiently in the hard wooden chair. Mallory was taking too long to get to the point.

"Mrs. Rogers," he interjected, "there were blood spots on the kitchen floor and on the doorway leading outside. There were more blood spots on the concrete stairs. After that it was hard to tell, because the driveway and parking area is a loose, dusty gravel. The blood spots seemed to lead out into the driveway, though we couldn't tell for sure. But it is obvious that there had been a fight or a struggle of some kind in that kitchen, and someone was cut in the process. The blood spots were small and scattered, but they were fresh. Someone either left by the back door or was carried out, we don't know which. That someone had apparently been cut, probably by the broken glass. Until we know otherwise, we are operating on the assumption that your daughter was one of the people involved in that struggle, and that she left the school building through the back door, probably against her will."

Depression descended on Carol and Bill like a pall being draped over a casket. Carol's hands began to tremble as Mallory picked up the narrative.

"Mrs. Rogers, our people are out there at the school right now. They have secured the area and are going over the building with a fine-tooth comb. They're looking for fingerprints, footprints, anything. Fortunately we got out there before anyone else had been in the building. We're working around the clock to cover the whole area before the kids come back in the morning. Our lab technicians have taken samples of the blood spots. We need to find out if you have any medical records or anything else that would give us Wendy's blood type. We also need to call her pediatrician."

Carol thought for a moment. It all seemed unreal. So much, so fast. She rose from the table. "Give me a minute," she said as she walked from the room, visibly shaken. Jeffrey was still in the doorway.

"Is there anything I can get for you, Mom?" he asked as C? walked past.

"No, I'll get it. I know where it is," she replied, disa into the hallway.

Bill watched his wife leave. Then he turned back to Mallory. "What do we do now?" he asked. "What's next?"

"We have asked the principal to get us a list of all the school employees and anyone else who might have had access to the building or who might have been there this afternoon," Mallory responded. "For openers, we'll contact all of the names we can get."

"Tonight?" Bill asked.

"Yes, tonight," Mallory responded, "or as soon as we can get to them. We want to talk with everyone by morning, at the very least with all of the cafeteria employees. It's important to get to them while their memories are fresh, before they get started talking to each other and garble everything up. You never know when someone might know something that will turn out to be the key that unlocks the whole puzzle."

"Then what?" Bill asked.

"Then we begin following up any leads that turn up from those efforts, and from the work being done by our lab people," Mallory answered.

Bill was silent for a moment. "Is there any hope?" he asked.

"There's always hope," Sanderson replied. "Look, I know it's hard not to jump to conclusions at a time like this. You're going to think the worst. But try not to do that. No stone will be left unturned. We'll find Wendy, I assure you of that. There's always hope. Always."

Bill Rogers looked up from the table. Carol was back in the doorway, standing next to her son, a small folder in her hand. Tears were streaming down her cheeks.

"God, I hope you're right," Bill said, looking up into his wife's tortured eyes. "I hope you're right."

4

The hour before dawn is a special time in the city. A curious stillness hovers over empty streets, creating a deceptive kind of calm. Most bars and clubs are closed; offices and stores have not yet opened. It is a period of limbo, a time when the busy, cluttered, crowded urban sprawl is poised between a much-needed rest and another day of hectic activity.

On this particular November morning the air was typically cold and damp. An early glow in the eastern sky softened the bite of the chill north wind as it heralded the approach of a new day. The starry canopy was just beginning to fade to gray, on its way to a bright morning blue. Most of the city's inhabitants were huddled in their warm beds, enjoying a temporary peace, gathering strength for the coming day.

But at the Rogers' home on Hillside Drive there was no peace, temporary or otherwise. No one was asleep. Lights were on all over the house, just as they had been all night long. Several policemen scurried about. Carol and Bill Rogers were still awake, still dressed in the clothes they had put on the morning before. Wendy Rogers's bed was still made up, untouched since Wendy had last left the house.

Twenty hours had passed since Carol had watched her daughter ride off to school. Twenty hours, most of which spent in agony, with no word. Each succeeding minute seemed like an eternity. Each ring of the telephone brought sudden anticipation, followed by yet another disappointment. Hope was dwindling fast.

At that same hour, patrol car 252 was parked along the curb on a suburban street several miles from the Rogers' home. The dome light inside the car glared brightly.

Inside car 252, Officers Morgan and Sanchez were checking another name off their list. For the past two hours they had been rousing people out of bed, disturbing their slumber, interrupting their peace. So far they had knocked on seven doors. Seven anxious, pajama-clad people had responded, but had known nothing. Seven alibis had been duly recorded, seven apologies extended. Only one name was left on the list. One more. Then the two officers could get some breakfast and go home. Officers Morgan and Sanchez were very tired, and very discouraged.

"Who's next?" Sanchez asked his partner. Morgan glanced down at his clipboard.

"Jordan. Frank Jordan," he responded.

"Where does he live?" Sanchez asked as he pulled the car away from the curb and eased down the deserted street.

"Eight twenty-six Cleveland Street, Apartment D." Morgan placed his clipboard on the seat beside him, then reached up and flipped off the dome light.

"Cleveland Street? Good God," Sanchez said. "That's way the hell across town. I thought you said we were almost through."

"This is the last name. What do you want me to do, call him up and have him meet us somewhere?" Morgan was too irritated to be gracious, and too tired to take any criticism from his partner.

"Great planning, Morgan," Sanchez muttered.

"Stick it in your ear, Sanchez," Morgan snapped back, leaning his head against the headrest and closing his eyes. In spite of his response, he wasn't really angry. Neither was Sanchez. They were both worn out, that's all.

They drove across town, moving along the deserted streets at ⬚berate pace, past yellow-flashing stop lights which would ⬚rn to alternating red and green. The silence was broken ⬚ to time by the crackling of their police radio. Both men only half-listened to the exchanges. The calls were all routine. Nothing exciting was happening.

Luther Morgan was a rookie, fresh out of the police academy, whereas Carlos Sanchez, with almost a year's experience, was a relative "veteran." They had spent a dull two months on the night shift together, encountering little more than an endless stream of streetcorner fights, public drunks, and squabbling spouses. But they really hadn't expected much more than that. They were on the bottom of the heap. This was just another in a series of scut-work assignments.

Cleveland Street was in Palmyra Heights, a sprawling area just north of the business district, a once-fine neighborhood that now hung suspended between periods of affluence. Its well-to-do former inhabitants had moved away long ago, and the city's young rich had not yet discovered its potential for redevelopment. Revival would inevitably come, if the wrecker ball didn't get there first. Meanwhile the neighborhood muddled along with a strange mixture of old folks who couldn't afford to leave and transients who rented rooms in the numerous boarding houses that were once stately old homes.

The large old houses that lined both sides of Cleveland Street weren't well marked. At one time, numbers had been painted on the curb that edged the sidewalk in front of the houses, but they had long since faded. Some front doors bore numerical markings, but most were hard to see, especially in the dim predawn light. Sanchez drove the car slowly down the boulevard as Morgan directed the spotlight first at one door, then the next, taking care to avoid aiming the bright shaft of light directly into the windows.

"That's it—over there with the torn screen." Morgan's light rested on a door that badly needed paint, as did most of the others.

Morgan switched off the spotlight as Sanchez pulled the black-and-white patrol car over to the curb and eased in behind an old white sedan. Morgan chuckled as he looked at its rear end, which still showed the effects of some past collision. An old hound was sniffing at the gap where the trunk lid didn't quite stay down. The dog scooted off just as the police car pulled up.

Morgan had the passenger door open before the car came to a complete stop. "Let's get this over with," he said as h out onto the sidewalk. Sanchez turned off the headlights, put on his regulation cap, and climbed out from behind the wheel.

The two officers walked up the front walkway, mounted the concrete steps, and stood in front of the battered door. The old house was dark and quiet. The door had no bell and no knocker, but the knob turned freely.

"What was that apartment number again?" Sanchez whispered as he stepped into the musty, dimly lit hall.

"Shit. I forgot," Morgan answered. "The list is in the car. I think it's Apartment D."

Sanchez took out his flashlight and aimed it at the first door they came to. A tarnished brass "A" hung askew from a single nail. A nameplate was suspended below the letter, but it was dingy and faded with age, and the name was illegible. Sanchez moved the beam of light across the hall to Apartment B, with the same general results.

"Wanna try upstairs?" Sanchez asked.

"Let's check around here first," Morgan replied. Then he paused. "Do you smell what I smell?" he said. It was more than just a mustiness, it was a strange, sickening kind of sweetness.

Sanchez followed his partner down the narrow hall to a small alcove where two more doors led to two more apartments. From the crack at the bottom of the door, they could see that lights were on inside one of the two. A flash of the light revealed the "D" they had been looking for.

"Well, at least we won't be waking this one up," Sanchez remarked as he put away his flashlight. Morgan rapped sharply on the door. There was no response. He knocked again. Still no response. He looked at Sanchez, who gestured his approval. It was time to identify themselves.

"Open up, it's the police," Morgan said in a firm voice, loud enough to be heard inside the apartment. There was still no response.

"Maybe there's nobody here," Morgan said. "What do we do now?"

"I'd hate like hell to have to make another trip out here," ˙anchez replied. "Maybe he's in the bathroom or something. ˙s he live alone?"

"˙e list didn't say," Morgan answered. He pressed his ear

to the door and signaled for Sanchez to be quiet. "I hear music, a radio or something."

Sanchez stepped up to the door and pounded on it with his closed fist. "Open up, it's the police," he shouted. Then he lowered his voice. "Open this door, you lazy bastard," he muttered.

Out of frustration, he instinctively reached for the doorknob and rattled it. The knob moved freely. The surprised officer glanced at Morgan, who smiled and shrugged his shoulders. Sanchez pushed open the door.

A thick, sweet smell rolled out into the hall through the open door. The room was filthy. Clothes, books, and papers were strewn everywhere. A battered end table at the foot of a well-worn couch was covered with empty bottles and drug paraphernalia.

Through an open doorway on the other side of the cluttered living room, the officers could see into a dimly lit bedroom. In the far corner of the bedroom, seated in a chair, was a young man dressed only in an undershirt and a pair of khaki slacks. His face was flushed and pock-marked. Stringy black hair hung loosely about his head. His piercing eyes had a glazed expression. He stared at the officers, one corner of his mouth curled upward. He didn't move, but just sat there and kept on staring. Morgan instinctively unsnapped his holster.

"Frank Jordan?" Sanchez called out. There was no response. "Are you Frank Jordan?" Sanchez tried again.

The young man slowly waved one hand, and continued sneering. Still he said nothing. Seconds ticked by. The officers didn't know what to do next. They were tense and ready.

The young man pressed his palms into the arms of his chair and slowly pushed himself up into a standing position. He steadied himself on the edge of the bed, then staggered across the room toward the doorway. Both officers unholstered their pistols.

The young man lurched and almost fell, but at the last second caught himself on the doorway and leaned against it for support. In the brighter light the officers could see that he wasn't armed. He just stood there, hanging on to the door frame, still smil... that sarcastic, mocking half-smile. Finally he spoke. His... were slurred, his tongue thick.

"Well, let's get this over with," he said.

As he spoke, he extended his wrists toward the officers, palms turned upward. When he released his grip on the doorway, he stumbled forward into the living room. Sanchez tried to catch him, but missed. The young man hit the floor with a thud and rolled over onto his back, his arms still extended, the smile still on his face.

It was at this precise moment that Officers Morgan and Sanchez noticed the spots of dried blood on the young man's pants.

‖5‖

Frank Jordan confessed immediately, even before he got up from the floor of his filthy apartment.

"I killed her. I did it." That was all he said.

Tears streamed down his face after making this announcement. But his wasn't the anguished cry of contrition, nor did he suffer the wracking sobs of guilt. It was more like the bursting of a wall that had been holding back a reservoir of tension that had been building in him for the past few hours. The dam simply broke and out came the flood, spilling all over him, engulfing him, as he sprawled on the dirt-encrusted rug. But the smile never left his face; hardness quickly returned to his features.

Morgan and Sanchez followed the procedures which had been drilled into them by their police training. At first they had been more shocked than Jordan; neither of them had really expected this assignment to produce any results, least of all something as important as this. It wasn't until much later that they would become aware of their own mistakes. At this point they felt nothing but excitement. This was big, real big.

Sanchez read Jordan his rights while Morgan called headquarters, using the telephone instead of the police radio avoid leaking their discovery to the press. Within min ends of the block had been cordoned off. The police secured the area and began the meticulous process of dismantling the small apartment inch by inch, searching for corroborating evidence. The search quickly spread to the old white sedan parked out front. Its battered trunk was given detailed attention.

In the meantime Frank Jordan quickly rebuilt his defenses. He refused to say anything to anyone, and never repeated his earlier admission. His resolve, and his nerve, returned at the same time; both grew stronger as the whirlwind of activity increased around him. He was the center of attention for the first time in his life and he savored every moment. His sarcastic, streetwise attitude made everyone angry. He arrogantly demanded his one phone call and demonstrated an uncanny awareness of the limits that the law placed on his interrogators, almost daring them to go too far and do too much. Thanks to the convoluted shortsightedness of the law, he had the upper hand, and he knew it.

It was a frustrating, maddening exercise for Morgan and Sanchez; and yet the more experienced officers fared no better. Even Al Mallory found it difficult to control himself in the face of Jordan's cockiness. He knew they had their man; they all did. He knew they could prove it, too. But they faced a far more difficult problem at this point. They had to find Wendy Rogers.

The toughest assignment fell to Tom Sanderson. Since all of the officers were needed at the scene, it became his job to contact Bill and Carol Rogers before the press picked up the news and spread it all over town. He drove as quickly as he could to Hillside Drive, rushing to get it over with, yet dreading having to face this poor family.

Sanderson felt physically ill. The lump in his throat was almost choking him by the time he eased his government-issue sedan into the driveway on Hillside Drive that had become so familiar to him during the past few hours. In the early-morning glow, the trim, well-kept house looked like a thousand others, well-lighted and full of activity, its inhabitants dusting off the cobwebs of the previous night and preparing for the new day. The irony wasn't lost on him. In a different time and place he the Rogers family might have been good friends. He might iving over here for a variety of pleasant reasons, instead of as the bearer of terrible news.

He tried to think of other things as he walked up the walkway. For an instant he managed to forget the nature of his mission, but the presence of an officer at the front door brought him back to reality.

The officer recognized Sanderson immediately and let him in. The house was deathly quiet as the two of them stood in the hallway, whispering to each other. The officer gestured toward the kitchen. Sanderson crossed the thick living room carpet, trying to think of what he would say. How could he soften such a blow? How could he make it better? Should he pierce their hearts slowly, or cleave them in two with a sudden burst of bad news? There was no right answer.

Carol Rogers looked up from her coffee cup. A low moan began, deep in her throat at first, building to a crescendo of agony as she saw the tears that were streaming down Tom Sanderson's face, tears he never knew were there.

"Oh, God, no!" she cried, even before he could speak. Words were unnecessary. She knew. As bad as it had been, there had been hope; now there was nothing. She felt as if a weight had descended upon her, crushing out her life, killing all of her joy.

She closed her eyes and sat there, completely unable to cope, much less comprehend. All she could do was to wish herself dead, but the merciful release of death would not be hers. She had no choice but to live, and endure.

‖TWO‖

The First Monday in April The Following Year

||6||

"**M**ay it please the court, that concludes the case for the defense."

Tom Sanderson thought he detected a hint of smugness in Martin McPherson's voice as the elderly defense attorney made his pronouncement and sat back down in the chair next to his client, Frank Jordan. Jordan's smile was still firmly in place, as it had been every day during the trial. McPherson ran one hand through his silver hair and looked over at the prosecution table.

There was reason for smugness. Martin McPherson had managed to make a real dogfight out of what should have been an airtight case. Using his consummate skill and drawing upon his invaluable experience, McPherson had spent the last several days twisting and turning the facts and manipulating the witnesses, trying with some success to make a cold-blooded murder look like an unplanned quirk of fate, characterizing it as an abomination of equal horror to the victim and the perpetrator. All the while he had been building up to his "grand finale," his last witness, Dr. Norman Green, the psychiatrist.

The state had long since been aware that temporary insanity would be the only defense. But the skill with which that defense had been presented was nonetheless a surprise. McPherson and Green had worked together remarkably well; they had planned and rehearsed with great care. Their personalities had become one, their questions and answers batted back and forth across the courtroom as if they were skilled combatants playing a tennis match.

Their effort had paid off. The jury had given its attention to Dr. Green's impassioned plea for mercy on behalf of his patient. Mercy was, after all, the bottom line.

In spite of Sanderson's objections, in spite of his strategically timed interruptions, in spite of his own equally skilled cross-examination, damage had definitely been done, though just how much he couldn't be sure. The Assistant D.A. tried not to let his feelings show as he returned to the lectern.

"Anything further, General Sanderson?" Judge Henry Coleman said, peering down from the bench. There was a tone of impatience in his voice, the same tone that had characterized his attitude toward the state's case from the outset.

Had Judge Coleman gone out of his way to make things difficult for the prosecution? Legal scholars might have denied that, but to Carol and Bill Rogers, it seemed like he had. Unburdened by any real knowledge of the intricate protections in favor of the accused that are built into the legal system, the parents of the victim had sat in awe for more than a week, becoming increasingly depressed as events unfolded before them.

All of the decisions, big and small, had seemed to them to be based on what was "fair" to the defendant, not on what was right. Everything, even down to the time of adjournment, had been cast in Jordan's favor. There had been ample time for Dr. Green's testimony on the preceding Friday evening, but McPherson had managed to get an early adjournment based on his client's alleged fatigue and strain. The real reason was obvious to everyone except the judge: The impact of this testimony would be much greater on Monday morning when the jury was fresh.

At McPherson's insistence, in order not to prejudice the jury against Frank Jordan, all vestiges of feeling and emotion had been barred from the courtroom. Tears were too obvious, anger was unheard of, even the slightest indications of grief were forbidden. To make matters worse, evidence was excluded—vital, important evidence, on grounds that seemed to Carol and Bill Rogers ridiculous.

Not only was Jordan's confession barred from the jury, but the officers had been severely reprimanded for entering the apartment without a warrant, and for "hearing" a confession without first advising Jordan of his rights.

"What could they have done, for heaven's sake. It all happened so fast. Whose side is he on?" Carol had asked Bill that question later, as they talked about Judge Coleman and all that they had seen him do.

Rightly or wrongly, Bill and Carol Rogers felt very much alone, and very frustrated. Like many other victims of crime, like thousands before them who had been burdened with tragedy only to find their tragedy compounded in the courtroom, they were rapidly losing faith in the system.

Wendy Rogers was their daughter. Her death was, first and foremost, their loss. But immediately after the funeral, they had surrendered control of this unfortunate situation, and had been plunged into a maelstrom of activity ostensibly choreographed by the district attorney's office, but dictated in fact by the machinations of a highly skilled defense attorney and the whims of an irrational judge whose lust for publicity was second only to his determination to protect the killer's rights. That was how they saw it. And few observers would have disagreed, least of all Tom Sanderson. He gripped the lectern and masked his anger as best he could, then addressed the judge.

"May it please the court, the state wishes to present its first rebuttal witness, Sergeant Lyle, Gordon Lyle, of the Metropolitan Police Records Division."

Judge Coleman leaned back in his swivel chair, a look of obvious disgust on his face. Martin McPherson lept to his feet instantly and began to speak without waiting for the court's permission.

"Your Honor, the defense wishes to object to this testimony and further wishes to discuss this matter in the absence of the jury."

Judge Coleman excused the jury. All twelve jurors trudged out of the courtroom for the umpteenth time, followed by th alternates. They were worn out from the experience of the ceding week and thoroughly bewildered by the constant ruptions. It seemed to them that they had spent more of the courtroom than in it.

The bailiff closed the door at the end of the jury box. Judge Coleman turned to Martin McPherson and nodded.

"Your Honor," McPherson began, stepping out from behind the table, "we have been through this before. The state was instructed during its case-in-chief that evidence of my client's past record would be admissible only if my client took the stand. Well, he didn't take the stand, and this is not proper rebuttal. Frank Jordan's character and veracity are not issues in this case. We strenuously object to this line of testimony."

"Wait a minute, Counselor," the judge said, raising a hand in the direction of McPherson. "General Sanderson, what is the purpose of this witness? Is Mr. McPherson correct?"

"Yes, Your Honor," the district attorney replied. "Sergeant Lyle will testify as to the prior record of Frank Jordan. He will show that this man has a history of arrests for indecent exposure, assault on young girls, and related crimes, leading up to a point in time just six months prior to the disappearance of Wendy Rogers."

"What's the relevance?" Judge Coleman asked.

My God, Carol Rogers thought as she covered her face with her hands. What's the relevance? I can't believe this. I just can't. She stood up, pushed back her chair, hesitated for a moment, then left the courtroom. Bill Rogers followed her into the hallway just as Tom Sanderson began his impassioned plea for inclusion of Frank Jordan's history as a sex offender. Sanderson knew it was fruitless, but he gave it his all.

Carol stood out in the hall and let her eyes adjust for a moment. It seemed almost dark out there in comparison to the courtroom, with all the bright television lights. She walked to a window at the end of the hall and stared down at the traffic below. In a moment she felt Bill's arm on her shoulder; her body remained rigid and unyielding.

"This is insane, Bill. It's absolutely insane."

"I wish I could tell you it isn't," Bill said, "but I can't."

"I just don't understand," she continued. "What are they trying to do? What's wrong with those people, anyway? How can they possibly be arguing about whether that man's record is relevant? How can that lawyer possibly say that credibility and character important? My God, Bill, how much more important can they be? That's the most important thing. He's a twisted, lying, deranged killer, and they say that's not relevant?"

"That's the law," Bill said without conviction.

"Screw the law," Carol responded with complete conviction. "Screw all of them." Bill recoiled at her uncharacteristic bluntness. He was at a loss for words.

He didn't have time to say anything anyway. At that moment a voice called from the doorway to the courtroom. It was the bailiff; it was time to go back in. The jury was about to return to the jury box.

"You go on," Carol said to Bill. "I'm not going. I can't take it anymore." Bill didn't try to argue, but left her standing there staring into space.

He hurried down the hallway and back into the courtroom. Everyone stared at him. Both television cameras followed him as he walked over and took his seat by Tom Sanderson at the prosecution table. The jury box was full; the witness chair was empty. Martin McPherson had obviously won another battle.

Bill leaned over and whispered to Sanderson, then Sanderson rose and spoke to the court.

"May it please the court, Mrs. Rogers is temporarily indisposed. We can continue without her if the court wishes."

"Call your next witness," Judge Coleman responded curtly, showing no apparent compassion for Carol Rogers's condition, whatever it might be. Bill wondered if this discourtesy was as obvious to everyone else as it was to him.

Bill looked around the courtroom as Sanderson returned to the lectern to begin the series of routine rebuttal witnesses which would wrap up the proof to be presented by the state. He tuned out the sounds around him and studied the three people who were seated at the defense table.

In the eyes of Martin McPherson he saw the glint of steel nerves, the glare of complete concentration, and a steadiness born of confidence. Bill disliked McPherson, but admired him in a strange way.

In the eyes of Frank Jordan he saw nothing but contempt, sallow, glazed-over expression of disdain that masked weakr and fear. Bill held nothing but hatred for this man.

The third person at that table was Ellen Hayes, McP'

associate counsel. She alone returned his gaze without turning away. Bill hadn't figured her out yet. The feeling he saw in her eyes didn't rise to the dignity of compassion, but at least it was a response of some kind, and compared to the demeanor of her co-counsel and their client, the difference was like night and day.

The Monday session dragged to a close without Carol. On Tuesday, she was back in her usual place, patiently enduring the arguments of counsel and the unbelievably tedious charge to the jury. Carol also focused on Ellen Hayes's expression, searching for a glimmer of empathy. It kept her from looking at Frank Jordan or Martin McPherson. She hated Jordan with every fiber of her being; McPherson wasn't far behind. Staring at them only increased her sense of outrage. When court ended that evening, she was relieved to be out of their presence at last.

7

What a way to end a day, Ellen Hayes thought as she pulled back the curtain and peered out into the darkness. A light rain continued to fall. She kept watching until Mrs. Mayberry, her elderly housekeeper, was safely in her car. As the car pulled away, Ellen switched off the porch light and let the curtain fall back in place.

Late evenings were not unusual for Ellen, but this one had lasted longer than most. As a trial lawyer she was accustomed to staying late enough to take care of any emergencies. But this day had gone on forever. She was grateful that Mrs. Mayberry had been able to stay late, even if the dear lady's irritation had made the last few moments a bit tense. Ellen had thanked her profusely and "stroked" her with praise, but it was clear that she was pushing her luck.

Ellen turned out all of the lights in the living room and walked back into the kitchen to make herself a cup of something hot. Perhaps it would help her sleep.

The copper kettle soon began to chirp its monotonous tune. Ellen took the hot water from the stove, poured it over a pile dark brown crystals in the bottom of her cup, and stirre mixture. She shook the droplets of water from the plas that covered the late edition of Tuesday evening's off the plastic, and placed the folded newspaper under her arm. With her free hand she turned off the lights in the kitchen, then she walked down the long hall toward her bedroom, carefully measuring each step, balancing the cup so as not to spill anything.

She paused at the first door. It was cracked open. A shaft of light from the hall sliced through the room and fell across a little bed. In the light's path she could see the back of her son's curly head. She pushed open the door and tiptoed quietly across the room, stood at the edge of the crib, and leaned over the tiny figure.

Ellen could hear raspy breathing over the steady hum of a vaporizer. The child seemed constantly to be nursing a cold. Ringlets of tousled hair were plastered against his perspiring forehead. His eyes were tightly shut, his forehead wrinkled, his mouth turned down at the corners in the faintest frown. His favorite bear was scrunched up in the corner of his bed, far from his grasp, and his blanket was in a wad at his feet.

"No wonder he is frowning," Ellen whispered to herself as she reached down and untangled the cover, folding it out of the way. "Don't worry, Chad," she said quietly. "Mommy's home." She patted his moist brow, then took the fuzzy, love-worn bear and tucked it up under one little arm.

"Lullaby, and good night," she sang softly, looking down at her son. How guilty she felt at moments like this. She longed to be able to spend more time with him. She hated it when the pressure of her work kept her away until after he had drifted off to sleep. Another day had passed her by, another day of her son's life gone forever, spent without her.

Ellen couldn't remember a time in her life when she hadn't known inner conflict of one kind or another.

She had been an only child. By all rights she shouldn't have had to worry about pursuing her parents for their attention, but she did so anyway. Ironically, her only competition had been herself.

She had been slow to develop physically. Her most painful memories were of long periods spent at the full-length mirror, staring at her awkward, gangly body, wondering if she would enjoy the soft curves and attractive shapeliness that she saw in other girls her age. Such comparisons were as in-for her parents as they were for her. Real or imagined,

Ellen was haunted by the belief that her parents were disappointed in her spindly legs, her shapeless chest, and her plain, freckled face. These thoughts fed upon themselves, producing in her a seriousness that only served to make her that much less attractive. Thus the vicious cycle continued.

Convinced that she was a failure in the eyes of her mother and father, Ellen sought acceptance in the only area she saw open to her. She turned to books and the pursuit of knowledge.

Learning had always come easy to her. She had been reading and writing long before she entered the first grade, rarely participating in the childish activities of her peers. As a teenager in the turbulent Sixties, she was as serious as the times in which she lived. She had a keen, inquisitive mind that refused to accept anything without asking questions and demanding plausible explanations. Teachers loved her and encouraged her intellectual curiosity. She flourished and bloomed in the classroom, finding there the acceptance that she sorely needed. With each new academic achievement, her parents' pride became more obvious. That made her work even harder.

But life was not all work and no play for Ellen. She bloomed in other ways as well. Gradually, the spindly legs grew into shapely limbs, the freckled face and straggly hair to a charming countenance crowned by beautiful auburn tresses that highlighted the freckles that lingered on her cheeks. The effect was one of beauty and innocence, a youthful freshness that conveyed both childish enthusiasm and womanly appeal.

The boys who had ignored her early on soon became young men standing in line to win her favor. But the die was cast for Ellen. The love of knowledge and a desire for excellence had been born at an early age, and nurtured to full flower during the lonely days of her youth. The young men of her generation were a day late and a dollar short. She simply had no interest in anyone who was unable to challenge her mind.

Near the end of her high-school days, two tragic events took place. Both were destined to have a significant impact on the course of her life.

First, her father relieved his middle-age stresses by leaving her mother for a much younger woman. Ellen witnessed in horror the crippling effect of this impetuous decision on her mother. The poor woman was devastated. Her marriage had been happy one day and destroyed the next, ending without warning. Aging noticeably overnight, she turned from a loving, caring, attentive mother into a bitter, hostile shrew. And Ellen bore the brunt of that change.

Ellen's mother had been wiped out financially as well. She was ill-equipped to face the task of supporting herself and her daughter. The poor, frustrated woman had no place to go for help, either financially or emotionally. The burden of this sudden responsibility took a terrible toll. More and more she lost her ability to cope, until one day she suffered a complete nervous breakdown. Then and there, Ellen vowed that she would never find herself at the mercy of a man.

Ellen's academic achievements saw her through college with little financial strain. She excelled as an undergraduate and had her pick of the best law schools. Fate decreed that she would wind up as a classmate of Todd Hayes. An editor of the Law Review, he was an equally aggressive student who saw in Ellen both beauty and intellectual challenge. They fell in love instantly, and a wedding soon followed. Unfortunately, though, Todd nurtured a traditional view of the relationship between husband and wife. Conflict intruded on their happiness almost from the start. He had never been involved with a woman whom he could not dominate. This was a new experience for him, and he had completely underestimated Ellen's determination for professional success.

During those years Ellen worked constantly to prepare herself to practice law. With a single-mindedness that Todd grudgingly admired, she nursed her ambitions and drove herself toward her goal. The first woman in her family to aspire to something beyond the traditional woman's role, she was determined to be a success. Then, just when the brass ring seemed within her grasp, she found out that she was pregnant.

At first she was angry. She and Todd began to fight openly over his expectations of her role as a mother. She resented the child even before he was born, and after Chad arrived, in spite of her genuine love for the tiny boy, she simply wasn't able to live up to her husband's expectations.

Todd regarded this failure as entirely Ellen's fault. Fed up, he left for good—and tried to take Chad with him.

Ellen won that battle, though, and retained custody. Now, at twenty-nine, she found herself with no choice. Like it or not, the responsibilities of career and motherhood were thrust upon her with equal force. It seemed so unfair, especially at times like this.

"I'm doing my best, dear little baby, I really am," Ellen whispered. "Someday you'll understand, you'll see." She kissed the tips of her fingers and pressed them against Chad's cheek, then quietly left the room.

In her bedroom, Ellen placed the coffee cup and newspaper on the night table by the bed. She turned back the blue coverlet, and fluffed up the pillows. Across the room she caught a glimpse of herself in the full-length mirror. Her auburn hair was damp and matted; streaks of mascara trailed down her face. Water spots from the rain still covered her dress. "You big-time trial lawyer, you," she said, mocking her bedraggled image. Then she patted her hair dry, changed into a warm flannel gown, and slipped beneath the sheets. Finally settled in, she took a sip of the tepid coffee, unfolded the paper, and began to read.

JORDAN JURY LOCKED UP

To the surprise of most observers, the jury in the Frank Jordan murder trial reached the end of the day without a verdict. At 6:00 P.M., Judge Henry Coleman finally ordered the ten men and two women sequestered for the night, ending more than seven hours of fruitless deliberation.

After more than a week of testimony and extended legal arguments, the case was finally submitted to the jury Tuesday, after Judge Coleman instructed the jury on the law before a packed courtroom and a television audience that took advantage of the rare opportunity to look in on the judicial proceedings.

Jordan, a 20-year-old high-school dropout, is accused in the brutal slaying of 12-year-old Wendy Rogers. Jordan has remained impassive during the long trial. His two lawyers, veteran criminal attorney Martin McPherson and his associate Ellen Hayes, argued strenuously that Jordan was insane at the time the crime was committed. According to their theory, he was not capable of being responsible for his actions, hence he should not be found guilty.

The controversy over the mental state of Jordan, who was twice arrested as a juvenile for sex-related attacks on young girls, has polarized public opinion in what was already the most publicized case in this city's recent history.

Argued strenuously, Ellen mused. She and McPherson had fought like dogs over that issue. Frank Jordan is no more insane than I am, she thought. She had boiled inside while listening to her boss urge the jury to let that deranged killer off the hook, all because he was allegedly incapable of making rational decisions while his hands closed around that poor child's throat and squeezed out her last breath. She resented having her name connected with that argument. She had told McPherson exactly how she felt in no uncertain terms. It was the final rift in their steadily weakening relationship. When this trial was over she would be moving to her own office.

Funny, she thought, every time I think I have established a good relationship, things just fall apart and I have to start over. She took another sip and read on.

The body of Wendy Rogers, daughter of Mr. and Mrs. William Rogers of Hillside Drive, was found stuffed in a drainage culvert off New Hope Road last November, following the most intensive manhunt in the city's history. For three days, hundreds of volunteers combed the Belleview area after the little girl disappeared from Belleview Middle School. She had been reported missing by her older brother, Jeffrey, a 16-year-old junior at Belleview High. Arriving late to pick her up, Jeffrey found his sister's schoolbooks partially hidden under the bushes lining the front walkway of the school. He alerted his parents, who later called the police.

Less than 24 hours after the girl's disappearance, police obtained a confession from Jordan, a construction worker who was part of a crew doing maintenance work at Belleview Middle School. But Jordan quickly retracted the confession and steadfastly refused to help authorities locate the child. Though both the confession and Jordan's juvenile record were later excluded from evidence and were not revealed to the jury, overwhelming circumstantial evidence linked Jordan to the slaying, prompting veteran court observers to predict a quick verdict. But a quick verdict has not come. Deliberation will resume at 9 A.M. tomorrow.

Ellen put the paper down. "The confession was later excluded from evidence. . . ." she repeated softly. "Just because the door wasn't locked, and the poor, unsuspecting police went on in without any warrant." It was almost as if Frank Jordan had figured out what was happening and had blurted out his confession before the police had time to realize what they had stumbled on to.

Ellen stared blankly into space. How can people ever have any confidence in a system of justice that contorts itself into convoluted postures to protect killers, while ignoring the plight of their victims she wondered. The article had reminded her all over again of the spontaneous admission of this brutal killer, his history of sex-related offenses, and how these vital facts would never be heard by the jury which would decide his fate. She felt the same nausea, the same revulsion that she had felt in court.

I'm lucky to be getting out while I still have my sanity, she thought. Tomorrow was it. She was moving out. McPherson would just have to accept it. Her decision was final, not just the passing whim of a capricious female.

"That's what he thinks, no doubt," she thought as she leaned her head back against the pillow and closed her eyes.

Ellen checked the alarm clock to be certain that it was properly set. It was nearly midnight. The whole thing would begin again in too short a time. She turned sideways, settled her head into the downy mass of pillows, and reached back with one arm to massage the mounting tension in her neck muscles. Then she closed her eyes and began a fruitless search for sleep.

She wasn't the only one who would be unable to find the healing balm of untroubled sleep this night.

‖8‖

"**H**elp me, help me!" Wendy screamed as the swirling black water splashed around her shoulders. One blood-soaked hand clung to a piece of broken wood to keep her from sinking. Her dark eyes were alive with terror, her face was contorted in anguish. Piercing cries could barely be heard above the roar of the water as she floated around in an endless circle, drifting closer and closer to the center of the deep black whirlpool. As she came near the shore, she extended her arm toward her mother, stretching it forward with all her might, but to no avail. She floated quickly by, pulled away from safety by violent currents that were beyond her control. Farther and farther she floated, farther and farther from sanctuary and rescue, nearer and nearer to the dreaded vortex. "*Mommy, Mommy!*" Wendy cried.

Carol Rogers bolted upright in bed, her eyes wide with fear, her heart pounding. Shuddering, she tightened her arms across her chest. In an instant, reality dawned. She was in her own bed, next to her husband. She looked at the clock on the bedside table. It was one-thirty in the morning. Wednesday had arrived early.

That nightmare, that awful, horrible nightmare . . . Would

it ever go away? She couldn't begin to count the times she had endured this same dream since Wendy's disappearance. It was always the same. Wendy clinging to a floating scrap of wood. Sweet, innocent Wendy, rushing by and reaching for help. So close, so real, yet inexorably floating toward the final depths while Carol stood helpless at the water's edge.

Carol looked over at Bill. His head was buried in his pillow. He was sound asleep, unaware of her agony.

She hadn't told him about her dream. There were other things she hadn't told him about, too—lonely afternoons driving aimlessly to and from the school where Wendy had spent her final day, the terrible heaviness she felt all day long, the times she would sit alone in Wendy's room, lost in painful memories. At times she was almost catatonic.

Bill could tell that she was upset and depressed. So was he. Somehow he didn't show it. He locked those feelings away in a tiny little box somewhere in the inner recesses of his heart, locked them up so tightly that none would ever escape. He showed nothing, and he shared nothing. Carol resented this deeply. She tried to understand, but couldn't. He had always been that way, but why now? Why at a time when she needed him most?

In retaliation, she cut him out of her feelings as well. Bill could not possibly help her, because she would never let him know how bad it was. Life went on for everyone else, but life had stopped for her on that fateful day. Life had stopped. Now she was just waiting for it to end.

For the first few weeks after Wendy's death, Carol had been haunted by her own imagination. She couldn't help but think about the last hours in her daughter's life. She conjured up visions of panic-stricken moments and unspeakable indignities, images that pursued her mercilessly until she finally found solace in forced activity. But in her quiet times, the visions returned with all their fury.

Carol sat on the edge of the bed and slid her feet into her slippers. She pulled her faded blue robe about her shoulders and walked out into the dark hall. Alone and isolated, she faced another in a long series of sleepless nights.

She switched on a light and wandered down the hall toward the staircase. At the top of the stairs she paused. The door to

Wendy's room was partially open. A shaft of light from the hall sliced through the room and fell across the bed. The bed was empty. Carol pushed the door open the rest of the way.

Wendy had been her parents' pride and joy from the moment she was born. A darling child, unmistakably female even as a baby, she was brought home from the hospital with a small pink bow taped to her little bald head. It matched the bow that Bill had tied to their mailbox to herald the arrival of their daughter.

Little wisps of hair soon grew into flouncy curls that bounced about as Wendy ran through the house, getting into everything. Mischief was her middle name, but anger was impossible when she flashed her impish, winning smile. Bill had always said that Wendy smiled with her whole face, not just her lips. He was right. She seemed to glow when she was happy.

Carol loved to dress Wendy up and show her off. Her wardrobe was filled with lace, ruffles, bonnets, and booties, and the ever-present ribbon in her hair. Carol spent hours dressing her daughter, talking to her, caressing her, tickling her, creating a bond between mother and daughter that would be abruptly torn asunder twelve years later.

Visions of piano lessons and ballet recitals filled Carol and Bill's dreams for Wendy. Lovely dresses and festive parties, good schools and great books, all this and more. They wanted the best of everything for their daughter, especially the best love and attention that they were capable of giving.

Carol sat on the side of the empty bed and ran her hand along the edge of the ruffled canopy. She traced the smooth surface of the tall bedpost with her fingers. The room looked just the way it had looked when Wendy left it, the bed still neatly made, the green quilted spread still home for an assortment of stuffed animals. Loyal friends, waiting for the owner who would never return.

"A big-girl bed! Oh boy, a big-girl bed!" Wendy had chortled, expressing her glee as she bounced up and down on the mattress for the first time, even before the sheets had been put on. It had taken some doing to make her calm down long enough to make up the bed. They had just known that she would love it. Somehow a little princess like that deserved a canopy bed.

Carol wandered over to the dresser and looked down at the small photo of Wendy posing in her Brownie uniform. Suddenly a wave of images crowded in on her. Bald-headed Wendy in her christening gown, letting out a wail as the tiny sprinkle of cold water rolled down her cheek. Wendy in a pink sundress, still in diapers, taking her first tenuous steps toward her father's outstretched arms and then plopping down on her well-padded bottom. Wendy with her first missing tooth. Wendy on the front porch, pencil case and pad in hand, on her first day of school. Wendy in the May Day pageant, dressed in white, sneaking a glance at the audience to see who was looking. Warm memories, good memories, experienced with pride and satisfaction.

In truth, all that Carol had ever really wanted for her daughter was the kind of childhood that she had enjoyed herself.

The third child of middle-class parents, Carol had been the first girl on either side of the family, lavished with love and attention by parents and grandparents alike. Blessed with an outgoing personality, she had responded by being equally loving and attentive. She was the center of activity in their home, a position she clearly relished.

Weekdays were spent at her mother's side, listening to her read, or walking in the nearby park. Carol would climb into one of the swings and cry, "Push me, Mommy, push me!" On weekends she became Daddy's girl, following him around as he did his chores, being his "helper" and his companion. Early memories were consistently warm for Carol: ballet and tap recitals, piano lessons, school plays—she was always involved, and her parents, beaming with pride, were always there.

Throughout her childhood, until the day she left home to live with her husband, Carol's parents saw to it that she attended church every week. They were strict fundamentalists, and they raised their children in the fear of the Lord. Faith had always been a vital part of Carol's life as far back as she could remember, and it still was.

Carol loved her two brothers, and they worshipped her. The boys were both excellent students, moving through high school and college with facility, paving the way for their younger sister. Carol excelled academically, earning straight A's in high school. She easily made the honor society, and graduated near the top of her class. High school was great fun in the late Fifties, a carefree time of bobby sox and circle pins, saddle oxfords and angora sweaters, Chevy convertibles and "Rock Around the Clock."

Carol had lived in a legendary time, though she had no way of knowing it then, and she had enjoyed it to the hilt.

In spite of her academic success, little effort was spent on selecting a college. She enrolled in a school in her hometown without giving it a second thought and began taking courses designed to provide her with marketable office skills.

There was no such thing as a "double standard" then, though she couldn't help but notice from time to time that there was a great deal of discussion about her brothers and their future careers, while her role as a future homemaker was taken for granted. That didn't matter. Marriage and family suited her nicely.

When Carol quit college after her sophomore year to marry Bill Rogers, her parents greeted the news with excitement. The tears they shed were tears of joy. Neither she nor they gave any thought to missed opportunities or wasted talents.

Marriage was fun. Bill was still a student, and Carol went to work to help put him through school. She enjoyed the company of other wives who were helping to finance their husbands' education. She looked forward to meeting Bill at their modest apartment at the close of each day. Bill graduated, and the two of them settled down to an enjoyable routine. With two incomes, they managed nicely for a year or two. Then came Jeffrey.

Carol loved Jeffrey deeply, even though she had secretly nurtured the desire for a girl all during her pregnancy. Lace and ruffles were out of the question, of course, but she dressed Jeffrey up as much as Bill would tolerate, and showed him off with great pride. As he grew older, however, she could see his interests drifting toward the things Bill enjoyed—fishing, hunting, sports—things that meant little to Carol. An emptiness still lingered in her life, a void that was finally filled when Wendy was born, only to be created anew in the fall of Carol's thirty-ninth year, when Wendy was wrenched from her life in a burst of unspeakable violence.

"Wendy, my baby," Carol whispered as she stood in the shadow-filled bedroom, letting her mind wander through the memories that permeated the room.

As always, the final memory returned to haunt her. Once again she felt the empty, helpless feeling of those three terrible days when the search dragged on. Once more she heard the grating sound of the cold, impersonal slab pulled out to reveal the gray, lifeless face. Once more she felt the final realization that it was Wendy, and it was over. Once more she surrendered to gut-wrenching, uncontrollable spasms of grief. Tears poured from her eyes, but no sound came forth. So deep was her grief that she couldn't even find relief in an honest cry.

The days leading up to the trial had been bad enough. But the six days in court had been horrible, unbelievable. For six days she had sat across the table from Frank Jordan, looking into his face. Here was a man who had brutally abused and killed her daughter. Everyone knew it. And yet for six days they had all been trapped in that courtroom, enduring public scrutiny, listening to the endless recounting of a horrible series of events, but hearing only part of the story.

Here was a man whose very lips had spoken of his guilt, and yet the jury was told only the smallest part of the truth while his skilled, highly paid lawyers eschewed justice and pleaded for freedom on the grounds of insanity. Insanity! Everything's possible in the name of insanity! No matter what might ever be done to Frank Jordan, his punishment could never compare to her own. She had been forced to endure the horror of this trial, forced to relive Wendy's death again and again until she could take no more.

"I'm the one being punished!" she cried out loud, clenching her teeth lest the sound of her rage escape into the still quiet of the spring evening and awaken her husband.

Finally she put the picture back in its place, exactly where Wendy had kept it. She stared at herself in the mirror, seeing red eyes encased in dark circles, skin puffy and blotched. She turned away, not wanting to look. She left the room and tiptoed down the stairs at a measured pace, finding her way to the small, tidy kitchen.

She knew where the gun was kept—it had been there for years. It was always loaded, though it had never been used. She stared at the cabinet door for several seconds, then stretched to her full height. She couldn't reach it. She pulled over a stepstool and climbed up, probing deep into the cabinet. Fumbling around for a moment, she found a small lump of steel wrapped in protective felt. She took it out of its hiding place.

"It's strictly for protection," Bill had told her on the day he brought it home. He showed her how to use it but warned her to be careful. "Don't take it down unless it's a real emergency. It's not a toy. Don't ever get it out unless you really need it."

"I need it. I really need it," she said out loud now.

She sat down at the kitchen table and placed the gun in front of her. Then she bowed her head and folded her hands in front of her like a small child in a Norman Rockwell painting. No words came. There was nothing left to say, not even to God.

Her large leather purse was on the counter next to the table. Rummaging around, she took out a pen and a small pad, placing a clean sheet of paper on the table. She looked at her silver pen for a moment, turning it slowly in her hand, watching the light dance off of its shiny surface. Then she began to write, haltingly at first. In a moment, she found herself writing frantically, as if possessed. The pen flew across the white surface.

She didn't hear Bill as he called her name down the staircase. She didn't realize he was coming until she heard the bottom step creak. I can't let him know, she thought. She tossed the half-finished note into the trash can in the corner, then stood up, her back to the dining-room door, the gun still tightly clutched in her trembling hands. Her eyes darted about; finally she folded her arms across her chest, with the gun stuffed up under one fluffy sleeve of her robe.

"Come back to bed, honey," Bill said as he stood in the doorway, blinking and squinting in the bright light. "Are you okay?" he asked, almost as an afterthought.

"I couldn't sleep," she said. He started toward her. Spying her purse sitting open on the counter, she shifted around quickly so that her back was toward Bill. With one hand she pulled the purse over and pretended to fumble for a Kleenex, and with the other she stuffed the gun into the purse. Then she pulled out a tissue and dabbed it against her tear-stained cheek, just as Bill's arm slipped around her shoulder.

The two of them stood together in the quiet kitchen for a moment. She leaned against him, tightening her fists into little balls to keep from trembling. Thank God, she thought. He didn't see it. She breathed a sigh of relief.

"Come on back to bed," he said. "I'll fix you something to help you sleep."

"I don't understand it, Bill. I just don't understand it. Why isn't it over? What could possibly be taking so long? I can't stand another day of this, I really can't."

Bill poured a jigger of vodka into a small glass of orange juice, then offered it to her. "This will help," he said.

"He's guilty, Bill, he's as guilty as sin. We know it, he knows it, everybody knows it. I don't think the jury will let him off. How could they? But they've been out so long. What in God's name could they be doing?"

"They won't let him off, honey. It will all be over tomorrow. You'll see." He handed her the glass. She took a sip of the tart liquid, holding it with both hands to keep it steady.

"I hope so, Bill. I hope you're right," Carol said as she walked into the darkened dining room and headed back upstairs. Bill turned out the kitchen light, leaving the still-open purse sitting on the counter.

9

At precisely 7:50 A.M. on Wednesday, on a side street one block from the municipal jail, Bess Jordan pulled her old Plymouth over to the curb and turned off the engine. She adjusted the rearview mirror to provide a view of her face. She wanted to look her best for her son.

Appearance had always been very important to her. She had tried to instill this attitude in Frank, but without success. "We may be poor," she would say to the boy as she washed behind his ears, or straightened out his collar, or parted his poker-straight hair, "but we can be clean, and we can be neat. And that's the way we are going to be, son, clean and neat." It had been like talking to a brick wall.

Typical of boys his age, Frank Jordan had invariably wound up in a state of disarray, clothes disheveled, hair sticking out in umpteen different directions. And just as invariably, almost every evening he had incurred his mother's wrath.

"Frank Jordan, you come in this house this minute!" Bess would demand, pointing an accusatory finger at her son. Sometimes she would march right into the middle of his play world without saying a word, unceremoniously snatching him up in front of his friends, grabbing an arm or twisting an ear with her strong fingers. She would lead him back home for a tongue-lashing and a good scrubbing while his friends stared in disbelief. Other times he would hear her braying voice calling from the back porch. It was the same routine, day after day. Naturally, Frank always dreaded his mother's return from work.

Bess Jordan had no choice but to work. She was their only support. But when she was at home, she was determined that Frank would have the same discipline and training as children with a full-time mother. She desperately wanted him to make something of himself, to rise above the circumstances of his birth, to pull himself, and hopefully her as well, out of their ghetto.

Bess stared at her face in the car mirror as she applied fresh lipstick. It was a pale pink, almost no color at all; like Bess herself, the makeup she wore was dull, lifeless, and nondescript. Her face had the shape and structure of real beauty, but the key ingredients were missing. She was a sallow woman with no vitality, no sparkle in her eyes, no rose in her cheeks. Years of monotonous drudgery had extinguished any flame that might once have illuminated her face. Random etchings of wrinkles had invaded from all directions, making her look much older than her fifty-one years. And to top it off, she had a perpetually stern and disapproving countenance, a "Don't you dare love me" expression that repelled warmth, affection, and kindness before they could be offered.

Bess examined a long cluster of gray hair that hung down beside her face, which had succeeded in escaping the tortuous bun perpetually imprisoning the rest of her hair. The bun was severe, and not at all flattering, but it was easy to do and it stayed in place. The ubiquitous bun had become a part of her personality; she could scarcely remember ever being without it. She reached up and hastily tucked the offending strand safely behind her ear.

Satisfied that there was nothing else she could do to improve her appearance, she positioned the mirror back in place, unbuckled her seat belt, and opened the car door.

The car, like Bess, was durable and dependable, but unadorned and colorless. She had walked on to a dealer's lot one day and simply bought the first sedan she'd seen. She didn't look around, haggle, or deal. She just turned to the salesman and said, "I'll take it." Paid cash, too. Full sticker price. Like everything else in her life, she didn't do it until she could afford it, and once she had saved up enough money to do it, she made her purchase without style or flair.

Bess closed the car door and checked to be certain that it had locked. After studying herself one last time in the car window, she glanced at her watch. It was almost eight. She must hurry. She would be able to visit with Frank for a few minutes, but only if she arrived promptly at eight. Court would open at nine, and Frank would be inaccessible.

She had visited him every day while he was awaiting trial, and every day during the trial, too. It was important to her not to miss this visit, or any other. She felt that it was her duty to be by his side, to show her support on a daily basis. That's what a good mother would do, she had thought. Not wanting to be late, she walked quickly toward the Municipal Jail Building.

In spite of her dour expression and prim lifestyle, there had once been a "brief shining moment" in Bess Jordan's life. There had been a time when her beautiful dark hair had fallen free and cascaded down her shoulders, spiraling into a myriad of waves and curls, a time when she had run barefoot through the grass and felt the cool breeze on bare shoulders, a glorious time of love and passion, long, long ago.

More than twenty years had passed since Harvey Jordan had walked into her life. By that time she had reached thirty and settled into single adulthood with the kind of melancholy resignation typical for unmarried women of her era.

As the youngest of three girls, she had watched with delight as her older sisters matured, finished high school, and entered into courtship. Her sisters were vivacious young ladies whose main problem was deciding which suitor to marry. Life for them had been a picture-book experience. Popularity came easy as they waltzed through youth on their way to their appointed destinies with motherhood. Whether that was really true or not didn't matter to Bess. That's the way it seemed, and the appearance of things was all she knew.

As she grew older, Bess examined her own life and remembered what her sisters were like and what they were doing at the same age. The comparison was inevitably disheartening. Nothing ever happened for her the way she wanted it to, or the way she felt her parents expected it to. Indeed, she saw herself becoming more and more of a burden to them, as well as an embarrassment. She didn't seem to have that special something that men found attractive. For the life of her she couldn't figure out why, but one thing was certain: she knew she didn't have it, and she had no idea how to get it.

Bess tried to talk to her mother, but without success. There was never any true understanding between them; it was never two women talking to each other with each hearing what the other had to say. The fine art of listening was lost on Bess's mother. It was as true then as it was now: Where there is no listening, there can be no genuine understanding, and certainly no meaningful communication.

Bess gradually developed a defense against the pain of alienation. She simply quit trying to talk to her mother, even though she continued to long for the woman's guidance. As for her father, he was the archetypal stern disciplinarian, the untouchable power-figure. She never felt comfortable enough to try to communicate with him in the first place.

Well-meaning friends tried to help. They encouraged her to have confidence in herself, and set her up with blind dates. But nothing seemed to click. High-school graduation came and went. Though she was a good student, college was never a consideration. In her world, women didn't go to college. She got a job in a dry-goods store and continued to live at home, consoling herself with the notion that it was her lot to take care of her parents in their old age—a noble but depressing task.

Then along came Private First-Class Harvey Jordan. He just showed up one day at the store where she worked. He was the handsomest man she had ever seen, and he asked her out immediately. She declined, knowing that her mother would never approve, but Harvey was persistent and quite clever. He found out where she went to church and showed up there one Sunday. How could Bess's parents possibly object to a man who came to church?

A whirlwind courtship ensued. Bess was a new person. Harvey was attentive to her needs. He cared about her feelings; he was the first person who had ever really done so.

He took her to all of the places she had never been. He swept her off her feet and into a world of parties, picnics, moonlight walks, and church socials. Tall and handsome, he was an impressive escort. She was very proud of him, and never missed a chance to show him off.

Romance was heady stuff for this thirty-year-old woman. She believed strongly in the institution of marriage, in the importance of virginity, and in all of the other "right" things. But he begged and begged. Though she knew better, she gave in for fear of losing him. He represented her last great hope.

Bess, herself, wasn't able to enjoy the experience, but Harvey certainly did, and as often as she would submit. Bess's mother had warned her not to "do it," that sex was dirty and nasty, and her mother turned out to be right. Bess soon felt used. She tried to talk to Harvey, but their discussions always turned into arguments, then into fights. Things went from bad to worse in a very short time.

Harvey Jordan never knew that Bess was pregnant. He had left the matter of birth control up to her, but hadn't told her. She knew practically nothing about the subject and had simply assumed that he would take care of such things.

Bess never knew that Harvey had been transferred. All of a sudden one day he was gone, as quickly as he had come. No note, no explanation, nothing. Mortified and unable to face her family and friends, she packed her bags in the middle of the night, withdrew her meager savings the next morning, and took the first bus to the city, where she remained until Frank was born.

Bess never saw her parents again. She couldn't face them. They considered her a disgrace, marking her off as a teacher might mark off a child who had left school and was never coming back. With a stroke of the will, she simply no longer existed.

Bess took on Harvey Jordan's name and created a fantasy to satisfy her son when he asked about his father. Unfortunately, the fantasy backfired. She portrayed Frank's father as such a saint that Frank naturally assumed his father's absence must be his mother's fault. Thus began a rift between mother and son that would never be mended.

Bess Jordan dedicated herself to her son. He was the only thing in the world that still mattered. She tried her best. She managed to feed and clothe them and to provide a roof over their heads, but that was only a small part of the responsibility that had fallen to her by default, and there was just so much time in each day.

Within the limitations set by her ability, she devoted as many hours as possible to Frank's nurture and discipline, sacrificing her own pleasures in the process. This added an element of martyrdom which further complicated an already complex relationship. After all these years of sacrifice, Frank's failure to amount to anything was a source of great frustration and concern. She had been upset enough by his bouts with juvenile authorities. Now, his apparent involvement in a horrible crime created a double burden for her to bear as she stood at the door of the municipal jail that morning, seeking admission. For all of that, she was determined to stand by her only son. Prodigal that he was, he was her own flesh and blood, and she would be his mother to the bitter end.

Deep in the bowels of the municipal jail building, Frank Jordan sat on the bare cot in the spartan atmosphere of his maximum-security cell. He knew that his mother was coming. He also knew that she would be on time. Of that he could be certain. She was always on time. Always prompt, always punctual, always dependable—everything that he was not. Frank Jordan hated his mother's guts.

It was all a matter of perspective. Bess Jordan thought that she had done her very best, and perhaps she had. But something vital had been missing. Sure, she worked her fingers to the bone to provide for him, but she reminded him of her sacrifice on a daily basis. She did everything possible to make him be all of the things she wanted him to be, but no matter what he did, nothing was ever good enough. Nothing ever gained her approval.

When Frank told Bess that he had landed a good part in the school play, she asked why he didn't get the lead. When he brought home grades of which he was proud, she reminded him that he could do better. When he dared to mention the name of a girl he liked, she told him that there was no girl in the entire school worthy of his attention. Nothing was good enough, no matter how hard he tried. He was unable to win her approval. He finally quit trying and rebelled against her authority completely.

Frank dropped out of school and got a job as a short-order cook, moving out of his mother's house as soon as he was legally able. He dated a series of women but never established a lasting relationship. Inevitably he would become angry with them. Though he didn't realize it, he almost always saw his mother in their actions, or heard her voice in their words. He would lash out and try to hurt them, unaware that it was really his mother who was the object of his wrath. No woman would put up with such erratic behavior very long, and none ever did.

The latest had been a thirty-three-year-old divorcee with two small children who had shared her trailer and her body with him until she could no longer put up with his outbursts. She had locked him out and left his belongings in the back seat of his car two weeks before the tragic death of Wendy Rogers. It was the last straw, a final rejection that exploded violently within him, creating a storm of emotion that finally found release in the tragic death of an innocent girl, whose name he had never even known.

Now Frank heard a key scratching around in the lock. The heavy metal door to his cell swung open. He knew what was happening; he didn't have to be told. It was time to go to the visitors' room. The woman he hated more than anything in the world, and the only woman he would ever love, had arrived for her daily visit, on time as usual.

‖10‖

few hundred yards away from
the Municipal Jail, in far more comfortable surroundings, Martin
McPherson was leaning against the doorjamb at the entrance to
Ellen Hayes's office, watching her sort through the contents of
her desk. McPherson's white hair was disheveled, his eyes red
and watery from too many sleepless nights. A gold chain extended across the front of his blue pin-striped vest. At the other
end of the chain was an old pocket watch, which he flipped open
with one hand.

"It's almost eight-thirty, Ellen. Judge Coleman wants us in
court at nine so that he can bring in the jury and give them
his famous pep talk. We need to leave here in twenty minutes
or so."

"I'll be ready," Ellen answered without looking up.

McPherson's office was in an old building directly across from
the Municipal Courts Building. Some years earlier he had bought
an abandoned warehouse and had remodeled it completely, one
of many smart moves on his part. Such properties were at a
premium now. He had rented most of it, but the showpiece was
his own suite of offices, located right in the center of the building.

His quarters were filled with antiques and collectibles, reflecting both affluence and good taste. "You don't want your clients to think that nobody else has ever paid you the kind of bucks you are charging them," he had once told Ellen, by way of justifying one of his more outlandish purchases. Thus he greeted his clients from an antique swivel chair drawn up to a massive roll-top desk; by contrast, Ellen's desk was plain, utilitarian, modern, and nondescript. But when she had crossed McPherson's threshold four years earlier as a neophyte lawyer, this cubicle had seemed like the most beautiful place in the world.

Fellow graduates at her law school had fallen all over themselves trying to curry favor with McPherson during his visit to the school to personally interview prospective associates. She had been surprised when he agreed to interview her, and stunned when he selected her to intern at his side. While one might find fault with some of the causes he defended, it was impossible to find fault with his skill as a defender. A few years at his side was equivalent to a lifetime of experience with most other law firms.

McPherson watched as Ellen took her diploma down from the wall, carefully wrapped it in newspaper, and placed it in one of the boxes that surrounded her desk. The silence was uncomfortable.

"What makes you think things are going to be any different anywhere else?" he asked quietly.

Ellen looked up. "Do we have to go through this again?" she moaned. "We've been over and over it. I have nothing else to say."

"Then just listen," McPherson said, entering the crowded room and sitting on the edge of her desk. "I've got some things to say to you, even if you don't have anything to say to me." Ellen kept on packing while her boss talked.

"Ellen, you've got a bright future. Clients like you. Many of them have started asking for you. You have an incisive mind; you get to the point as quickly as anyone I've ever had up here. I just can't see you throwing all of this away for a hole-in-the-wall office with a phone that probably won't ever ring. I really think you're making a mistake."

"I'm not cut out for criminal law, Mac, and you know it. I guess I'm just too sympathetic."

"Sympathetic, hell," McPherson snorted. "I'm just as sympathetic as you are. Your problem isn't sympathy, it's bleeding-heart idealism."

Ellen bristled. This was the standard catchall McPherson used for anyone who disagreed with him.

"Ellen, listen to me," he continued. "You're being unrealistic. This is life, real life. You're a defense lawyer. You've got a job to do. Your responsibility is to put together the best possible defense for your clients. If you really want to search for truth, go get yourself some incense and a white robe and go live on a mountain. If you want to practice law, here or anywhere else, you've got to forget all of that and learn to work within the system."

"To hell with the system," Ellen snapped back, immediately regretting her intemperance and disrespect.

"That's easy enough to say," McPherson retorted, apparently unabashed, "but the system works. It may be crazy, it may be convoluted, it may seem unreal and unjust sometimes, but it works, better than any system has ever worked before. Unless you know something that nobody else knows, it's gonna keep on working, too."

"Look, Mac," Ellen said, softening her voice, "your system is about to return a not-guilty verdict against a twenty-year-old reprobate with a history of weird acts, who snuffed out the life of a poor little girl whose only crime was being female and alone in her own school. He's guilty! We have known that since the very first day we met him! And yet for the last several weeks our goal in life has been to make it absolutely impossible for the jury to put him away. And the hell of it is that we just might succeed. I don't know how that makes you feel, but that makes me sick! At this moment the last thing on my mind is singing the praises of your precious system."

"Guilt is a relative term, Ellen, you know that," McPherson answered. "In the legal sense he isn't guilty until the jury says so. The real question is whether the state is going to needlessly execute a young man who really wasn't in his right mind, who really wasn't capable of making moral choices, or whether we are going to institutionalize him and put him where he can get some help. What possible good can we do by 'snuffing out,' as you so bluntly put it, two lives instead of one? What will that accomplish?"

"It would take one more killer off the streets, that's what," Ellen responded. "Mac, you know as well as I do that there is no guarantee that the state will keep him even if he is sent to the mental institute. They sure as hell won't cure him. We know that without asking. They haven't cured anyone in years. They mean well enough, but they don't have the money or the staff. They'll examine him every few months, and then as soon as they think he's able to function in society, out he goes. That could be six months, maybe a year. Hell, it could even be less. I just can't live with that. He shouldn't ever be out on the street again."

"You're talking about extremes, about what might theoretically happen, Ellen. That's not fair, and it's not realistic either. You know damn good and well that's not going to happen. If they ever get him, the state's gonna keep him."

"How can you be so sure?" she replied. "I'd give anything if I could believe that, but I can't! There's no way to predict what those psychiatrists will say, and you know it. Your Doctor Green is a prime example."

"Norman Green is an excellent psychiatrist," McPherson retorted. "His credentials are impeccable."

"He's a hired gun," Ellen replied. "He'll say whatever he thinks you want to hear. He's nothing more than a medical pimp. His calling card should read 'Have Opinion, Will Travel.' "

McPherson's face reddened. He straightened up to his full height and took Ellen's shoulders in his hands, staring down into her distraught face. "Ellen, you'd best be careful. You're going to say something you'll regret later."

Ellen looked up into the face of her mentor. She really liked and admired him, though at times they fought like cats and dogs. Martin McPherson gave his all for his clients, leaving absolutely no stone unturned. He was the consummate advocate: tough but ethical, aggressive but fair, totally dedicated to his cause. She admired that, even coveted it for herself. But so often she found herself trapped between her training as an advocate and her inevitable empathy for the real people involved in her cases.

"I'm sorry, Mac," she said softly, taking his hands in hers. "I don't want to hurt you. I really don't. I admire you. You've been good to me. You've given me opportunities I never dreamed possible, and I'm grateful. But I just don't think this is the life for me. I've got to step back and take another look. I've got to get away from this pressure and try to sort out all that has happened to me. You've given me a wonderful opportunity to learn, but I'm ready to do things my way. I know you can see that. Can't you?"

The question was never answered. The buzzer on Ellen's telephone suddenly broke the silence. Ellen pressed the "local" button. "Yes?" she queried.

"Is Mr. McPherson in there?" It was his secretary, Lorene Fulcher.

"I'm right here," McPherson answered.

"It's ten till nine, Mr. McPherson. You told me to remind you," Lorene Fulcher said.

"Thanks, we're on our way," McPherson replied. "Let's go, Ellen," he said, extending his hand toward her. "Time to go watch old Coleman do his thing."

"Mac," Ellen said quietly, "thanks for everything. I'm grateful to you, I really am. It's been one hell of an experience."

"You're welcome," he answered, smiling, picking up her suit jacket and holding it for her while she slipped her arms into the sleeves. The two of them walked together down the short hall to his office, where he picked up his leather briefcase.

Outside, in the glare of the morning sun, they waited for a break in the busy traffic, then crossed Broad Street to the plaza in front of the courthouse, blending into the flow of human traffic climbing the wide granite stairs. Together they entered the Municipal Courts Building through the great bronze doors. Like most of the people who would come in and out of that massive building on this business day, they were oblivious to the huge bronze relief carving of blind justice that graced the front facade.

11

"Members of the jury, I hope you had a pleasant evening, and I hope you are ready to go back to work. But before you return to the jury room to deliberate, there are a few things I need to say." Judge Coleman put down his notes and slowly removed his reading glasses, holding them in front of him as he swiveled his chair toward the jury box. He didn't need any notes at this point. He knew what he was going to say.

The judge's enormous black leather swivel chair was perched behind the dark mahogany judicial bench that had served as the focal point of Division Two of the Criminal Court since the Municipal Courts Building was completed in 1936. The massive building was designed in "courthouse classic" architecture, a styleless conglomeration of the most cumbersome features of Greek, Egyptian, and Roman traditions. In short, it was a monstrosity.

The old courtroom seemed especially somber this morning. For the first time in several days, the temporary television lights which had been strategically placed in the chamber were not turned on. There was no need for the public to view this morning's routine proceedings.

"Members of the jury, the bailiff tells me that when you were sent to dinner last night, one of you mentioned to him that you were deadlocked. I need to ask you about that. But first, I need to know which one of you has been elected foreman?"

"I am the foreman, Your Honor." The answer came from a man in the middle of the back row. His location indicated that the jury had taken his election seriously. More often than not the person seated nearest the judge ends up being elected foreman, simply because this is the seat where the foreman sits in most fictional courtroom scenes.

The bailiff motioned for the foreman to stand. Judge Coleman slipped on his glasses and glanced down at the seating chart on the desk in front of him. A few awkward seconds passed before he located the right name.

"Mr. Prentiss, as foreman, I want you to tell me what the last count was yesterday evening, before you went to your evening meal. I don't want you to tell me which way the vote went, whether the majority voted for guilt or innocence, that wouldn't be proper. Just tell me the count."

"Your Honor," Arnold Prentiss responded nervously, "the last vote was nine to three." A murmur swept through the packed gallery.

Judge Coleman rapped his gavel down and the noise stopped. "Mr. Prentiss," the judge continued, "again, be careful not to give me any details, but please tell me one more thing. Has the count been nine to three for a long time, or are you making progress?"

"I believe we are making progress, Your Honor," came the reply. From the looks on the faces of the other jurors, it was apparent that there was no unanimity on this point.

"Very well, thank you, Mr. Prentiss." The judge removed his glasses, and turned his attention once again to the entire jury. Mr. Prentiss, not knowing what to do next, finally sat back down.

"Members of the jury, several days ago, after considerable questioning and agonizing, you were selected from among your peers to take on the awesome responsibility of deciding this case. These excellent lawyers have spent the last few days demonstrating a high degree of skill, and I must say that both the state and the defendant have been represented in a first-class manner." Judge Coleman adopted a dignified, sonorous tone, befitting the seriousness of the occasion.

"He thinks the television cameras are still on," Martin Mc-

Pherson whispered to Ellen Hayes. They were seated next to each other at a long table facing the jury box, at a right angle to the judge's bench.

The judge continued. "The taxpayers of this community have a considerable sum invested in these proceedings. The families involved have paid a heavy price in emotional involvement and time. The lawyers and the witnesses have done all that they can do. The state, the defendant, and the taxpayers of this community all want a final decision of this case. That can only come from you. It *must* come from you. There is no reason whatever to expect that any future jury will be better able to decide the fate of Frank Jordan than you are. I am going to send you back in there, and I want you to stay there and wrestle with this thing until you come up with a decision."

Ellen turned to her boss and spoke in a stage whisper. "He isn't supposed to do that. Surely he knows that the Supreme Court doesn't allow judges to pressure juries into compromise decisions!"

McPherson leaned toward Ellen, turning slightly so as to block the judge's view of his response. "Coleman has never been one to let the law get in his way," he observed dryly. They both swiveled back toward the judge, who was continuing with his instructions.

"Don't sacrifice your beliefs and don't give in to pressure. Each of you should be your own juror and follow your own conscience. But listen to one another. Respect one another's opinions and try to reach some unanimous decision, if you can do so in good conscience. Remember what I told you before. Your verdict must be unanimous, but it must also be the considered verdict of each and every one of you individually."

Judge Coleman leaned back in his chair and faced the lawyers. "Anything else, gentlemen?" he said. Martin McPherson and Tom Sanderson stood to respond. Ellen remained seated. The judge's deliberate use of the masculine gender was an affront to her. Whether it was intentional or not wasn't important. That kind of slight never failed to irritate her, no matter how frequently it happened.

"Nothing further, Your Honor," Sanderson answered.

"Nothing for the defense, Your Honor," McPherson stated.

"Very well, then. Members of the jury, you may return to

the jury room to resume your deliberations. As I told you before, if you have any questions, or if you reach a verdict, just knock on the door to get the bailiff's attention." Judge Coleman then stood up; everyone else followed suit. "Court is in recess until further notice, gentlemen," he announced.

That's two in a row, thought Ellen disgustedly. What a male chauvinist ass!

Judge Coleman's chauvinism was no surprise. She would never forget her first encounter with him, several years ago. She had been assisting McPherson in a small case. Judge Coleman happened by the counsel's table shortly after the case was concluded. He shook hands with McPherson and congratulated him on the victory, then put his arm around Ellen and solicitously patted her on the shoulder. At the time she chalked it up to her youth and inexperience. By now she knew better.

Tom Sanderson picked up his briefcase and retrieved his raincoat from the rack. He chatted briefly with Carol and Bill Rogers, then slipped out of the courtroom through a side door, avoiding the confusion that reigned in the gallery. Frank Jordan, who had been sitting next to Ellen, was escorted out through another door by a policeman. Carol and Bill weaved their way through the crowd to join their son, Jeffrey, and Joe Holman, their minister and friend, who had come to wait with them.

Tom Sanderson walked briskly down the hallway, his shoes clicking out a rhythm on the old marble floor. He brushed aside questions from a small group of reporters who followed him down the hall, pulled open a heavy mahogany door, and entered the reception area of the D.A.'s office, tossing a quick greeting in the direction of Helen Hawthorne, the receptionist, who was on the phone. Sanderson picked up his messages and moved on past her toward his private office, but she quickly hung up and called after him. "General Sanderson," she sang out, using his formal title as an Assistant District Attorney, "General Douglas wants to see you right away." From the way she emphasized "right away," it was obvious that she delighted in delivering this ultimatum.

Damn, Sanderson thought to himself. All I need is to have to face him now.

Tom Sanderson's feeling of chagrin was exacerbated by the

irritating tone of superiority in Helen Hawthorne's voice. Hawthorne was a fixture in the office. She had watched three district attorneys and two dozen young assistants come and go over the years. Sanderson regarded her as a busybody who thrived on conflict. She seemed to take an inordinate amount of pleasure out of watching young lawyers flounder around in ignorance. Hiding behind the protection of tenure and civil service, she dished out misery to the staff and rudeness to the general public. Why she hadn't been fired years ago was a mystery to him.

Sanderson moved quickly down the narrow hallway to his small private office. His own secretary, Mary Ann Harper, a much more pleasant sort, was at her typewriter, intensely involved with her work. She didn't see him until he was almost past her.

"How did it go? Any news?" Harper asked.

"The jury reported a nine-to-three split, and Coleman gave them his dynamite charge," Sanderson answered. "They've gone back to deliberate. Beyond that, heaven only knows what's happening." He stepped into his office, put his briefcase on the desk, and headed for his rendezvous with Carlton Douglas.

At thirty-four, Tom Sanderson was an upwardly mobile young man; he had already gone remarkably far. Tall, strikingly handsome, with just the slightest trace of premature gray at the temples, he exuded the confidence of one who knows what he is doing and where he is going.

After a distinguished law-school career that included membership in Order of the Coif and a place on the Law Review staff, he had turned down several prestige firms, choosing to gain immediate trial experience by joining District Attorney Carlton Douglas's staff nine years ago. A skilled and convincing advocate with an enormous capacity for work, he quickly rose to first-assistant status.

As first assistant, Sanderson handled the toughest, most visible cases. The Wendy Rogers murder was the juiciest in a long line of plums that had come his way. Though his future looked bright, there was no consensus as to the direction that future might take. But for his loyalty and indebtedness to Carlton Douglas, he would be an odds-on bet to run for district attorney someday. Other rumors had him lusting for the mayor's seat, perhaps even the governor's. Nothing seemed too out of reach for Tom Sanderson.

Carlton Douglas was standing behind his desk. His door was open. He saw Sanderson coming down the hall and motioned for him to come on in. Sanderson took a seat at the end of the vinyl couch nearest to Douglas's old wooden desk. The furnishings were typical government issue—adequate but certainly not impressive. Douglas's face was tense. He was obviously concerned.

Carlton Douglas was an able administrator. At forty-eight, he was in his second term as district attorney. He liked the job and he intended to keep it. What he lacked in courtroom skill he made up for in administrative savvy. He tried few cases himself, choosing instead to surround himself with bright, aggressive assistants.

At first, the press had been critical of him for not personally handling cases in court. Most reporters, though, had no real concept of the enormous administrative headaches involved in running such an office. But Douglas had survived that initial criticism. By pitting his assistants against one another and carefully parceling out choice assignments to the most aggressive and successful, he had amassed an enviable won-lost record and had secured for himself the respect and support of the community.

In recent months Carlton Douglas had been leaning heavily on Tom Sanderson. The Wendy Rogers case was the most highly publicized prosecution ever undertaken by his office. Far beyond his concern for the victims and the community, Douglas had a personal stake in victory. Losing this case could be the first step toward defeat in the next election. He felt responsible for his assistants and wanted to support them as much as possible. But above all else he wanted to win.

"What's going on down there, Tom?" he asked now. "Is everything under control? Sounds like this one may be slipping away from us."

Sanderson tried to explain what was happening, but there wasn't much to say.

"The jury is hung at nine to three. We don't know the split. I've got to believe the nine are for conviction. There isn't any way they could be voting to let that animal loose."

"I hope they're not, Tom," Douglas growled. "I thought we had a lock on this case. Not even McPherson should be able to get this guy off, but that jury has been out too damn long. The mayor's on the phone, the newspaper is on the phone, everybody in town is calling. The prophets of doom are already licking their chops. I swear, I think some people thrive on bad news. I'll tell you one thing, Tom, if we lose this one, this whole damn town's going to be wanting my scalp."

"What do you want me to say? I'm sorry?" Sanderson responded. "You know as well as I do that we've done everything we could." He rose to leave. "If the jury finds him not guilty, it'll be on their consciences, not ours."

"I know that, Tom," Douglas answered, "but if we lose this case, everybody in town will be trying to figure out some way to claim that we blew it. Look, all I ask is that you cover all of your tracks and don't leave anything out. Nothing. Don't let me down, understand?"

Sanderson left Douglas's office as quickly as he could. His face was red, his ears were ringing, his nerves were on edge. He had already felt bad enough about what was happening in court; his boss had made him feel even worse. He admired Carlton Douglas and wanted to do his best. It would have been easier for Tom if the veteran D.A. had just bawled him out and let it go at that.

Why in hell doesn't he just go ahead and chew me out? Sanderson mused. Why lay on a guilt trip? At this point, he had endured just about all of the pressure he could stand.

‖12‖

Back in the sanctuary of his private office, Tom Sanderson jerked off his coat and threw it over a chair. He slumped down into the chair behind his cluttered desk and began to sort through a three-day assortment of mail and unanswered calls. He tried to concentrate on the task at hand, but his mind kept replaying the frustrating scene in Carlton Douglas's office. In a few moments, he was interrupted by the intercom buzzer. It was Mary Ann.

"General Sanderson, Ellen Hayes is here to see you. She's out front in the reception area."

"What in the world would she want with me?" he muttered. "Just a minute," he responded into the intercom.

Good lawyers admire and respect tough opponents, and try not to let their legal controversies bleed over into personal conflicts. But at this particular moment, Tom Sanderson was deeply distressed over the possibility that he had let Carlton Douglas down, and even more worried that a deranged killer might be slipping through his fingers and back out into society. He was in no mood to fraternize with the enemy.

Out in the reception area, Ellen stood to greet him.

"What can I do for you?" he asked, in a voice that expressed as little sincerity as he could muster without sounding hostile.

Ellen wasn't expecting to have to talk in this public area. She looked around; everyone in the cramped space seemed to be staring at her. "I really wanted to speak with you privately, if you have a moment," she said.

"I really don't," Sanderson answered curtly. "As you can no doubt imagine, I've been tied up the last few days, and I've got a mountain of mail to wade through."

Ellen's face colored. "Look, Tom, we have a job to do just like you do—"

"I don't envy you," Sanderson snapped, cutting her off in mid-sentence. "Thanks to your 'doing your job,' as you put it, Frank Jordan may go free. You and Mac may be able to live with that, but I for one think it will be a crying shame if that maniac ever walks the streets again. Now if you will excuse me, I really need to get back to work."

Sanderson turned abruptly on his heels and left, leaving Ellen standing alone next to Helen Hawthorne. The old woman looked up and smiled, but there was no warmth at all in her expression. Ellen felt enormously self-conscious. Finally she walked stiffly toward the doorway which led to the public hall.

Ellen had come to this office to express her sympathy for Sanderson's clients, and to tell him that she was leaving Mc-Pherson's office and going out on her own. But she never got to open her mouth or say the first words. "Stupid fool, I should have known better," she mumbled as she pushed open the heavy door. She almost ran head first into Carol Rogers, who was coming into the D.A.'s office, along with her husband, son, and minister. Ellen's and Carol's eyes met briefly; they quickly passed each other by.

Tom Sanderson returned to his office and tried his best to get some work done. It wasn't easy. Ellen Hayes's visit took center stage in his mind, and refused to yield to any other thoughts. He had come on too strong, and he knew it. He was chagrined. Promising himself he would make it up to her when he saw her again, he went back to work, trying his best to focus on the task at hand.

He was interrupted once again by the intercom buzzer. "General Sanderson, Mr. and Mrs. Rogers would like a word with you, if you have a moment." He really didn't have a moment, but by this time he was resigned to the fact that he was not going to be able to control the events of this day.

"Of course, tell Miss Hawthorne to send them on back."

Sanderson rose from his chair and hastily moved some files from the couch. In a moment the door opened; Bill and Carol filed in, followed by their son, Jeffrey, and Joe Holman. Carol was the first to take a seat. She stared straight ahead, seemingly detached from all that was happening around her. Bill was the first to speak.

"Tom, Carol and I want you to know that no matter what happens, we're grateful for all you have done. We know how hard you've worked on this case. Whatever happens, we are satisfied."

"I appreciate that, Bill," Sanderson responded. He *was* grateful. He wanted this kind of support, and he needed it.

"What do you make of this, Tom? What's the jury up to, anyway?" Joe Holman asked.

"I don't know," Sanderson replied. "It's beyond me to understand. Even the nine-three split is a mystery. I can't conceive of three people being convinced that Jordan isn't guilty, but that's got to be what's happening. There's no way you'll ever convince me that the nine are for innocent, not even on the insanity issue. I just don't believe that can happen."

"But what if it does?" Jeffrey Rogers asked, raising the question that was on everyone else's mind. "What if the jury does find him innocent? What then? Can we appeal?"

"No, Jeff, there's no appeal from a verdict in favor of a defendant in a criminal case. The state never gets a second chance," Sanderson responded.

"Why not?" Jeffrey didn't understand. Neither did any of the rest of them.

"When a person is accused of a crime, put to trial, and found innocent for any reason, then our Constitution protects that person from having to go through that process a second time. Sometimes injustices result, I suppose, but for the most part that's a good principle. When you think about it, if that weren't the case, an oppressive government could ruin the lives of innocent people by subjecting them to a series of trials for the same crime. That would amount to persecution."

"I guess I understand, but I don't like it," Jeffrey replied. "It may be a good principle, but somehow when you are the victim, the good principle doesn't seem so good." At the moment Sanderson couldn't agree more. After a pause, Jeffrey continued, "If the jury does find Jordan insane, then what will happen to him?"

"He'll go to the state mental-health institute, where he'll be kept in their maximum-security area for as long as he's mentally unstable. That could easily be the rest of his life," answered Sanderson, intentionally emphasizing the positive. This was no time to be reminding these distraught people of the other options, although he was worried sick about how quickly Frank Jordan might be back on the street.

"He could be out in a year, maybe even less," said Carol, repeating what she'd heard in the news about the trial. Her expression remained vacant and dispassionate.

"That could happen, Carol," Tom Sanderson responded gently. "But you need to realize that it isn't likely to happen. If Frank Jordan is as sick as the psychiatrists think he is, then there is no quick cure. It is far more likely that he'll spend years in there, maybe even the rest of his life."

"But the fact remains, he could be out in less than a year. You can say that's remote, and you can say it won't happen, but it still could, and you know it." Carol's words were slow and deliberate, but her voice rose as she spoke. "What kind of justice is that?"

Bill Rogers squirmed and looked around, his eyes moving quickly from one face to the other. Then he stood up. "Look, Tom has things he needs to do. Maybe we had better get out of the way."

"Where are you folks waiting?" Tom asked.

"Out in the hall. We're just hanging around wherever we can," Bill answered. "If we had time we'd go for a walk, but the jury could be back at any minute, and we feel like we need to be close by."

"Come on, I'll find you a quiet spot." Sanderson took Carol's arm and the others followed, walking together down the narrow hall to a door which opened onto a small conference room. The room was empty. Sanderson cleaned the clutter off the table. "No one will bother you here. If you need anything, let Mary

Ann know. I'll send for you when the court calls us back." He went out into the hall, closing the door behind him, leaving the four of them alone.

Minutes stretched into hours. Lunchtime came and went. Joe Holman went out for hamburgers and soft drinks, but Carol and Bill only nibbled at their food. Empty coffee cups began to pile up. Tom Sanderson looked in every so often, unaware that each knock on the door produced a sudden sense of panic, followed by immediate deflation. Bill Rogers and Joe Holman tried to make small talk, but with little success. Conversation seemed irrelevant somehow. In spite of their best efforts, Carol showed little interest in idle conversation. She was traumatized by the agonizing delay.

At one point in the afternoon she broke her long silence.

"Joe, when this is all over you are going to have to explain to me where God fits into all of this. For the life of me, I don't understand."

"What do you mean, Carol?" Joe answered, sitting by her side, taking her hand in his.

"It is inconceivable to me that a God of love, the God you preach about, would let something like that happen to one of his innocent little children," Carol said, looking at her friend through moist, red eyes. "It just doesn't fit. If God exists, if God really cares, and if he really has the power to change things, then why did he let this happen?"

"I have no magic answers, Carol, you know that. That same question has been asked a million times before. I guess that when God loved us enough to give us freedom to be ourselves, to live our lives and make our choices, then that necessarily meant that he gave us the freedom to make bad choices and bad decisions. Sometimes those choices and decisions hurt other people, even hurt them to the point of taking their lives. But, Carol, you must understand that if God didn't give us that freedom, then we wouldn't really be human, would we?"

"Is the freedom worth the pain?" Carol asked.

"I don't know. Sometimes I wonder. But I'll tell you this, I believe that God hurts just like we hurt when one of his children goes astray, and I believe he weeps just as we weep when some innocent angel is the victim of an abuse of that freedom. I can't prove it, and I can't explain it, but I really believe it."

"Oh, Joe, I want so badly to believe that myself, but right now I just can't." Carol gripped Joe's hands and looked into his eyes. Her face was a portrait of anguish, reflecting the enormity of the burden that she felt. To her, the weight of the world was on her shoulders, and hers alone. Across the room, Bill Rogers sat upright in one of the wooden chairs, his arms folded across his chest, his eyes taking in the scene in front of him. His face bore no expression, but his mind was filled with thoughts. He wanted to say something, but didn't know what. He wanted to get up, to go over to Carol and put his arms around her, but he couldn't, he just couldn't. So he sat there, rigid and expressionless, staring dispassionately at the woman he loved.

Suddenly the door opened. It was Tom Sanderson. His suit jacket was back on; his tie had been straightened. It was apparent that this wasn't a false alarm. The time had come.

"The jury has reached a verdict. They're ready to report. It's time to go back to the courtroom."

Carol Rogers stood up and picked up her purse from the scarred old tabletop. Bill reached for her arm. They walked together out of the district attorney's office and into the long hallway which echoed with activity. But the only noise Carol could hear was the rapid hammering of her own heart as it raced out of control. She was filled with dread and anticipation as they approached the courtroom door.

13

A long, white van, nearly the size of a city bus, was parked on the back side of the courthouse. It had no windows and only one door. A gaggle of cables emerged from a small hole in the top of the van, stretching like a giant umbilical cord across the sidewalk to the outer wall of the courthouse, held above crowd level by crude wooden stands. The entwined mass then snaked its way up the old building's side and into an open window on the top floor. There the various cables parted, eventually finding their separate ways to the cameras, light stands, and microphones that would record today's courtroom proceedings for posterity.

Inside the van, two engineers attended a vast array of screens, gauges, and dials. Cameramen and lighting technicians sat in an open area at one end of the van, playing cards, reading books, and otherwise avoiding boredom while waiting for something to happen. When the time came, all of them had to be ready to roll. Boredom was the price of preparedness.

At precisely 4:35 P.M. the unmarked door of the van bolted open. Three men raced down rickety portable stairs, crossed the sidewalk, and entered the courthouse through a service door. Inside the van, one engineer, serving as director for the remote feed, put on a headset and began to talk to his counterpart at the studio. The other engineer switched off the van's inside lights and began turning various knobs and dials. As promised, advance word had come directly from Judge Coleman's office. The television crew had been given ten minutes to get everything turned on and in place. Ready or not, it was time to go. This was real life. Real emotions hung in the balance. Television's rigid schedule could not be accommodated under such circumstances. This ten-minute concession would be all there was. It was "show time" in the Criminal Court.

"We'll be coming your way in less than ten minutes, pal," the director in the van said to his counterpart in the studio. "Use the number-four intro, and run it in about nine minutes and thirty seconds. Then we'll switch to a broad shot of the courtroom and wait for something to happen. That's all I know right now."

"We'll be ready," came the response from the studio several miles away. "Too bad they didn't string this along a while longer so we could use it as part of the regular evening news. Wouldn't that have been one hell of a lead story?"

"Don't say that too loud—Coleman might hear you," the director responded only half-jokingly. "The way he's been hamming it up the last few days, it wouldn't have surprised me for the bastard to lock the jury up until prime time, just so he could get the exposure."

"The number-four intro is on cue," came the report from the studio. "We'll run it in nine minutes unless you tell us not to."

Earlier in the day the pool reporter selected for this assignment had taped four different "stand-ups," or taped introductions for the live feed which would come later. The television people had tried to cover all the possibilities. The number-four intro was the one to be used if the jury returned before dinner to render a verdict.

Carol and Bill Rogers followed Tom Sanderson through a side door into the courtroom. The deputy sheriff standing guard nodded pleasantly at Carol as she passed by. Immediately after their arrival, four huge lights were turned on in the courtroom. The designers of this courtroom, like most in America, never considered such outlandish possibilities as the presence of cameras to record trials; the lights, the cameras, and all of their attendant paraphernalia were clearly intruding on sacred ground.

Their presence created a carnival atmosphere which added to the discomfort of the participants.

Carol and Bill made their way to the prosecutor's table and took seats next to Tom Sanderson, who was closest to the jury. Bill sat next to Sanderson, Carol nearest the podium. Over at the defense table, Martin McPherson sat closest to the judge, with Ellen Hayes near the podium, leaving an empty chair for Frank Jordan, who wouldn't be brought in until it was almost time to open court. The less time he spent in court, the less risk of problems.

The spectators' gallery was jammed, just as it had been during the entire trial. The front row was set aside for family members and involved parties, such as Jeffrey Rogers and Joe Holman. Bess Jordan, occupying a front-row seat near the defense table, was primly dressed in a navy blue suit, with a simple white cotton blouse buttoned to the neck. Her face was drawn and tense. There were dark circles around her eyes. Like Carol Rogers, she showed the effects of weeks of stress and tension.

After a brief moment, a door swung open in the paneled wall next to the bench. The bailiff entered first, followed by Frank Jordan and a guard. Jordan was dressed in gray slacks, a blue-and-gray-checked sport coat, and an open-collar shirt. Though his clothes were neat, their cut and fabric proclaimed their inferiority. His hair was disheveled, as usual, and he gave the appearance of one not accustomed to being clean and dressed up. He looked very young, and very bewildered, in spite of his tough veneer.

Jordan's plastic smile was, as always, firmly in place. His hands were out in front of him, wrists cuffed together. A few moments before he entered the courtroom, a guard had removed ankle shackles which he had worn on the trip over from the jail. Now, the same guard removed his handcuffs. There would be no sign of restraint devices when the jury came in, nor would there be such things as prison garb, or visible weapons on the guards.

Frank Jordan looked over at his mother and managed a brief wave before taking a seat between his lawyers.

"All rise," the bailiff commanded. Everyone stood immediately. Judge Coleman entered, mounted the bench, and stood behind his large leather chair, holding a file folder under his arm.

"Open court, Mr. Bailiff," Judge Coleman said.

"Oyez, oyez, oyez," intoned the bailiff, following a tradition that stretched back through the years, far beyond the creation of this particular court. "Division Two of the Criminal Court is now open, pursuant to adjournment. All persons having business before this honorable court draw nigh, give attention, and ye shall be heard." He bowed his head and continued. "God save this state, the United States, and this honorable court," he said, then quickly raised his head. "Judge Henry Coleman presiding. Be seated, please."

Everyone sat down, including the judge himself.

"Ladies and gentlemen," the judge began, "I understand that the jury wants to deliver its verdict. Before the jury comes in, I want to warn each and every one of you that I will not tolerate any outbursts. I have asked the sheriff to post guards at the public doors. No one will be allowed to enter or leave the courtroom from the time the jury comes in until I have dismissed them and they have been escorted from the building. Their job has been tough enough, and when they are finished I don't want them to be subjected to harassment from the lawyers, the press, or anyone else. Is that clearly understood?" The judge slowly looked around the courtroom. "All right, Bailiff, bring in the jury."

The bailiff disappeared behind the door at the end of the jury box. He soon returned, and held the door as the jury marched in, single file. Arnold Prentiss, the foreman, held a small slip of paper in his hand.

There are people who make a living studying human behavior. Some claim to be able to make accurate predictions as to what a jury will do, drawing conclusions about each juror's ultimate decision based on his or her mannerisms, body language, and the like. Others claim to be able to pick both the foreman and the initial split based on the jurors' reaction to key testimony. Still others swear that you can look at the faces of jurors as they enter the courtroom to deliver the verdict, and tell by their expressions and the presence or absence of eye contact what their verdict will be. On this particular occasion the behavioral scientists would have had a field day. The jurors collectively presented every possible degree of emotion and every conceivable facial expression as they entered the box.

The first juror looked directly at Frank Jordan. One or two glanced in the general direction of the prosecution table. Most either stared straight ahead in an awkward attempt to reveal nothing, or looked down in an equally stilted manner. They all appeared disheveled and worn out. At least one of the women had apparently been crying, and possibly some of the men. None of the jurors wanted to be there—that much was obvious. It had been a very long and very trying two days of deliberation. After what seemed like an eternity, they all took their seats.

"Members of the jury, have you reached a verdict?" the judge asked.

The foreman stood erect and glanced down at the piece of paper he held in his hand. "We have, Your Honor," he responded.

Judge Coleman turned to the defense table. "The defendant will please rise to receive the verdict of the jury." Frank Jordan stood, flanked by his lawyers. Turning back toward the jury, the judge continued. "Mr. Foreman, what is your verdict?"

Arnold Prentiss looked down at his slip of paper again. "We, the jury, find the defendant not guilty, by reason of insanity."

The courtroom burst into chaos. Martin McPherson, flush with unexpected victory, offered his hand to Frank Jordan, who was smiling broadly, his first sincere smile since the trial began. Ellen Hayes stood transfixed. Bess Jordan rushed through the swinging gate to embrace her son. The bailiff quickly separated the two of them and led her to a seat next to the wall. Judge Coleman hammered down his gavel several times, trying to regain control.

Carol Rogers slumped back in her seat. She felt as though she had been slammed head first into a stone wall, at high speed. Every fiber of her being felt crushed. She was paralyzed by disbelief, unable to do anything except stare straight ahead.

Bill Rogers turned toward Tom Sanderson, his mouth hanging open in total dismay. Sanderson stared straight ahead, his teeth and fists both tightly clenched.

"Order, order!" Judge Coleman shouted, continuing to pound away with his gavel, obviously very angry. "I must have order at once!" After a moment, the loud banging finally had the desired effect. The room became quiet.

The judge began to speak. "Mr. McPherson, you and Mr.

Jordan please be seated for a moment while I poll the jury. And I expect you to keep your client and his mother under control. Is that clear?"

"Yes, Your Honor," McPherson replied.

The judge swiveled around to face the jury.

Tears were pouring down Carol Rogers's cheeks. Her initial disbelief was rapidly giving way to anger. She leaned down beside her chair, picked up her large leather purse, and placed it on her lap, opening it up to search for a fresh tissue with which to stem the flow of emotion. She took out an empty purse-sized pack, tossed it aside in despair, and continued to rummage deeper into the huge pocketbook.

"Members of the jury," the judge said, "I told each of you at the beginning of this trial that the verdict had to be *your* verdict, that you had to be morally comfortable with the result. For that reason I'm going to ask each of you to state your verdict individually for the record." Judge Coleman took out his jury chart and looked down at the names, then began to poll the jury. "Mr. Berger, what is your verdict?"

"Not guilty, by reason of insanity, Your Honor," Berger replied without hesitation.

"Mr. Cartwright, what is your verdict?"

As the polling continued, Carol stared down at her open purse. The bright courtroom lights revealed the little chrome pistol which her rummaging hand had just uncovered in her purse. When she saw it, her heart suddenly started pounding away inside her chest. The judge continued asking each juror for confirmation of the verdict.

"Miss Blakemore, what is your verdict?"

Carol reached into the purse, grasped the small pistol with one hand, and released the safety with the other. She covered the weapon with both hands and looked at her husband and Tom Sanderson. They were busily exchanging whispered comments. The judge was almost through. The last juror's name had been called.

"Not guilty, by reason of insanity, Your Honor."

Judge Coleman paused, appearing momentarily dismayed, but quickly regained his composure and turned his attention to the defense table. "Will the defendant please rise?" Once again Frank Jordan and his lawyers stood up, just as Carol Rogers's trembling hand slowly tightened around the handle of the small gun. Carefully and deliberately she lifted it out of the purse. Frank Jordan was still smiling, looking straight at the jury. Immediately behind him, his mother was crying tears of joy.

"Mr. Jordan, you have heard the verdict of the jury. The verdict of the jury now becomes the judgment of this court. . . ." Judge Coleman prepared to pronounce the final judgment.

For months to come, the incredible events of the next few seconds would be hashed and rehashed over a thousand cups of coffee and a thousand Bloody Marys, by those who were involved and by countless others who were only spectators. Everyone would have an opinion, but no one would have an explanation. This sort of thing simply could not happen in a modern courtroom in the late twentieth century, certainly not under the watchful eye of live television.

Countless bailiffs, police officers, and deputy sheriffs were within a few feet of the defense table. They were all armed, trained, and supposedly alert. Carol Rogers was right in the thick of things, not shuttled off to the side. She was the center of attention, the object of public scrutiny, an unfortunate victim of violent crime to be gawked at and pitied by the public at large. There was plenty of time for someone to notice, for someone to react, for someone to break the inexorable chain of events that started when the courtroom lights first reflected off of the shiny chrome surface of the weapon as Carol lifted it from her purse. But no one noticed. No one reacted. Not until it was too late.

For the briefest instant it was as though time was suspended in this cavernous chamber for everyone except Carol Rogers. In one swift, deliberate move she raised the small pistol past the edge of the table, leaned forward, and rested her elbows on the hard wooden surface. All of her feelings were on hold momentarily except for an incredible sense of blind determination. The barrel of the gun was pointed straight at the gloating face of Frank Jordan.

". . . that you be committed to the custody of the state mental-health institute, where . . ."

Exactly as she had been taught by her husband, Carol squeezed the trigger with a deliberate, even pressure, smiling slightly while she did so. Suddenly there was a burst of smoke. Sparks flew from the barrel. A loud report echoed through the room as a violent explosion inside the pistol propelled a tiny ball of lead through the air with lightning speed and deadly force.

The first bullet covered the distance between Carol Rogers and Frank Jordan in a split second. Attracted by the sound, Jordan glanced over toward Carol. His expression changed to stark terror as the bullet struck him in the throat, tearing through his flesh. Blood spurted from a punctured artery.

Carol squeezed the trigger a second time and then a third, sending two more explosions resounding throughout the room, and two more deadly missiles streaking toward the defendant.

Jordan's hands reached upward in a futile gesture of defense as the second bullet ripped through his clothing, hitting him in the shoulder, forcing his body to turn toward the left. The third bullet caught him in the middle of the chest just as he completed the turn.

Now it was Bess Jordan's turn to be paralyzed by disbelief. She started screaming as her son reeled toward her. He opened his mouth as if to speak, but only a deathly gurgle came forth as he collapsed to the floor at his mother's feet, staring up at her with unseeing eyes.

"My God," Ellen Hayes whispered as she stared at the scene before her.

Martin McPherson leaned down toward the jerking body of Frank Jordan. He wanted to help but didn't know what to do. Bess Jordan just stood there, immobilized, her uncontrollable screams barely rising above the mass of confusion. Several people were rushing toward the crumpled body of her son.

Carol Rogers sank back into her chair, still holding the pistol in a deathlike grip. Her curious smile slowly yielded to the grotesque mask of agony. She began to sob uncontrollably and lowered her head to the table. Her body jerked with spasms as the grief she had suppressed for so long finally came to the surface. For the first time since her daughter's death, she cried out loud. Bill reached out and pulled her toward him. Tom Sanderson gently removed the pistol from her hand.

‖14‖

"**G**ood God Almighty, would you look at that!" the director whispered into his headset, leaning closer to the monitors to get a better view.

He and the engineer stared in disbelief at the incredible scenario unfolding before them. On one of the tiny screens they could see people frantically working over the body of Frank Jordan. A police officer was administering two-man CPR with the help of a deputy sheriff. Between breaths, the deputy tried vainly to find a pressure point that would stem the flow of blood from the wound in Frank Jordan's neck. On another screen Tom Sanderson could be seen taking the gun from the hand of Carol Rogers. Her face remained buried in Bill's shoulder.

Every muscle in the director's body was strained tight from tension as he struggled to keep everything working in spite of the confusion. He was on automatic pilot; his one goal was to get the best possible picture on the air.

"Pick that damn thing up and move it around if you have to, but whatever you do, keep Jordan's body in sight," he said to the harried operator of camera one. "Stay with him as best you can. Number two, follow the woman at all cost. If either of you get in a tight spot or get blocked off from view, we'll try to switch around. The tape is rolling. Whatever you do, for God's sake, don't get unplugged."

When the first shot rang out, most of the jurors had jumped behind their chairs or had fled the jury box entirely. Judge Coleman had ducked under the bench as soon as he realized what was going on.

Ellen Hayes, just on the other side of Frank Jordan, had been strangely immobilized by it all, as if she was a spectator and not in any danger from a mis-aimed bullet. She had stood in place, staring at Carol Rogers for a moment, feeling nothing but shock and disbelief. Finally, galvanized into action, she began helping to move the heavy chairs and tables to give the officer and the deputy room to administer aid to Jordan.

Tom Sanderson couldn't believe what he had seen.

"My God," he whispered, his eyes darting back and forth from Frank Jordan to Jordan's mother, then back to the dying young man. Then he thought of Carol.

"Are you all right?" he called out as he grabbed her slumped shoulders. It was all he could think of to say. "Here, let's get her up," he said to Bill Rogers as the two of them pulled upward on her almost lifeless body.

Carol seemed to be in a trance. Joe Holman broke through the restraining cordon, jumped over the rail, and took one of her arms. Sanderson led the way as they fought through the crowd, making their way to the end of the jury box, through the door, and out into the small hall that ran along the back of the courtroom.

Sanderson borrowed a key from the bailiff and unlocked the jury-room door. He herded Carol, Joe, and Bill inside, and told them to wait for him there. Locking the door behind him, he worked his way back down the crowded hall, located a deputy sheriff, and instructed him to stand guard at the jury-room door and not let anyone in or out.

By the time Sanderson made his way back into the courtroom, some paramedics had arrived with a stretcher. Assisted by Martin McPherson, they put Frank Jordan's body on the stretcher and began the slow journey through the crowd. One of the paramedics skillfully inserted an I.V. needle into Jordan's arm and walked alongside him, holding a bottle of life-sustaining fluid aloft.

Sanderson's attention was suddenly diverted. A hand was grabbing at his shoulder. It was Jeffrey Rogers. His face was flushed. He had been crying.

Sanderson nearly cried himself. Instinctively he pulled the boy close to him, then quickly let him go.

"Do you know where my parents are?" Jeffrey asked.

"Follow me," Sanderson replied, leading him back through the crowd and into the small hall, which was still tightly packed with people. Reporters screamed out questions as the two of them wedged their way through. Sanderson motioned the deputy aside and unlocked the jury-room door. This time the force of the pressing crowd pushed him inside along with Jeffrey. Seeing their predicament, Joe Holman rushed over to the door and helped Sanderson force it closed against the crowd.

Jeffrey rushed across the room toward his mother, and as they embraced he burst into tears.

"Oh Mom, Mom . . ." was all he could say. He drew back and looked into her reddened eyes. He had wanted to be a comforter instead of the one needing comfort, but it wasn't working, not at all. They embraced again.

Tom Sanderson paced up and down the small room. His heart was racing; his mind was crowded with thoughts. Just moments before, the jury had been in here, debating the decision that had served as the catalyst for an incredible series of events. Now the room was in disarray. Crumpled notes and half-used pads littered the long table top; the twelve wooden chairs were scattered about. So was Tom Sanderson's mind. He didn't know what to do next.

In one corner, on a small wooden stand, he found a coffee pot. The coffee looked old and thick, but it was still hot. He pulled a cup from an opened plastic bag, filled it halfway with the dark, steaming liquid, and took it to Carol Rogers. She held it tightly, her hands visibly shaking.

"You'll be safe in here for a few minutes," Sanderson said to the four of them, trying to sound in control as he looked around the room. "There's still some coffee left, and the bathroom's over there," he added, pointing to a door at the far end of the room. "I'm going to try to find out what's going on, and see if I can get some help to clear these halls. The deputy here will be posted outside. But there's always a chance he might have to go do something else. Whatever happens, don't open the door or let anyone in here. I have a key; I'll let myself back in." Sanderson put his hand on Carol's shoulder. He started to say something else but stopped. He really didn't know *what* to say at this moment.

He unlocked the door as quietly as possible, gripped the handle, and motioned for Bill, Joe, and the deputy to come help. As if on signal, he pulled the door open. He and the deputy stepped out into the crowded hall; the other two pushed the door shut.

By this time, two uniformed policemen were systematically removing people from the jammed hallway. Both of the doors leading from the hall to the courtroom had been closed off and were now guarded. Moving through the crowd, one of the policemen caught Sanderson's eye.

"General Sanderson, the judge wants to see you right away. He's in his office." The policeman pointed toward the door to the judge's chamber.

Sanderson's heart stopped. "Thanks," he mumbled, weaving his way through the diminishing crowd. He entered the judge's chambers, then pressed himself against a back wall, making himself as inconspicuous as possible. No one greeted him or acknowledged his presence. He said nothing.

Judge Coleman was standing behind the ornate, carved mahogany desk, his judicial robe still draped from his shoulders. He was talking on the phone, but nodded at Sanderson without smiling. Carlton Douglas sat on the maroon leather sofa that faced the desk, his expression stern and an uncharacteristic hostility in his eyes. Police Chief Buck O'Conner walked over to Sanderson and put his hand on his shoulder.

"Yes, Your Honor," Judge Coleman was saying. "Thank you for the offer. Chief O'Conner is here now, and several of his men. I believe we have everything under control. Apparently it was Mrs. Rogers, acting alone. She just went berserk. There was nothing organized, or anything like that."

There was a pause while the judge listened to the mayor's comments. He rapped his fingers on the desk and looked around the room. Everyone else stared at him.

"Thank you again. If anything else happens, you will be the first to know, I assure you. Good day, sir." He hung up the phone and breathed a sigh of relief.

"What did he say?" Carlton Douglas asked, looking at the judge.

"He offered to send more police, the militia, whatever," Coleman answered. "He is righteously outraged. He's holding an impromptu press conference, apparently."

"Grandstanding as usual," Douglas mused. "Always the conscience of the community, the grand gesture after the fact. If we could have gotten any money from his administration for electronic passageways to screen people as they enter court, this never would have happened. Where was he when we needed him? And now, when the horses are all out of the barn, he wants to send help! Big deal!"

"Where is she now?" Coleman asked, turning to Tom Sanderson. "Is she in custody?"

"I put her and her family in the jury room," Sanderson answered, his voice unsteady. "She isn't going anywhere. I have a deputy sheriff at the door. Besides, she couldn't get through that crowd if she wanted to. She's safe for the time being."

"Her safety isn't what concerns me, Tom," Coleman stated grimly. "I don't want her getting out of here until we decide what to do."

Suddenly, for the first time, it occurred to Sanderson that Carol Rogers was in deep, deep trouble. Up until that moment his only concern had been for her welfare. Keeping her in custody wasn't something he'd thought about. At least he'd locked the door. He hoped the deputy hadn't left his post.

"Where's the gun?" Coleman continued.

Again Sanderson's heart nearly stopped. Before he could think of an excuse, Chief O'Conner answered the question.

"One of my men has it. It's in a safe place."

Sanderson quietly eased out a sigh. That was another detail he hadn't bothered to think of. He had given the gun to an officer, but in the confusion he couldn't remember which one.

"What kind of gun was it, Chief?" the judge asked.

"It was a Browning, .22 caliber automatic," O'Conner replied. "It has an accuracy range of maybe twenty feet, at best. She was either damn lucky, or she had been training for weeks. She held the thing like a pro." He looked at Sanderson. "You were right there, Tom. What happened?"

"I . . . I don't know." Sanderson was clearly embarrassed. "I never saw the gun until the shooting started. Her husband and I were talking, and the next thing I knew sparks were flying everywhere."

"What do you mean you never saw it?" Carlton Douglas demanded. "Hell, you were only two feet away from her. She practically had to hold the gun under your nose, and you never even knew what was going on? Oh, that's great. That's just great . . ."

"Calm down, Carlton," Judge Coleman interjected. "Believe me, if you had been there, you wouldn't have known any more about what was going on than he did, or than I did either, for that matter. Hell, the second I saw that gun I went under the bench as fast as I could. Everybody in that room had one thought, and one thought only—survival! If you had been there, you would have been under the podium." Judge Coleman was smiling.

"This is not a joking matter," Douglas responded. "A young man is dying and many more could have easily been hit when that woman opened fire. She was your responsibility, Tom. She spent the morning in our office conference room, probably using our blackboard to diagram her strategy." The district attorney glared at his assistant. "Anyway you look at it, this whole mess is your responsibility. I sure as hell don't think it's asking too much to suggest that you pay attention to what's going on, and to at least follow up with some reasonably intelligent investigation."

"Come on," Sanderson retorted curtly, bristling at the sarcasm of his boss. "You know damn well there has hardly been time for investigation." He hadn't expected such immediate hostility, either toward Carol Rogers or himself. "Besides, what more do you need to know? Unless someone pulled the plug, this whole fiasco was played out on live television, before hundreds of thousands of witnesses. If you can't win a case like that, then perhaps you don't belong in office!"

"That's quite enough, gentlemen!" Judge Coleman immediately ended the matter, but the underlying hostility remained. It was obvious that Carlton Douglas held his first assistant personally responsible. Sanderson was beginning to wish that he hadn't become so intensely involved in the lives of the Rogers family.

The door to the judge's office opened again. This time it was

Martin McPherson. He was ashen-faced. Dried blood splattered his clothing.

"What is it, Mac?" Coleman asked.

"I just got word. Jordan is dead. He never made it to the ambulance. He'll be pronounced D.O.A. when they get through with him, but they're holding off any official announcement until you decide how you want to handle it." McPherson sank into one of the wingback chairs that flanked Coleman's desk.

"Carlton, I'm going to leave the press up to you and Chief O'Conner," said the judge. "Meanwhile, we have some business to attend to. Chief, did you bring a warrant?"

"Yes, Judge, here it is." O'Conner handed over the small slip of paper. "What's her full name, Tom?"

"Carol Jeffreys Rogers," Sanderson answered, swallowing a lump in his throat. "What are you charging her with?"

Coleman looked at him, somewhat incredulously. "Premeditated murder, of course. What choice do I have?" He turned to Douglas. "Carlton, I'm putting Jordan's mother down as the official prosecutor."

"Don't do that, Judge," said Martin McPherson. "Bess Jordan is too upset right now. She's in no shape to deal with this."

"Who can we use, then?" Douglas asked.

"Well, it needs to be someone who was there, who saw what happened," McPherson answered. "Otherwise the warrant will be technically defective. Lord knows we don't need that, not in this case." The irony of this advice wasn't lost on the others in the room. Martin McPherson had spent a lifetime searching for such technical deficiencies, repeatedly using them to defeat the state's efforts to put his clients away.

"Okay, you're right. I'll put you down for now, Mac. You saw everything. Somebody has to sign this. I want to get that woman in custody as quickly as possible. We can substitute the Jordan woman when the grand jury hears the case. She should be the one in court when this thing comes to trial. Here, sign this." Coleman slid the paper over to McPherson, who signed it and handed it back. The judge added his signature, and held the slip out to Chief O'Conner. "Get one of your men to serve this, Chief. Sanderson will show you where she is."

"Judge, if you don't mind, I'd like to do it myself," Sanderson said, reaching for the warrant.

"I'll do it, Tom. You come with me," O'Conner said, taking the warrant. They both looked over at Judge Coleman, who nodded his approval.

When they arrived at the jury room, Sanderson waved the deputy aside and unlocked the door. Carol Rogers was still sitting in the corner, exactly where she had been when he'd left a short while ago, still staring blankly into space. Bill Rogers was at her side, holding her hand. They both looked up when Sanderson and Chief O'Conner entered.

"Carol," Sanderson said, kneeling in front of her, "this is Police Chief O'Conner. We have something we need to do. There's no need for you to say anything, just listen. And try to remember, he's only doing what he has to do. Do you understand?"

She nodded.

"Carol Jeffreys Rogers," the chief began in a quiet voice, "it is my duty to tell you that you have a right to remain silent. . . ." Carol's eyes widened. She looked up into the chief's face. The cold reality of what she had done finally began to sink in, as the chief continued to remind her of her rights as an accused murderer.

‖15‖

Carol sat on the edge of the narrow cot and shivered slightly in the cool, dark stillness. A dull pain throbbed in back of her eyes, radiating first around her head, then down her shoulders. Her throat felt scratchy, her back ached, her shoulders slumped with fatigue. She hadn't slept all night. She hadn't even tried; she'd been afraid to yield to the temptation, afraid that if she surrendered herself to sleep in this barren, ugly, graffiti-scarred cell, she might never awaken, might never be able to leave this place with her sanity intact.

But her physical discomfort was nothing compared to the agony in her heart and in her mind.

Numbness had characterized the hours following her arrest. As if her mind were wrenched from her body, she had been an unfeeling spectator to a grim series of events, existing only because she had no choice, buffeted from place to place by unfeeling strangers, gawked at as if she were a freak. Withdrawal had been her only defense.

Bill had stayed with her through much of the tedious booking process. Thank God for Bill; he had been her only link with reality. The two of them had been escorted down a service elevator and out a back entrance of the courthouse. Police regulations had to be followed; no exceptions could be made. Thus she had suffered the indignity of crossing the public street with her arms in front of her and her wrists bound together by handcuffs. Her trip from the courthouse to the jail building across the street had been quickly discovered by the press; by the time she and her entourage had reached the jail, their way had been blocked by an array of photographers and reporters.

Thanks to the efforts of the sheriff and his staff, the booking process had been carried out in private. Her belongings were inventoried, and she was issued a styleless gray jail dress. There were forms to fill out, fingerprinting to endure, and a mug shot to be taken. By this time Claiborne Bennett had arrived in response to Bill's frantic call. As attorney for Bill's employer, he was the only lawyer Bill knew well enough to call. His presence was a great comfort to them both. His inexperience in such matters was of little concern; his presence was all that mattered.

At ten o'clock in the evening, the absolute latest hour possible, Bill had gathered Carol's belongings and left, unable to watch as the matron led Carol down the concrete corridor toward an empty cell. Though he couldn't see her being led away, the hollow sound of her footsteps on the concrete floor would echo in his mind forever.

In spite of the consideration shown to her by the sheriff, in spite of the kindness of the matron, and in spite of her knowledge that she would be free again in the morning after the preliminary hearing, Carol had never in her life heard anything so ominous, so frightening, or so final as the metallic clanging of the barred door of her cell as it closed for the night, locking her in. The sound had echoed off of the bare walls and resounded throughout the deepest recesses of her brain, slamming cruelly against the walls of her mind. Once alone, she had stood in the middle of her cell, stripped of all identifying characteristics, another dull, nameless face in a dull, shapeless dress, locked up for the night. There had been no way she could surrender to sleep.

During the incredibly long night the numbness had finally worn off, giving way first to fear, then to panic. It was all so incredible, so totally and completely unbelievable. Yet it was real. She couldn't calm down. There was simply no way to bring her feelings under control. She had sat on the edge of the bed for a while, then paced up and down, dredging up her recollections of the day's events. It had all happened so fast! She still couldn't comprehend it completely. Her mind had replayed the scenario a thousand times during the night as she shifted around in search of comfort, worlds away from her warm home and loving husband. Her mind had raced along in high gear. Sleep, even stillness, had been out of the question.

Now, as she sat in the dark, listening to the rhythmic breathing of the person in the next cell, every nerve in her body was standing straight up, at full attention, as if waiting for something else to happen. It was as though she had just finished a race and was unable to cool down, unable to rid herself of the adrenalin high. Every time she thought about all that had happened, her heart sped out of control, and yet she couldn't help herself. She had thought of nothing else for hours.

Even as the third bullet was still in mid-air, still racing toward its target, Carol was already wishing she hadn't done it. Not out of concern for Frank Jordan; he was nothing to her. Indeed, it had been the sight of his smirking face that had pushed her over the edge. No, it was because she instantly realized the impact it was going to have on her life, and on the lives of the people who loved her and trusted her. In rapid succession, in a matter of split seconds, she had experienced a great sense of release, an overwhelming sense of revulsion, and a horrible, indescribable regret.

If she could have stopped the hands of time, if she could have stuffed the tiny grains of sand back up into the hourglass, she would gladly have done so. But once the first shot was fired, it was too late. Indeed, from the very moment that she first forced the tiny trigger past its point of no return, it was too late. No power on earth could have raced ahead of that first molten ball of lead and directed it from its destiny.

Now here she was, sitting on the edge of a steel cot, her feet on a cold concrete floor, her eyes staring blankly at an unadorned block wall. She pulled the drab wool blanket up around her shoulders as another shudder racked her body.

Carol had never stopped to consider the meaning of freedom before. It was something she had always enjoyed and had always taken for granted. Suddenly all of her freedom was gone, even if just for a short time. Her waking and sleeping, her coming and going, even something as menial as turning off the light, were all controlled by someone else. Throughout this entire incredible experience, that awful moment when the cell door clanged shut would stand out for Carol as her darkest moment, the time when she had felt the most desperate, the most alone. But it was almost morning now, and she had survived.

At six-thirty A.M., the official arrival of Thursday morning was heralded by the sudden glare of the bare bulb in the ceiling of her cell. It was turned on without warning. The bright light snatched her mind from the brink of disorientation and jerked her back into the horror of reality.

A breakfast tray was delivered shortly thereafter. It sat on the floor, untouched. Just as she had done almost all night long, Carol simply marked time, waiting for this incomprehensible ordeal to end.

This can't be real, she thought to herself. There is no way, just no way.

Violence was foreign to her nature and abhorrent to her Christian faith. And yet in the space of less than twenty-four hours she had contemplated taking her own life and had killed another human being. The incongruity of it all numbed her. It was as though she would awaken from this nightmare, have a good cry, perhaps even a laugh at the absurdity of it all, and it would be over. But that was not to be. All vestiges of normalcy had fled from her life with the speed of light, even before the sound of gunshots had ceased echoing off of the bare courtroom walls.

Carol rubbed one bloodshot eye with a corner of the rough blanket. Out in the hall she heard footsteps. They seemed to be coming her way.

A few minutes earlier, Bill Rogers and Claiborne Bennett had presented themselves at the entrance to the visitors' room and signed the register. Visiting hours didn't start until ten o'clock, but Bennett had checked in as the official legal counsel for Carol Rogers. As her attorney, he would be allowed to see her at any time except when lights were out, ostensibly for the purpose of preparing a defense. He and Bill had come as early as they could.

At sixty-two, Claiborne Bennett was a distinguished corporate attorney and senior partner in the firm of Bennett & Silverstein. And though he'd come to the municipal jail at this early hour, just as he'd come the evening before, he had no intention of defending Carol. His many years as a corporate lawyer had taken him far afield from the rough-and-tumble arena of the defenders of criminals, and he wanted no part of it. His gray-flannel existence had prepared him for the boardroom, not the visitors' room at the local jail.

Bill Rogers's call had come as a surprise, but Claiborne Bennett had been more than glad to help. He was familiar with the situation. He had followed this tragic chain of circumstances with great interest and even greater sympathy, from the brutal killing and the discovery of Wendy's body to the incredible turn of events in court. Like the rest of the community, he had been outraged over the murder of that innocent child and had shed no tears over the death of Frank Jordan. Now he found himself right in the middle of the maelstrom. The excitement and notoriety that came with this role were foreign to him, but not unwelcome.

As the footsteps approached her cell, Carol stood nervously at the edge of her bunk, staring blankly at the metal door and listening to the sound of a key being inserted into a lock. The large door swung open.

"Mrs. Rogers, your lawyer and your husband are here to see you," the matron said. "Come with me please."

At the first sight of Bill, Carol broke into a run, her arms outstretched. They embraced for a long time. The tears she had been saving all night flowed onto his shoulder. All he could think to do was to pat her shoulder, and to say, over and over, "There now, it's okay." It was just what she needed.

Carol told Bill about her night. She made it sound better than it was, out of sympathy for him. Then they talked about what would happen later in the day.

"Carol," Bill said, "Mr. Bennett will represent you at the preliminary hearing. After that, we'll have to find a lawyer experienced in criminal cases."

Carol turned toward Claiborne Bennett with a pleading look in her eyes.

"Bill's right, Carol," Claiborne Bennett said reassuringly. "It's just not something I'm familiar with. Believe me, you'll be better off."

"What's going to happen today, Mr. Bennett?" Carol asked.

"At eleven o'clock, Judge Wentworth has scheduled a preliminary hearing, Carol," Bennett replied. "That's a hearing given to every person accused of a felony, to make the state show that they at least have enough evidence to establish a presumption of guilt. It's the law's way of being sure that innocent people aren't arrested without cause and then hidden away in jail while the state tries to build a case."

"Does the state have to offer any evidence?" asked Bill.

"Yes, but the prosecutors usually put on as little proof as they have to in order to convince the judge that there is probable cause to keep the accused under arrest and send the case on to the grand jury. Obviously the state doesn't want to tip its hand any more than it has to."

"What do we do at the hearing?" Carol's voice was anxious. "Am I going to have to say anything?"

"We could put on proof, but we probably won't," Bennett responded. "Unless the defendant's evidence is pretty sure to carry the day, such as when there's an iron-clad alibi or something like that, I'm told it's best not to do anything. You won't have to say anything, and you should just keep quiet unless I tell you to speak. It seems to me that under the circumstances we should just waive the proof and agree to have the case go to the grand jury. Let's face it—you don't have to be an experienced criminal lawyer to know that the state has a lock on this preliminary hearing."

"Then why have the hearing at all, why go through all of that?" Carol asked.

"It's just part of the required procedure, Carol. It's what has to happen, just like your having to wait in jail until the hearing can be held. After the case is bound over to the grand jury, Judge Wentworth can set bond. Before that, he can't. He doesn't have to set bond at all, but in all likelihood he will in this case. My responsibility, and probably the only one I am qualified to handle in this court, will be to convince the judge that you are a responsible citizen, and that you will show up for trial if they let you out on bond. We want it set as low as possible, of course. You'll have enough hassle and expense without having to give a small fortune to a bondsman. I can't make any promises, but I'll do my best."

Bill glanced over at his wife. Dark circles rimmed her eyes; she looked haggard and drawn. He felt so sorry for her, and so helpless himself. He had barely begun to comprehend all that had happened, and had no idea what to do or say next. Almost by instinct he reached over and took her hand. Her eyes told him she was glad that he had; at least they were in this together.

"What do you know about Judge Wentworth?" Bill asked.

"I only know him by reputation. Everything I hear is good, though. I understand he's smart, tough, and fair. Under these circumstances, that's about all you could ask for." Bennett rose and motioned for the guard in the hall to come unlock the door. "The sheriff has given Bill permission to stay with you until they're ready to bring you over to the hearing. He'll come over with you then. He brought you the clothes and other things you asked for—they'll let you change before you leave here. If there's anything else you need, call me at my office. My secretary will know where to find me. Otherwise, I'll see you in court at eleven."

"Thank you, Mr. Bennett," Carol said.

"We really appreciate your help," Bill echoed, shaking the elderly attorney's hand.

"You're both welcome. I just wish there was more I could do. Remember, Carol, I'll do the talking when we get to court. Don't say anything unless I tell you to, no matter what." The guard opened the door; Claiborne Bennett quickly left.

‖16‖

Later that morning, Carol and Bill were escorted back across the street to the Municipal Courts Building. Carol stared at the ground as she walked; Bill helped lead her along. Even though her arms were now tucked in front of her, with a sweater draped over the offensive handcuffs, she felt conspicuous and embarrassed. She didn't want to see the stares of strangers. She couldn't stand it. She forced herself to focus on the ground in front of her, but prying eyes pricked at her consciousness. She knew they were there, and she was helpless to avoid them.

The Division One courtroom was jammed with spectators by the time they arrived. There had been standing-room-only for at least an hour. Word of this hearing had spread throughout the courthouse; there had been talk of little else since the cataclysmic events of the previous day.

As soon as official notice had been received that Carol's preliminary hearing would be in Division One, technicians had begun to transfer the television equipment from Division Two, across the hall. The two courtrooms were mirror images of each other, with their main doors just a few feet apart. With little time to spare, everything had been moved. Now the bright lights were back on; the stage was set for the morning's hearing.

In a few moments the bailiff appeared, stepped up to the judge's bench, and tapped sharply on the wooden surface with the judge's gavel. The sudden noise brought everyone to immediate attention.

"All rise," the bailiff cried out.

Everyone in the courtroom stood and faced the bench. Judge Randall Wentworth emerged from the door to the right of the bench, ascended the stairs, and stood behind the judge's chair. His keen eyes surveyed the courtroom as he glanced from face to face. His stern expression served as a clear warning to any who might dare breach decorum in his courtroom.

"Open court, Mr. Bailiff," the judge commanded.

At age fifty-four, Randall Wentworth was the very model of a jurist. He was a distinguished black man, his tawny skin accentuated by bushy gray hair which tapered down to full sideburns that were almost white. Blessed with a booming voice that commanded attention and respect, and piercing eyes that had been known to stare right through ill-prepared lawyers, Wentworth was the first black to be appointed to the criminal bench in this state, and his credentials were impeccable. In four years on the bench he had earned the respect of lawyers and litigants alike by being fair. Still, he ran a tight courtroom. This hearing was to be no exception. Without fanfare, he got down to business.

"Call the first case, Mr. Bailiff," said the judge.

"Case number 83503, State versus Carol Jeffreys Rogers. Charge: Homicide. Status: Preliminary hearing," said the bailiff in his most dignified voice.

"Who represents the defense?" the judge inquired.

Judge Wentworth peered at Claiborne Bennett over his reading glasses as the elderly lawyer stood up. "I do, Your Honor, Claiborne Bennett of Bennett and Silverstein."

"Mr. Bennett, do you intend to remain of record in this case to its conclusion?" The judge's question was not unexpected. Wentworth knew that Bennett's "eminence" was not in the criminal area. When a lawyer allows himself to become counsel of record in a case, there is much more involved than the simple declaration of an attorney-client relationship. Being counsel of record also creates a court-attorney relationship. The attorney becomes an officer of the court, and cannot abandon the cause without the court's permission.

"Your Honor," Bennett responded, "with the court's permission it is my intention to represent Mrs. Rogers only at this hearing. I have advised her to obtain counsel with more expertise in this area for the further handling of this matter."

"Mr. Bennett," the judge responded, "there are no temporary lawyers in this court. We will enter your name as counsel of record in this cause. As such, you will be totally responsible for the handling of this matter until such time as you are formally relieved of that responsibility. If and when you are replaced by another lawyer, it will be necessary for you to prepare and submit to the court a motion to be allowed to substitute counsel, and an order signed by yourself and the new lawyer. Of course that motion will be given every consideration at the appropriate time, but I cannot rule in advance. In any event, until such a motion has been made and granted, this court must hold you fully responsible for the defense of Carol Rogers. Is that clear?"

"Yes, Your Honor," Bennett answered quietly, somewhat flustered.

"Who is going to represent the state?" the judge then asked, turning toward the prosecution table. Carlton Douglas stood. Tom Sanderson remained seated.

"Your Honor, I will personally handle this prosecution for the state," the district attorney stated, pausing for effect. He looked over at Claiborne Bennett, his face communicating subtle contempt. "From beginning to end," he added.

Judge Wentworth was silent for a moment. He removed his reading glasses and began to clean them, taking time to let Carlton Douglas's surprising revelation sink in. Douglas's aversion to the courtroom was well known to the judge. Finally he replaced his glasses, shook his head, smiled, and went on with the proceedings.

"Very well, let District Attorney Carlton Douglas's name be entered as counsel of record for the state," he said.

The gauntlet had been thrown down. Carlton Douglas had committed himself to the fray.

"Is there anything that needs to be handled preliminarily, gentlemen?" the judge asked.

"Yes, there is, Your Honor," Claiborne Bennett replied, standing up once more as he began to speak. "The defense wishes to waive a preliminary hearing in this matter and let the case be bound over to the grand jury."

"Very well," the judge responded. He wasn't surprised. "What about bond, Mr. Bennett?"

"Your Honor," Bennett answered, "we respectfully request that bond be set relatively low." He stepped away from the lectern and looked at the judge as he spoke. "Your Honor, we realize that the charges are serious, very serious, indeed. But the purpose of bond is to insure the appearance of the defendant in court at the proper time. It should be obvious to this court, just as it is obvious to me, that this woman is a dependable, solid citizen with deep roots in this community. Her husband's work is here. Her son is in school here. Her family needs her at home, and she needs to be there."

While Claiborne Bennett spoke, Carol Rogers looked over at the defense table. Carlton Douglas was leaning forward on his elbows, his gaze frantically alternating between the judge and Bennett. The look on his face was one of pure hatred. There was fire in his eyes; his jaws were clenched shut. A shudder ran down Carol's spine; she looked away quickly.

Then her glance fell on Tom Sanderson.

He was slumped back in his chair. She saw a sadness in his expression, as if he couldn't believe what was happening. Carol had seen that look before. She had seen it in court, in fact. She had seen it on Ellen Hayes.

"No good cause would be served by retaining her in jail at the taxpayers' expense," Bennett continued. "I can personally assure you that when it comes her time to stand before the bar of justice, like any good citizen she will be there. I will see to that as an officer of this court whether I am still counsel of record or not. But in the meantime she is entitled to the presumption of innocence, as much so as any defendant who ever stood before this court. I respectfully urge, on her behalf, that bond be set at a reasonable amount."

When Bennett finished, Carlton Douglas rose to speak. Judge Wentworth waved him back down.

"Gentlemen," the judge began, "in all candor I already know what I am going to do. There is no reason whatsoever to belabor this. The statutory minimum bond in homicide cases is ten thousand dollars, and that's what I am going to set. I have no doubt that this will be sufficient to secure the defendant's presence at the proper time." He paused for a moment to emphasize what was to follow. "However, I am going to set a special condition to the bond, Mr. Bennett. Your client must make her final selection of a lawyer within one week. I cannot leave the matter of permanent counsel unresolved any longer than absolutely necessary. I plan to set this case right away. There is no need for a delay, and I want to get this matter concluded. This entire community *deserves* to have this matter concluded. Is that clear?"

"I understand completely, Your Honor," Bennett replied. "My client will have that matter attended to within the week."

"Anything further, gentlemen?" the judge then inquired.

"Nothing, Your Honor," the two lawyers said, almost simultaneously.

"Adjourn court, Mr. Bailiff." The judge rose and left.

That was it. In ten minutes the hearing was over. Judge Wentworth's reputation as a no-nonsense judge was thoroughly vindicated. Everyone involved in this case now knew, without question, that Randall Wentworth would be in command of the proceedings. He would be fair, but he would be firm. Once he had decided on any question, that would be it. This courtroom would be no place for the faint of heart.

At the defense table, Carol Rogers and Claiborne Bennett rose to leave. Carol turned to look for Bill. Her attention was drawn instead to a familiar face in the gallery. She recognized Ellen Hayes, and wondered why she had come. The two women looked at each other for an instant. Then Claiborne Bennett took Carol's arm and led her off to the clerk's office, to arrange for her bond. Bill Rogers caught up with them in the hall.

"What do we do now?" Bill asked.

"The first thing is to post bond," Bennett replied, cutting his eyes toward one of the photographers who dogged their steps. "We can call for a bonding company representative to meet us at the clerk's office—I got several names from a friend. Or if you prefer, we can try to work out a deposit, or put up the equity in your house, or try to figure out something else to keep from losing any money on the front end. It might take a while, but it would be worth it to me. You decide. Whichever we do, we'll be able to leave as soon as arrangements have been completed. We can send someone by the sheriff's office to pick up your things later. Then, after bond has been arranged, the first order of business will be finding the right criminal lawyer. We've got to act quickly on that one. Frankly, it's clear to me that Judge Wentworth will jerk your bond in a minute if you don't have someone in a week."

"Do you have any idea who we might talk to?" Bill asked. "I don't know any lawyers at all."

"I wish you would stay on. I dread the thought of dealing with a total stranger," Carol said.

"Believe me, it wouldn't be fair to either of you for me to impose my ignorance on you," Bennett responded. "I've asked around and I can give you some names, but you two should go on home this morning and let Carol rest awhile. Later we can get together and discuss some of the possibilities. You won't have any trouble finding the right lawyer—every criminal lawyer in town is drooling over this one. Public exposure is the lifeblood of their craft, and this is a highly visible case. We should be able to pick and choose."

When they finally arrived at the clerk's office, Bill was allowed to assign the equity in their home as security instead of posting a bond. In a few moments they were fighting their way back through the crowded hall and out the front door of the courthouse to the waiting car which Bennett had arranged. Scurrying past clamoring reporters, they climbed into the back seat and were quickly whisked away.

Carol and Bill were grateful for a few quiet moments, each of them lost in thought. Finally Bill spoke.

"Carol, we need to deal with this lawyer problem today. It can't wait until later."

"Why not?" Carol exclaimed. "I've just got to rest this afternoon. Why can't it wait? Mr. Bennett said we could take some time to work this out."

"I won't be here tomorrow," Bill answered. "I'm supposed to leave in the morning for the product show. I have a nine o'clock flight. I'll be gone for a week. You know that."

"I forgot," Carol responded. Her heart ached; her expression plunged toward sullenness. She hadn't forgotten. She just hoped that he would have better sense than to leave at a time like this.

Bill lowered his voice to keep the driver from hearing. "You know I don't have any choice. The world may be able to stop for some people, but if we expect to eat, I've got to show up at that trade show and get as many orders as I can."

"Nobody's indispensable, Bill," Carol retorted without lowering her voice. She didn't care who heard her. "They could handle it just fine without you, and you know it. You just want to get away. That's your way of doing things. When trouble comes, you just close your eyes and get away. You carry on as if nothing has happened, until you finally convince yourself that it's true. Well, something has definitely happened, and you can't avoid it!"

Carol turned away from her husband and stared blankly out the car window. At this point she had been drained of all spirit. She had no desire to fight with him.

"Good God, Carol," Bill whispered, leaning his head back against the seat. "Do we have to go through this now? I'm doing the best I can. You know that."

"I don't know anything," Carol responded. "And I don't care. You go ahead. Do what you have to, or what you want to. That's what you always do, anyway." She turned her face away from him and bit her lip.

The car moved quickly along the quiet streets. Inside, the air was thick with tension.

"You could at least have waited until we got home," Carol said, still avoiding Bill's gaze. He didn't reply. He never did; their communication was almost always one-sided.

"It's not the trade show, Bill," she said. That was true. She knew how important it was. Indeed, their income for the coming year would depend to a great extent on his success at this show. "It's not that at all."

Then what is it? he thought. But he didn't say anything, just gritted his teeth and endured the passing moments. What good would it do? he mused. It always ends the same way.

They continued to ride along in uncomfortable silence.

"You needn't worry about a lawyer. I already know who I'm going to use," she stated flatly.

"Who?" Bill asked.

"Ellen Hayes," Carol answered.

"That's not funny!" Bill shot back.

"I'm not kidding," Carol responded, struggling to keep calm.

"I like her. She's smart, she's well trained"—Carol paused for a moment—"and she's a woman. That's important to me."

"This is serious business, Carol. It's not something to take lightly. You'd be crazy to deliver yourself into the hands of your enemies. You just missed killing Ellen Hayes by inches. If you were stupid enough to ask her, she would laugh in your face."

"Can we discuss this," Carol said, "or would you prefer to just vent your spleen?" The driver's face reddened as the conversation continued.

"Look," Bill answered, forcing his voice down. "Let's drop this for now. You rest this afternoon, and we'll talk about it again tomorrow morning before I leave. This is no time to deal with something this crucial."

"Bill, I'm serious about this. I got the feeling during our trial that Ellen Hayes was sympathetic, that she understood what I was going through. And I don't think a man could possibly understand, not really. I sure don't want to have to try to make one understand. I'd rather have someone who can think like I think from the very first. I don't need someone who can make fancy speeches and raise technicalities but has no idea how I feel about all of this."

Carol shifted in her seat, turning her back away from her husband, and stared idly out the window. Bill closed his eyes and tried to concentrate on other things. He hated conflict; Carol was right about that. And she could be the most stubborn woman in the world when she set her mind on something. Had he been watching her while she spoke, he might have recognized something familiar, something he detested. It was in her facial expression. It was something he had seen many times before, a kind of benign, satisfied expression that always appeared when her mind was made up, when she was comfortable with a difficult decision. It was a look that invariably infuriated him, because she only used it when there was nothing in the world he could do to make her change her mind.

‖17‖

Friday morning arrived all too soon. Carol rolled over in bed and fumbled with the alarm, finally managing to shut it off. Bill was already up. She could hear him moving about downstairs. She rolled her feet over the side of the bed and sat there for a moment, mentally picking the cobwebs out of the corners of her brain. She peered out the window at the first streaks of morning sun. At least it looked like it was going to be a pretty day.

She felt somewhat better, except for a bit of a headache. She had slept all night long—fitful sleep at best, but better than nothing. She heard the rattling of pots and pans in the kitchen, tossed on a robe, ran a brush through her hair, and went downstairs to join Bill. It was almost seven-thirty. Soon she would have to take him to the airport.

Bill had already assembled breakfast. Carol poured herself a cup of coffee and sat down across the table from him. Jeffrey was just finishing a bowl of cereal.

"Feeling any better, Mom?" Jeffrey asked. He looked over at Carol with genuine concern.

"I think so, honey," Carol answered, stifling a yawn. "I guess I would have to feel somewhat better, considering how bad I felt yesterday. I think I could sleep another twenty-four hours and still not get rid of this grogginess, though."

"Why don't you go on back to bed," Bill suggested. "I can take a cab to the airport."

"No, I want to drive you. I don't mind," Carol replied. "Just let me finish this coffee and I'll slip something on. It won't take a minute."

Bill would have preferred to ride to the airport alone, since the last thing he wanted was to continue their confrontation.

Jeffrey got up and put his dishes away. He gathered his schoolbooks and papers, kissed his mother on the cheek, and headed out the door. Carol rubbed a finger across her cheek at the spot where he had kissed her. She cherished that kiss.

"He's such a sweet boy," she said to Bill, "and so affectionate when I really need it. Sometimes he seems far more sensitive and understanding than you do."

"You didn't wait long to start up this morning, did you?" Bill said, tossing the paper down onto the table.

Carol stared down at her coffee while Bill ran upstairs to do some last-minute packing. She held the china cup between her palms and let its warmth radiate into her hands. She blew the dark liquid ever so gently, watching little circular ripples form on the surface of the cup, then quickly disappear. Then she looked around at her kitchen. It was a cheerful, comfortable room, decorated in yellows, greens, and whites. Most mornings, after her family had departed, she would sit in the breakfast nook for a while before starting her daily routine. It was a good place to organize her thoughts. She loved to sit in peaceful silence and look out the full-length window, watching the morning sunlight filter through the large maple trees, following the flight of the cardinals and towhees as they came and went.

The sunlight cast an irregular pattern of light and dark on the fresh spring grass and illuminated the flower bed against the back fence. The first shoots of spring crocus had begun to burst through the crusty surface of the earth. It was a time of new beginnings, of freshness, of promise for the future. Carol hoped that this was an omen of better things to come.

As she sat there nursing her cooling coffee, she thought how this was the very spot where she'd sat two days earlier, in the middle of the night. This same room that now warmed and comforted her was the very place where everything had started. How ironic it seemed that she could have sat in this spot feeling so alone, so depressed, wanting to take her own life, and now, two short days later, it had become, once again, her place of refuge.

"Time to go, Carol," Bill called out as he came down the stairs. The sound of his voice broke her mood. Her tranquillity dissipated instantly.

"I'm coming," she said as she stood up. She quickly rinsed out her coffee cup and placed it upside down on the drying rack. She grabbed her purse from the counter, the same large leather purse she'd carried to court. Then she dashed upstairs, threw on some khakis and a sweater, stepped into some flats, grabbed her cardigan, and hurried back down to the waiting car.

The two of them drove along the streets in silence, past rows of attractive, middle-class homes. Large trees lined the curving roadway, shading most of the front yards. Most of the lawns were well kept and manicured, the homes well developed with shrubs and plantings that reflected years of care. Carol loved this area. The homes reflected pride of ownership. Whenever she turned off of the main thoroughfare and onto the winding residential street that leads to the little lane on which they lived, she felt that she was entering another world, a quiet, sheltered world. She especially needed that feeling now.

"I'm sorry, Bill," she said as she watched him drive along. "I'm sorry I said what I said this morning. I'm sorry about yesterday. I know it's tough on both of us," she added. "I really do."

Bill said nothing, but reached over and placed his hand on top of hers.

He turned the car out onto the busy, commercial thoroughfare that marked the eastern boundary of the residential area. The station wagon slid quietly along the pavement, passing rows and rows of business establishments—fast-food outlets, gas stations, small stores. An ugly proliferation of commercial signs lined both sides of the street. From this perspective the world looked vastly different. It even smelled different. The contrast heightened Carol's longing for the protective environment of home. She really didn't feel like being out this morning.

"Carol," Bill said, breaking the silence, "we really need to resolve this Ellen Hayes thing."

"What's there to resolve?" Carol asked defensively. She was caught by surprise. She hadn't expected him to bring it up. She could feel her protective shell closing around her, cutting off communication. His hand moved away from hers.

"Well, for one thing, I need to know what you are going to do. I don't want you to do anything foolish while I'm gone."

That's typical, she thought to herself. He assumes that I won't handle things right without him here. She hesitated for a moment before responding.

"If you stay home, then you'll know what I'm going to do. It's just that simple. I can't wait; you know that. The judge has given us a deadline." Carol's bluntness surprised Bill; it surprised her even more.

Bill aimed the cumbersome wagon up the entrance ramp to the interstate, and accelerated to a speed that would let him blend in with the moving traffic. The wagon cruised along in the right-hand lane while cars zipped past on the left.

Bill was quiet for a few moments. As they started to veer off onto the access road leading to the air terminal, he summoned up his courage and began again.

"Carol, I don't want to get into a fight with you this morning. I can't take that, not right now," he said. "But regardless of how you feel about me, you owe it to yourself not to do anything foolish. Ellen Hayes only has one positive characteristic—she's a woman. She's too young, too inexperienced, and too involved in this situation already. From every possible perspective she is the worst choice you could make. If you do something rash like that, you might well regret it for the rest of your life. You've just got to listen to reason. We can find out about the other women lawyers in town who handle this kind of case, if that's what you want. We can talk on the phone. I'll be available. But please don't do anything stupid. That's all I ask, for your sake as well as mine. Please, promise me you won't."

Carol didn't respond. Bill pulled the wagon up to the curb in front of the ticket area of the airport, stopped in front of an outdoor baggage counter, and got out of the car.

"Call me tonight and we'll talk," she said as she slid over into the driver's seat.

If Carol hadn't already been determined to see Ellen Hayes, the idea would have become permanently implanted in her brain the moment Bill told her not to do anything stupid. Stupid! It was his favorite word. He never gave her credit for having an ounce of sense, except when she agreed with him.

Bill pulled his large suitcase out of the tailgate. A porter came and offered to assist him. Bill was fumbling through his pockets for his tickets when he heard the car's engine. He stared in surprise and disbelief as the station wagon pulled away from the curb and headed out of the gate area.

If he had been able to see Carol before she drove off, he would have seen the tears welling up in her eyes. "What in the hell do you expect, hugs and kisses?" she said to herself.

Carol turned off the car radio. She was in no mood for music. She rode along the access road in silence, retracing the route they'd just come in on. Reaching the interstate, she maneuvered herself into the flow of traffic. As usual, cars whipped by her on the left as she cruised along at the legal speed limit. Apparently I am the only one on the interstate who has chosen to obey the law, she thought to herself, amused at the irony of it. At about that moment a sports car came up on her left and darted in front of her, rushing to make the exit which they were both approaching fast. Carol pressed down on her brakes and slammed her horn as the sports car barely missed the front of her wagon.

"Dammit, watch where you're going, you fool!" she shouted out. Then she turned red, embarrassed at her uncharacteristic outburst. "What's happening to me?" she cried out. Her fists gripped the steering wheel tightly. She jerked at it as if to give it a good shake. "What am I becoming?" She bit her lip to keep from crying out loud.

Carol drove off the interstate and down the thoroughfare toward home. Soon she found herself back in the welcome ambience of her neighborhood, far from the noise and confusion. She drove along the winding street that led toward home, past the comfortable, inviting houses, past the well-clipped hedges just beginning to show new growth, past the oaks, maples, and elms that gave the neighborhood its distinctive appearance, past little dogs chasing each other back and forth, up and down the sidewalk. But when she reached her street she didn't turn. Instead she drove on along the winding road as it snaked its way up a large hill and then back down into a valley filled with more homes, more shade trees, and more stability and comfort.

She drove the station wagon up a steep driveway which gradually leveled off. Two giant oak trees formed a protective umbrella, almost totally obliterating any view of the blue sky and morning sun. The sparse grass along each side of the driveway was still moist with dew. Several squirrels scampered up the large tree trunks as they heard the sound of her car. Carol pulled over, put the gearshift lever in park, and turned off the motor. She sat with her arms folded across the steering wheel, her head resting on her arms.

After a moment, she grabbed her purse, threw her sweater around her shoulders to ward off the morning chill, and walked along the driveway toward the front of the large white building. Double front doors were flanked by frosted-glass side windows. She tried one of the burnished brass handles, but it was locked. She tried the other; the heavy door swung open and she slipped inside. As the door closed behind her, she passed a small sign propped up on a tripod in the darkened narthex:

WELCOME TO
BELLEVIEW PRESBYTERIAN CHURCH
JOSEPH HOLMAN, MINISTER

‖18‖

Joe Holman eased his Toyota up the rear driveway of Belleview Presbyterian Church. Though he didn't see Carol's car, he would not have been at all surprised to find someone at the church at this hour. People often sought the solace of its quiet beauty. That pleased him; he had planned it that way.

Eight years earlier, he had startled his governing board by insisting that the sanctuary be unlocked twenty-four hours a day, seven days a week. "It's a sanctuary," he'd told the incredulous group. "We need to let it be what the name implies, a place of safety, comfort, and refuge. We can't predict when anyone will need to be close to God. This place must be open and available at all times." The board had voted with him, but it was close.

Sure, there had been an occasional wino or two. And there had been enough minor vandalism throughout the years to keep the tongues of Holman's detractors clacking with gossipy criticism. But through the years literally hundreds of people had come to the beautiful old building to seek comfort, to pray, to communicate in their own way with their maker, or just to be left alone in one of the seemingly last quiet places left on earth.

Carol had come alone to the sanctuary on more than one occasion, especially since Wendy's death. She knew that she could depend on its availability. As it was on this particular morning, one of the big front doors would be unlocked, and she would be welcome and safe inside.

Holman parked his car in the space marked *Pastor* and entered the education building. As he walked through the darkened fellowship hall, the clicking of his heels echoed off the block walls. It was a hollow, empty sound. One of his early resolutions had been to refurbish this assembly area, to soften it with some carpet, perhaps draperies, too. But it seemed that there was never enough money to go around. Year after year more important things had come up.

Sometimes it seemed to Holman that his ministry was nothing but a constant stream of administrative duty—begging for money, dealing with personnel problems, moderating heated arguments over pointless theological squabbles. He longed for a place where he could simply minister to the needs of his flock and leave the administrative headaches to others. Unfortunately, Belleview was one of those "in-between" churches—big enough to need a myriad of services and programs, but not quite big enough to support a large staff.

Holman switched on the light in his small, interestingly cluttered office. Books and pamphlets lined the shelves and spilled over into stacks on the chairs and tables. Old sermons, notes, and memos covered the top of his desk. But Holman knew exactly where everything was, and exactly where everything belonged. The worst thing that could happen to him would be for someone to move everything around under the guise of "straightening up."

Joe Holman had come to Belleview eight years ago. This was the third church he'd worked at, and it was by far the largest. In all three he had endeared himself to the congregation. Diminutive in stature, he was energetic and enthusiastic, and had a keen sense of humor which helped him keep both himself and his vocation in perspective. People instinctively trusted him, men and women alike.

After glancing over his correspondence, Holman headed over to the storage area which was located on the other side of the sanctuary building. But instead of taking the long route, he decided to cut through the sanctuary itself.

He didn't notice Carol right away, hidden as she was in the darkness near the rear. She remained motionless as Holman came in, so immersed in her own thoughts that she didn't even see him when he entered.

Holman started across the sanctuary to the door on the other side but instinctively paused. Something was amiss. He looked around.

Through the tall windows he could see newly leafed-out trees rocking slowly back and forth to the rhythm of the morning breeze. Sunbeams played in the soft light that filtered through the leaves and streamed through the windows, forming irregular patterns along the carpet and the backs of the pews.

A huge cross silhouetted against a large picture window dominated the wall behind the choir loft. A smaller brass cross stood on the communion table in the altar area. It was turned slightly to one side, destroying the symmetry of the setting. He climbed the steps to the altar and started to correct this one minor imperfection. It was at that moment that he heard the cry from far back in the hall.

Holman walked slowly along the maroon carpeted center aisle, and sat down in the pew in front of Carol. He just sat there, saying nothing. Carol didn't move; she sobbed quietly and sniffled. Holman took a Kleenex from his pocket and held it out toward her as she lifted her head. Her eyes were red and watery, her face deeply flushed. She had been crying for some time.

"Here," he said, offering the tissue.

"Thanks, Joe."

They both sat there for a moment, saying nothing.

Carol felt no embarrassment at being seen like this. She had been with Joe before in times of deep distress. She was comfortable with him. He was the first minister with whom she had ever enjoyed this kind of relationship. It was a unique experience, one which she treasured.

Finally, she pulled herself together.

"I needed that, I really did," she said, smiling weakly through her tears.

"Sometimes the best thing in the world is to just let it all hang out," Joe said.

"Right now I really don't have any choice," Carol responded, pausing to sniff once again. "I can keep things bottled up just so long, then I begin to explode. Small explosions at first, then big outbursts like this one."

"You are entitled to a good cry if anyone is," Joe said. The two of them sat in silent stillness for a few moments, the quiet broken only by the noise of an occasional car passing by the church building.

"You know, Joe, I sometimes wonder if life will ever be the same again. I know time heals wounds, but I don't know that I will ever get rid of the feeling that the weight of the world is on my shoulders," Carol said. "And it isn't just the heartache. That alone would be bad enough. It's me. All of this is changing me, Joe, and I don't like what I'm feeling, or who I'm becoming. I bite Bill's head off as if he's to blame for everything. Heaven only knows how Jeff sees me now. At times I'm barely civil. They don't deserve that. They deserve better. None of this is their fault. It's just that I don't seem to have anything left to give anymore. I'm drained. I'm completely empty, and I see no hope for anything better."

"I can tell you that time *will* make things better," Joe responded, "but that won't make you believe it. You've just got to ride these feelings out as best as you can. I'll help; so will Bill, and Jeff, and all of your friends. One day you'll discover to your surprise that you feel a tiny bit better. That will be the new beginning. It won't happen overnight, but it will surely happen. God never gives us more than we can handle, Carol, he really doesn't."

"Do you really believe that, Joe?" Carol asked. "Do you really believe God gave all of this to me? Do you really believe God had anything to do with Wendy's death, and with all that's happened since?"

"Do you?" Joe asked, returning the question.

"I don't know what I believe anymore, Joe," Carol answered, looking at him with an expression of tortured anguish. "I used to believe God was in control, that he really did see the tiniest sparrow when it fell from the sky, that he could change things in our lives, in my life. But I'm not so sure anymore. I haven't done anything to deserve all of this. I really haven't."

She paused for a moment and shifted around, searching for a more relaxed position.

"I remember that night after Wendy died, a woman came up to me at the funeral home and told me that I should be grateful, because Wendy was with God, that she was happier now, and that God had needed her more than I did. I know she meant well, and she was only trying to help, but I just wanted to grab that woman by the shoulders and shake her as hard as I could. I wanted to scream at her, to tell her she was crazy, to tell her that the God I love isn't that cruel, that he would never have done something like this." Carol smiled and wiped her eyes with the Kleenex. "Poor woman. She didn't have any idea how close I came to letting her have it."

"I don't know what God does and doesn't do, or what he can and can't do, Carol," Joe said, "but I do believe he can help. I guess it isn't a question of God sending us what we can handle really. But I do believe God will give us help to handle whatever comes our way, if we will let him."

Carol didn't answer. She stared down at her hands and picked at the little wad of tear-soaked Kleenex, nervously twisting it into spirals, pulling off little pieces one by one. After a few moments she spoke again, her head still bowed, her voice quieter and more restrained.

"Joe, I will wish forever that I hadn't shot that boy, I really will. But it's not because I care about him. I don't. I care about what all of this is doing to me, to Bill, to Jeff, and our life together. I feel no remorse for that boy whatever, and that worries me. I'm not glad he's dead, but I'm not sorry, either. I just don't care. I hated him for what he did, and I don't care that he's dead. I didn't think I was capable of not caring, of not feeling anything. But that's exactly what has happened. I feel absolutely nothing. That worries me, Joe, that's not like me."

"You're being too hard on yourself, Carol," Joe replied. "You really are. You're measuring yourself against an unrealistic standard. You're not perfect, and you never will be, but you are human, and you have been deeply hurt. There's nothing wrong with you, or with what you're feeling. You are a human being with human reactions. You need to quit analyzing yourself. Let yourself feel what's really there, and quit worrying about what you think ought to be there. Don't you see? Human emotions and human responses are natural. They aren't good or bad, they are natural. When you start trying to label them as 'okay' and 'not okay,' you get into trouble. You need to start accepting your feelings instead of passing judgment on them, and on yourself as well."

"My head understands, but my heart is having an awfully hard time with this," Carol responded, smiling weakly.

"Just remember, Carol," Joe continued, "it's not your feelings that get you in trouble, it's denying that you have them. As long as you admit your true feelings and try to keep them in perspective, you'll pull through. And I can help. So can Bill, and so can Jeff, because we all love you, and we care about you." He took her hand and gave it a squeeze.

"Thank you, Joe. I really mean it. You've been a big help. Now if I could just feel better about Bill," she added, almost as an afterthought.

"You want to tell me about it?" Joe asked.

"Oh, it's nothing, really," Carol answered. Then she quickly changed her mind. "That's not true," she said. "It really is something. Bill and I got into a fight yesterday and almost weren't speaking this morning. We fought about what lawyer to hire. I have one in mind, one I want to talk to, but Bill doesn't think it's a very good idea. He told me so right off. He backed me into a corner with his attitude, so I reacted too strongly and told him off. Then one thing led to another. I know I could give in, and maybe I should, but this is important to me. I want who I want."

"Who is he?" Joe inquired.

"He? Good grief, you sound just like Bill." Carol smiled at Joe. "It's not a he, Joe, it's a she. It's Ellen Hayes."

Joe was quiet for a few seconds.

"I see the problem," he said. "Why do you think she's the right person? And would she take the case?"

"Frankly, I don't know, Joe. All I really want to do is talk to her. But I do know enough already to know that I want a woman. That's important. I don't think a man could ever put himself in my shoes, or understand what I've been through."

"I can understand that, Carol. But Ellen Hayes . . . ?" Joe's voice trailed off, leaving his own question unanswered.

"I just have this feeling, Joe. I think she's the one."

"Then go talk to her, Carol," Joe said, his voice conveying genuine conviction. "Go talk to her. You're the one with the most to gain or lose, and you're the one who's got to live with the consequences. I don't know whether she's right or wrong. I have an opinion, but I don't really know. But I do know, just as sure as we're sitting here, that you won't be satisfied until you at least talk to her."

"What about Bill?" Carol asked.

"Bill loves you, Carol," Joe responded. "He may not agree with you, but I know he loves you, and he is going to support you in whatever decision you make, if you think it through and really believe in what you are doing."

"I hope you're right, Joe," Carol whispered. "I sure hope you're right."

‖19‖

Carol and Joe went to the more comfortable surroundings of Joe's office, where they talked for some time. Carol continued to do most of the talking, but that really didn't matter. She was arriving at a turning point, perhaps even the "new beginning" that Joe had referred to. At the very least she was taking the first step.

Up until then, Carol had been letting her feelings control her life. It had been as if she were alone in a small boat, lost in a turbulent sea, bobbing up and down on wildly undulating swells, completely at the mercy of insidiously silent waves of emotion that threatened to capsize her and pull her under. But this morning she had finally begun to sort out and recognize her feelings and emotions. With Joe's help, she was able to identify those feelings for what they were, and to realize that her emotions were capable of destroying her.

"Your feelings are real, and they are true," Joe said to her several times during the morning. "The very same God that made laughter also made tears. Your feelings may be negative, and you may dislike them, but they aren't bad. Not at all."

None of her pain was eliminated. The agony and loneliness she had felt over the loss of her daughter was still as real as ever.

The depression was still as deep, the anger still as violent. Resentments and disappointment would still be a part of her life, but now they were recognized for what they were. She now understood that she had to be in control of her own existence in spite of those feelings.

She was still adrift on the stormy sea, and she would be there for some time, but there was a major difference. She was no longer lost. She no longer felt alone. And she realized that she had never been truly alone but had only felt that she was. Now she understood for the first time that others could help her, that they really wanted to do so, if only she would let them. With Joe's help she had finally placed one small, tentative hand on the rudder that guided her life. From now on she would plot her own course through the storm of her emotions, working with her feelings instead of against them.

As she drove back out the church driveway, under the protective canopy of the old oak trees, she thanked God for Joe Holman and for the impulse that had caused her to come there on that morning.

Safely home, Carol stretched out across her bed for a while. She was very tired, but she didn't sleep. She was too busy thinking back over the past few hours. It occurred to her as she lay there that she had rejoined the living, but that she had an enormous amount of work to do before she would be able to really enjoy life again.

After a very long time, she sat up in bed. "I might as well start somewhere," she said as she glanced over at the alarm clock on the bedside table, "and this is as good a time and place as any."

It was three o'clock. Today was Friday, a school day. In another half hour or so Jeff would be coming home. For as long as she remembered, she had looked forward to greeting her children on their arrival from school. She would prepare an afternoon snack for them and sit with them while they ate. This was their time together, the time when she found out what was really going on in their lives. These had been times of great joy to her, and she missed it very much.

It was during one of these afternoon sessions that Jeff had first shyly admitted a special affection for the girl who sat across from him in his history class. At another, Wendy had proudly announced that she had captured a part in the school play. Both of the children had been given opportunities to brag, gripe, complain, and ask for help. This was their time; they had Carol's full attention.

Even when Carol couldn't be there, she would still leave them a snack, and perhaps a note encouraging them to carry on without her. It had developed into a wonderful tradition, giving birth to treasured moments, rich memories, and strong ties between mother and children. Now Carol realized that in the midst of her self-pity over the loss of Wendy the wonderful tradition had come to an abrupt halt for Jeff as well. How tragic, she thought. How unfair to him, and how unnecessary it now seems. And *this* is the day to do something about it.

When Jeff came home from school and saw her seated at the kitchen table, he grinned from ear to ear. It had been a long, long time since he had seen an honest smile in this house.

If he had other plans, he never let on. He pulled up a chair and sat down. They talked. Nothing intense, nothing profound, just talk. It was a good experience for both of them. Neither stopped missing Wendy. That emptiness was still there, just as it would be for a long time to come. But they unconsciously acknowledged that life was still there to be enjoyed by those who lived. It didn't have to stop, no matter what had happened.

In a few moments Jeff got up from the table, gave Carol a hug, and headed out the door, still smiling broadly. It was a warm moment for Carol, as if the tiniest corner had been turned, the tiniest bit of progress made. As she watched her son run through the backyard, she found herself crying once again. But this time the tears were expressions of thanksgiving for her son who was living, and not tears of grief for the daughter she would never see again.

Later that night, Carol lay alone in her bed. The light was still on; an open book lay on the covers beside her. Her eyes were closed, but she wasn't asleep.

The phone rang. She picked up the receiver.

"Hi," she said. She knew who it was.

"Hi," Bill said. "You okay?"

"It depends on what you mean by okay," she said, shifting to one side and tucking the phone down under her neck so that she could talk without holding on to it.

"I'm afraid I wasn't much good to you, Carol," he said. She didn't respond.

"Look," he continued, "I love you. You know that. I know I don't always show it, but I love you. I'm just doing the best I can in a bad situation," he said.

"I know that, Bill," she answered.

"Anyway, I've thought things over," he went on. "I think I understand about Ellen Hayes. I still don't agree, but I understand."

"What do you understand, Bill?" she asked.

There was a long pause before he answered.

"I understand that it's your decision, not mine," he finally said. "I understand that I can't run things from hundreds of miles away. And I understand that I wish to God I were home, holding you in my arms, showing you how I feel," he added. "I would give anything if I was just able to do that."

Carol smiled. A tear crept over the edge of one eye and wandered down her cheek.

"But most of all I understand that you need my support, and not my criticism," he said. "You've got enough battles to fight without that."

Carol nodded and closed her eyes while he talked.

Later, as she listened to the steady, rhythmic ticking of the clock, she began to map out a plan in her mind, a definite course of action, a blueprint for recovery. It would work, she just knew it. The people were right, and the idea was right. She would think about it and let it jell over the weekend. Then on Monday, if she still felt the same way, she would have at it!

Carol finally drifted off and slept all night long, a deep, untroubled, comfortable sleep, the first she had experienced in many months.

‖20‖

Carol awakened on Monday in good spirits. The enormity of the task ahead was still uppermost in her thoughts; the burden of depression was still her constant companion. But she had found a new strength. Her resolve had survived the weekend. She was determined to make contact with Ellen Hayes this very day.

First she called Claiborne Bennett to set up an appointment. She wanted to see him in person, to explain her decision and seek his blessing. She reached him on the first try, a feat which many of his contemporaries in the legal profession believed to be impossible. Bennett was more than willing to talk and suggested that she come to town immediately. Delighted to be underway with this important project, she quickly showered and dressed, and headed straight for his office.

Bennett & Silverstein occupied the top floor of the First Merchants' Bank Building. It was an older building, a massive monument of granite that towered over one of the city's busiest intersections. Carol parked nearby and walked to the building, enjoying the sights and sounds of the city. It made her feel alive again to be out among these people. She entered the building through the brass front doors that led directly into the spacious bank. Everything about the bank was strong and solid, from shining marble floors to burled walnut desks, from vaulted ceiling and marble columns to ornate mahogany and brass tellers' cages which bustled with activity. Elegant antiques were thoughtfully placed about the large hall. Carol had forgotten how impressive the old place was.

Claiborne Bennett's offices were equally impressive. Like the bank, which his firm had represented for many years, his suite exuded an aura of stability. Upon entering these austere surroundings, one either felt confident or overwhelmed. There was rarely any in-between.

Carol got right to the point and told him exactly why she was there, using the opportunity to test the validity of her own reasoning, telling Bennett many of the same things she had said to Bill earlier. She described Ellen's apparent sensitivity and suggested that Ellen might be able to understand better than most lawyers how Carol could have reacted as she did to the death of her child. Bennett listened patiently, without any noticeable change of expression.

"Have you discussed this with Bill?" he asked her when she finally finished.

"Yes I have," she replied. "He and I talked about it before he left."

"Left? Where has he gone?" Bennett asked.

"A trade show," Carol replied curtly. "He left the morning after my release. He'll be gone for a week."

The silence was awkward. Bennett finally spoke. "I'm surprised he didn't tell me," he mused.

"I'm not," Carol interjected. He'd rather do anything than face trouble head-on, she thought to herself. "Anyway we talked again last night on the phone," she added. "I'll have to be honest with you. He isn't in favor of it, but he told me he would support whatever decision I make. He suggested that I call you and talk to you about it."

Bennett wheeled his chair around and faced the large window that dominated the wall behind his desk. He looked out at the impressive view of the city. It was his city, the place where he had been born and raised, the place where he had started out with nothing and made his way to the top of a tough profession. For a moment he was lost in thought. Then he swiveled back around toward Carol, looking straight into her eyes.

"Carol, I can't recommend the Hayes woman. I know nothing about her, good or bad. The truth is she hasn't been around long enough for anyone to really know anything. She hasn't had time to establish a track record. All of her experience has been as Martin McPherson's sidekick—obviously she's had a good teacher. And she's female; that seems to be important to you. Whether that's an asset or a liability depends on your point of view, I suppose. Most of the female lawyers I know are young, and most of them don't have much experience. She's probably logged as much criminal court time as any of them. Anyway, that isn't much to go on."

"If you can't recommend her, then who would you suggest?" Carol asked. "Do you have a better idea?"

"Well, I'm coming to that, Carol," Bennett replied. "I'm going to surprise you, I expect. I really don't have a better idea. I think you should go ahead and talk to the Hayes woman before you decide. It may turn out that she is the best choice under the circumstances."

"I don't understand," Carol said. "That seems a bit contradictory, doesn't it? You say on the one hand that you can't recommend her, but on the other hand you say I ought to talk with her. Why?"

"I don't mean to confuse you," Bennett responded. "I'm just thinking out loud. You see, in one sense I can't recommend her, because I don't know all that much about her. But in another sense it is almost imperative that you see her and talk to her. In a case like yours, where you're so intensely and personally involved, and where there's so much at stake, the relationship between the client and the lawyer is almost as important as the skill of the lawyer. In fact, it may be more important."

Bennett rose from his chair and walked around to the front of his massive desk. He leaned back against the desk, folded his arms in front of him, and looked down at Carol as he continued to speak.

"Carol, it is absolutely essential that you have complete trust and confidence in your lawyer. In addition, your lawyer has got to feel so strongly about you, and about your case, that he or she is willing to sacrifice his own needs and wants for the good of your cause. There has to be a real commitment from both of you. You have to put your life in the hands of that person and completely trust them to handle the case with skill and care, and that person must believe in you completely and experience your ordeal with you. From what I've heard you say, you may be able to develop that kind of relationship with Ellen Hayes. But one thing is for sure, you will never be satisfied until you've talked to her and found out for yourself. You can't just walk away from that idea now. If you do, you'll spend the rest of your life second-guessing your decision."

"You're right," Carol said, "absolutely right."

"Then talk to her. By all means, talk to her. Here, let's find out where her office is." He reached for the telephone to buzz his secretary.

A few moments later the two of them were out in the bright mid-morning sunlight, headed for Ellen Hayes's office.

Ellen's modest suite was in one of the newer, smaller buildings three blocks west of the First Merchants Bank Tower, just about the same distance from the courthouse as the old bank building. The building was clean and modern, but its thin walls were covered with a nondescript vinyl and its tile floor already showed signs of wear.

Ellen's name was not on the directory across from the bank of elevators, but Bennett's secretary had told Carol to go to the eighth floor. Carol pushed the up button.

"Would you like for me to come up with you?" Bennett asked.

"No, I want to handle it from here by myself," Carol answered. "Thank you. I really appreciate your help."

The elevator arrived; Carol got on.

"Call me and let me know what you decide, Carol. I really want to know," Bennett said.

"I will," Carol said as the doors slid shut.

The elevator sat where it was for a moment. Carol finally realized that it wasn't moving. She hadn't pushed any of the buttons. Grateful that no one had been there to see, she pushed the button for Ellen Hayes's floor. The motor sprung to life; the car glided slowly upward.

On the eighth floor, Ellen Hayes was scurrying about, making things as presentable as possible. Carol Rogers's call had caught her off guard. She really hadn't known how to react. Why would she be coming up here? What did she want?

From the inception of the Frank Jordan case she had admired Carol Rogers. Here was a woman who had endured the ultimate loss, only to be subjected to the relentless, indiscriminate stares of the curious, and the incessant, merciless glare of the public spotlight. Through it all she had seen in Carol a serene composure and quiet dignity that made her a person to be admired.

Carol's violent outburst in the courtroom had not changed that image. Indeed, far from being frightened or concerned for her own safety, Ellen had reacted with a disbelief which quickly gave way to admiration. She had not shared the outrage of Judge Coleman or the indignation of Martin McPherson. Instead she had seen the killing of Frank Jordan as an act of courage, the revenge of a woman wronged, the final response of one who had simply had enough. In her heart she had admired Carol Rogers for taking action, violent though it was, against the evil represented by Frank Jordan.

But she still didn't understand why Carol Rogers wanted to see *her*.

Ellen looked around the small room. It was hopelessly cluttered. Boxes were stacked everywhere, furniture was scattered about. For the most part, everything was still standing where the moving men had dumped it.

She had been in this office for only two days—barely time to move in, much less to unpack or to accomplish anything. She had no secretary, so she was doing double duty. The outer office was even more chaotic and disorganized than her private domain, if that was possible.

Ellen's train of thought was interrupted by a sharp rapping at the door. She pushed one more box out of the way, took a final look around, then crossed the small reception area and opened the door. She looked into the face of the woman she had been seeing from a distance in court. They stared at each other for a moment. Finally Ellen broke the silence.

"Come in, Mrs. Rogers," she said, extending her hand.

Carol hesitantly entered the small room. Because of the disarray, there was no apparent seating area. She didn't know where to go, or what to do. Ellen sensed her discomfort.

"Come on back here," Ellen said, pointing toward the inner office. "You'll have to excuse all of this mess. I just moved in here two days ago, and I haven't had time to straighten things out or to get any help." She moved a box from one of the chairs and motioned for Carol to be seated. "Make yourself comfortable. Do you need an ashtray?"

"No thank you, I don't smoke," Carol replied.

"Good," Ellen said. "I have no idea which box has the ashtrays, and I hate smoke."

Ellen walked around the cluttered desk. She started toward her desk chair, then changed her mind and shuffled a few more boxes and liberated another chair, arranging it so that it faced Carol. The more intimate setting might make the situation more comfortable for both. Ellen sat down. The two women looked at each other. The silence was awkward.

Looking back, Ellen would have a difficult time expressing the emotions she felt as she sat across from Carol Rogers. On the one hand she was intensely curious, of course. She wanted to know what Carol wanted, but more than that she just wanted to know the woman better. But she also felt a sense of uneasiness that bordered on genuine fear, fear that Carol might be blaming her for all that had happened and might have come here to give expression to that blame.

"Mrs. Rogers," Ellen finally said, "I'd love to be supercool about this whole thing, but the fact is that I am dying of curiosity. Let me be blunt. Why are you here?"

"I will be equally blunt," Carol responded, grateful for the chance to get to the point. "As you already know, I killed Frank Jordan. I have been arrested, and my case is going to the grand jury. Barring divine intervention, I'll be tried for murder. I need a lawyer. That's why I'm here." Carol took a deep breath. There. She had said it. The ice was broken. She waited for a response.

"You want my advice?" Ellen asked incredulously.

"I have all the advice I need," Carol replied. "I need a lawyer. I need a good, tough, sensitive, understanding lawyer."

Ellen sat quietly for a moment.

"Mrs. Rogers," she finally said, "you've got to be kidding."

21

Carol hadn't expected such a reaction. Perhaps she had expected Ellen Hayes to be excited at her coming, to be thrilled at the prospect of representing her. Perhaps she hadn't really thought it through. Certainly in her preoccupation with her own point of view, she had overlooked the possibility that Ellen Hayes might not take this seriously. Carol instantly felt deflated.

Just turning the corner had been a major accomplishment, and it had taken a major effort. For many months Carol had been a victim of life rather than a participant. Without knowing it, she had become the steel ball in a morbid game of pinball. In an instant she had been torn from a safe, predictable existence and unceremoniously deposited in an altogether different stream of life, propelled along out of control, subjected to rapid changes and shock-producing events, unable to make any real choices or decisions because of the impact of events that were being forced upon her.

When she had finally regained even the tiniest bit of control, she experienced an immediate feeling of relief and elation, all out of proportion to the size of her personal victory. She had engaged in a dangerous and unrealistic self-delusion, suddenly deciding that everything was going to be all right. The expression on Ellen Hayes's face, and the concise, pointed words she uttered, brought Carol back into the real world.

"Mrs. Rogers, you've got to be kidding!"

Carol hardly knew how to respond. She backpedaled instinctively.

"I didn't necessarily mean that I want *you* to represent me," she said. "I just want to talk to you about it, to get your advice, that's all." Carol's mind was confused. She was searching desperately for a neutral point from which to begin again, but most of all wishing she hadn't come at all. Pride forced her to stay until she could make a graceful exit.

"Why me?" Ellen asked. "Why do you want advice from me?"

"I don't know. Frankly, I wish I hadn't come here," Carol answered, wringing her hands nervously, staring down at the floor. This last comment slipped out inadvertently, but it was the most honest thing she'd said since arriving here. She bit her lip. The last thing she wanted to do at this moment was to lose control.

Ellen could sense Carol's discomfort but did nothing to bail her out. In truth, she really didn't understand what Carol was thinking or feeling, or why she had come. Whatever time it took, she was willing to wait it out just to find out what this was all about.

In another place and time these two women might have been friends. They had much in common. Both were intelligent, attractive, and quick-witted. Both had a large capacity for warmth and understanding. Both were fortunate enough to have a good sense of humor, and smart enough not to take themselves too seriously. Both had demonstrated considerable competence and skill in their chosen fields. There was only one significant difference: One was well educated, the other was not.

To the outside observer that difference might be imperceptible. To Carol Rogers, it meant fewer options, fewer opportunities, and a reduced sense of self-worth. It was that misplaced self-impression that was the source of her defensiveness in Ellen's presence.

"Mrs. Rogers, I didn't mean to be rude, I really didn't," Ellen said, softening her voice. "When you called, I probably should have told you not to come. But I didn't. I was curious; I wanted to meet you and hear what you had to say. Frankly, I have wanted to talk to you ever since the trial began, but I didn't think it was appropriate to do so. I didn't think you would come to see me. But when you called, it became your idea. That made it okay."

"What did you want to talk to me about?" Carol asked, feeling a bit more comfortable.

"I wanted to tell you that I was sorry that your daughter had been killed, to tell you that I cared about all that you were going through. I have a child of my own. I think I know how I would feel if anything happened to him. I haven't been through it, but I think I understand. During that trial I had a job to do, and I did it as best I could. But I wanted you to know how I felt. I didn't say anything to you, because it never was the right time or place."

"How old is your child?" Carol asked.

"He's two. His name is Chad," Ellen answered, smiling as she spoke. "In all modesty, he is darling. I have a picture of him here somewhere." She walked over to a box marked "desktop" and rummaged around until she found a small photo in a silver frame. She handed it to Carol.

"He's precious," Carol said. "Who takes care of him for you?"

That question, innocuous though it seemed, telegraphed an inner conflict which Carol had never resolved. She had always believed herself capable of success, capable of doing important things, capable of being an "Ellen Hayes," but had never found anything more important than being with her children. She didn't fully understand women who could have babies and then shuffle them off to the care of someone else so that they could pursue career goals. She was old-fashioned in that respect, and not ashamed to admit it. At the same time, she was jealous of such women.

"I have a housekeeper, a lovely woman who comes every day," Ellen replied, taking no apparent offense. "I'm very lucky to have her, believe me. Since my divorce I've had no choice but to work. Even if I wanted to stay home with Chad, I really don't have that freedom anymore."

"I didn't mean to pry," Carol said, realizing that her question might have communicated disapproval. "I wasn't trying to be critical. I'm sure you are doing your best under the circumstances. It's none of my business anyway. I know that."

"That's all right," Ellen said. "I don't mind talking about it.

Believe me, there are times when it just kills me to go off and leave him. But it's a no-win situation. I want children; I also want a career. I fought my way through nineteen years of school for a career. I couldn't just walk away from that, either. I found myself between a rock and a hard place, as they say. There was no right answer. I just have to do my best, and I think I am." She paused for a moment and smiled. "But enough of that. I shouldn't be boring you with my personal life. I'm sorry."

"No apology is necessary. Your feelings are important to me," Carol stated, her confidence beginning to return. "They tell me that my initial impression of you was accurate."

"What was your initial impression?" Carol asked. "I'd love to know."

"Well," Carol answered, "during the trial I saw you as a sensitive person. I knew intuitively that you had sympathy for my situation. I could see something in your attitude, something in the way you handled yourself. It made me feel good about you, even though you were on the other side. No, 'good' is too strong, but it kept me from feeling badly toward you. That's the reason I came here. I really thought that there was some chance that I could like you, that I could trust you, and that you could help me."

"How could you possibly feel comfortable with me as your lawyer? After all, I tried my best to defend the man who killed your daughter. It just doesn't make sense. Forget about what I think. How in the world can *you* reconcile that?" Ellen placed the picture of Chad on her desk and looked at Carol.

"I'm really not certain yet," Carol answered. "During the trial I found myself almost as angry at you and Martin McPherson as I was at Frank Jordan. I couldn't understand how the two of you could believe that he was unaware of what he was doing. Most of all I couldn't understand how you could do anything at all that might result in him being free to kill someone else. I just didn't see how you could do that and still live with yourselves."

"Which makes it all the more difficult to understand why you are sitting here talking to me about something so important as your own defense," Ellen interjected.

"How could you sleep at night, defending that boy as being insane?" Carol asked in a more emotional voice.

"Whoa, wait a minute. Slow down," Ellen said forcefully,

holding her hands out in front of her. "I'm not about to get into that. If you came here to try to get me to defend my representation of Frank Jordan, then you're going to be disappointed. I have no apologies to make, no explanations, no defense."

Ellen's response brought the conversation to an abrupt halt. Carol hadn't anticipated such a reaction. Caught off guard, she changed the subject.

"Forget about Frank Jordan for a moment," she said. "Forget that we were on opposite sides. The real question is how, or whether, you could defend me, in light of the fact that I did what I did. After all, you were there. You saw it, I'm guilty. There's going to be no hiding from the truth."

Ellen thought for a moment. "I haven't said that I would, or that I could. But if I did, I assure you I wouldn't suggest to a judge or jury that you're innocent. Obviously that would be impossible."

"I'd be the laughing stock of this town. I know what I'm up against," Carol said. "That's why this choice is so important to me. I need someone who can see beyond the facts and understand the emotional issue, someone who can make the judge and jury feel what I felt, so they can understand why I did what I did. I need someone who can convince them that they might have done the same thing themselves. That's the only chance I have. I'm in deep trouble, Ms. Hayes. I have no defense, and I know it. I try to act like everything is going to be okay, and I try to stay calm, but on the inside I'm going to hell in a handbasket."

"I'm not so sure you don't have a defense, Mrs. Rogers," Ellen said. "I'm not sure at all."

"Good grief! They have the whole thing on television," Carol responded. "What possible defense could I have?"

Ellen hesitated before she answered. "Insanity," she said.

Carol bristled. She glared at Ellen but saw no sign of sarcasm or mockery.

"We're off to a great start," she said. "You begin by not taking me seriously, and finally get around to telling me I am insane. No way! Uh-uh! There isn't any way I could deal with that. You've got to know how I feel about that kind of legal manipulation. Besides, you've used that trick too recently. You couldn't get away with it again."

"I don't think you understand, Mrs. Rogers," Ellen said calmly.

"Insanity is not a legal concept, nor is it a trick. It's a real medical issue, about a real medical problem. Mental illness really can affect the ability of a person to be morally responsible for his acts. Insanity is not a bad defense, nor is it necessarily a good defense. But it is a real defense. It's a fact of life." Ellen paused awkwardly. "Unfortunately, while it's a concept that applies to good people like yourself, it can also apply to scum like Frank Jordan, with unfortunate results."

"I hear you, but I don't understand," Carol said. "What do you mean? Explain it to me."

"Look at it this way. There are two basic reasons why people who commit crimes are put in jail. One is to protect society, because they are dangerous people. In your case we can pretty well discount that. You're obviously not a dangerous person. But the other reason is to punish the guilty. The law is built on the concept that guilty people should be sent to prison. That may seem simple, but it's not. There's no black and white. Everything is fuzzy and gray."

Carol looked intently at Ellen and waited for her to continue.

"The problem is how you define guilt. What makes a person guilty? Two things, really. A person is guilty if he knew that what he did was wrong but did it anyway. That's the first half of the formula. Yet a person can be held *responsible* only if he had the ability to keep from doing whatever it was that was wrong. That's the other half. If either of those two elements is missing, there can be no guilt. At least not in the legal sense."

"That's a tough concept," Carol said.

"I know it is," Ellen continued. "It's hard enough for lawyers to understand. It's no wonder laymen think we deal in semantic manipulation. It would be much easier if legal guilt was the same as being the one who did it. That would simplify our system of justice, but it wouldn't necessarily be right. Frank Jordan was the 'one who did it' in Wendy's case. You are the 'one who did it' in his case. If our goal is to get the 'guilty' off of the streets, the answer is simple: Punish you both. But if our goal is to punish only those who are guilty in the moral and ethical sense, then we must have some means of determining whether people who commit crimes are mentally able to make moral and ethical decisions."

"But how does this apply to me?" Carol asked.

"In a specific sense, I don't really know if it does apply," Ellen answered. "That's not for me to say. We would have to find out. But in a general sense, there are two possibilities. When the verdict was read out, your worst fear was realized. You suddenly believed that the man who killed your child was not going to be punished. You became obsessed. You lost control. Either you acted on impulse, or you didn't act consciously at all. Either you were so driven by your emotions that you couldn't have stopped yourself if you had wanted to, or you sort of shifted to 'automatic pilot' and had no real grasp of what was going on."

"I certainly knew right from wrong," Carol interjected. "I knew it wasn't right for me to kill that boy."

"Sure, you know that now," said Ellen. "And you probably knew it beforehand. But did you really know it at that precise moment? That's a pretty complex question. Insanity doesn't have to be permanent, you know, it can be a temporary thing. It can be very brief, but very real. The ultimate question is your state of mind at the instant you performed the act."

"Temporary insanity," Carol whispered as if she were testing out the words to see if she could live with them. "I don't know, I just don't know."

"I don't either, Mrs. Rogers," Ellen stated. "All I'm saying is that it's a possibility. It's something we would have to make a decision about. We can't just arbitrarily eliminate anything that might help you. Temporary insanity may be your very best chance, in spite of how uncomfortable it may make you feel." The level of enthusiasm in Ellen's voice had definitely increased.

Carol smiled. "You said 'we.' Does that mean you are going to take my case?"

Ellen paused for a moment.

"I want to think about it, Mrs. Rogers. This is all happening so fast. I want to be sure this is what I want to do. You ought to do the same thing. Let's sit on this for at least a day or so, to be sure we aren't getting into something that either of us will regret later. I want to work through the conflict in my mind. I think I feel good about it, but a lot of people are going to ask a lot of questions, and I want to be certain that I am completely satisfied."

"Maybe you're right. Maybe we do need to think about it," Carol said, rising as if to signal an end to the meeting. "But for my part, I'm already comfortable. I am a great believer in following my instinct. My gut feeling about this has been positive from the first moment. It may seem illogical, and it may not make sense to others, but it fits. I already know that. I really don't expect to change my mind, no matter how long I think about it."

"There are some other things you should consider," Ellen said as she walked Carol to the door. "I know this is your case, and you are the one with everything to lose. But I'm the lawyer. You've come to me for help. The only way I can help you is if you understand from the beginning that I'm in charge. You will be consulted, of course. I'll listen, and if you feel strongly about something, I'll probably decide the way you want me to. But I'm going to make the decisions, and you are going to have to do what I tell you to. Any problem with that?"

"No problem," Carol said.

"Good. And there's one more thing. We need to be thinking about a psychiatrist. If I take the case, I want you in the hands of the best possible doctor. I'll get some names to you after I've decided what I'm going to do. I'll run the names by you before we make a decision, and if you have any suggestions, feel free to speak up. But I'll decide. I've got to be comfortable with the choice."

Ellen extended her hand toward Carol. "Thank you for coming in, Mrs. Rogers," she said. "Considering the circumstances, you have paid me a very high compliment. I really appreciate it."

"You're welcome," Carol said, taking her hand. "By the way, I'd feel much better about this if you would call me Carol. If we're going to be working together, and I hope we are, then let's be a little less formal."

"Thank you, Carol," Ellen said, a smile on her face. "And I'm Ellen from now on. Even if we don't work together, we can still be friends."

Carol returned Ellen's smile, then left. Alone in the hall, she waited patiently for the elevator. When it finally came, she entered the small car, pushed the button for the first floor, and leaned back against the wall as the door slid shut. She closed her eyes and breathed a sigh of relief.

"One down, and one to go," she whispered to herself.

‖22‖

Shortly after ten the next morning, Ellen Hayes left her office and headed for a meeting with Judge Randall Wentworth. At ten-thirty the jurist would take a break from the trial in progress in his courtroom. Ellen had just enough time to run by Claiborne Bennett's office to pick up the order permitting Bennett and his firm to withdraw as counsel for Carol Rogers.

Even as the carpeted elevator carried Ellen up to the top-floor suite of Bennett & Silverstein, Bennett's secretary was feeding the order into the word processor, watching little green words march up and down the small screen like well-behaved soldiers in a video game. In an instant, the final product, perfect in every detail, would roll out of the rapid printer.

"I'm going to get one of these machines someday," Ellen remarked as she admired the finished document a few minutes later.

"I don't know how we ever did without them," Bennett responded.

His law partners would have loved that comment. Their firm would have enjoyed such sophisticated equipment years earlier had it not been for his legendary unwillingness to spend money. Around the office, it was said only half jokingly that if all of the decisions had been left up to Bennett, the entire suite would still be equipped with inkwells, quill pens, and rolltop desks.

Claiborne Bennett signed the document, then wished Ellen success with the case. Ellen had just enough time left to make her meeting with Judge Wentworth.

Ellen had heard the rumors about the judge, and did not look forward to meeting with him in chambers. The brief wait in the stark hallway outside of his office heightened her apprehension.

When she was finally ushered in, Wentworth was pacing nervously behind his desk, still in his robe, obviously in a hurry. She handed him the proposed order, which he read without comment and signed with a flourish.

"Miss Hayes," he said as he handed the document back, "please take this to the clerk's office and have it entered in the minute book. Then enter your name as counsel on the docket sheet. I plan to move this case along as quickly as possible. In a few days my clerk will call you about possible trial dates. If you have any pre-trial motions, I want them filed at least two weeks before trial so I can dispose of them. I want all preliminary matters cleared up in advance. We are going to get on with this trial."

"I'll be sure to take care of that, Your Honor. Thank you," she responded.

That was it. No sign of approval or disapproval, no social amenities, nothing. Ellen was unable to tell whether the judge had any personal feeling about her involvement in the case, but she knew for certain that he was in command. He'd certainly made it clear that he was going to move things along. Her work was cut out for her. She carried the signed order to the Criminal Court Clerk's office feeling a sense of relief. Her first solo encounter with the legendary Randall Wentworth had been without incident. Not many young lawyers could claim such good fortune.

Ellen pushed open the glass door to the Clerk's office and took her place at the counter, patiently awaiting the next available clerk, impervious to the hustle and bustle around her.

A moment later the order was filed. Ellen's copy was time-stamped, then she signed the docket book on the appropriate line.

As she closed the heavy book, Ellen felt the presence of someone behind her. Stepping back, she almost bumped into Martin McPherson.

"Ellen, how are you?" he said.

"Oh, you startled me!" Ellen laughed.

"I'm sorry," McPherson said. "But I didn't realize it took that much concentration just to sign your name." He smiled as he spoke.

"Well, Mac, you never know. Someday a student of history may be studying these pages. I just want to be sure they know who I was. Now in your case . . ." Ellen flipped the book open to another sheet she was familiar with. She pointed to his signature, an illegible scrawl.

"Touché," McPherson said, smiling. "I'll try a little harder next time."

Ellen placed her papers in her attaché case. She and McPherson walked out of the Criminal Court Clerk's office, into the bustling hallway.

"Ellen, do you have a few minutes?" McPherson asked.

"Sure," Ellen answered. "What's up?" She really didn't have time to spare, but she wanted to accommodate her former employer.

"Let's go downstairs to the cafeteria," McPherson replied. "I want to talk to you a few minutes. I'm buying."

"That's an offer I can't refuse, boss," Ellen said. "I wouldn't want to miss seeing you part with a buck. You sure didn't do that when I was working for you!"

"That's not funny," McPherson snorted, laughing out loud. By this time they had arrived at the bank of elevators. They stepped into a waiting car. When they arrived at the basement level, they zigzagged through the crowded hall to the cafeteria.

Ellen took their briefcases and looked around for a table while McPherson went to get the coffee. Privacy was out of the question, but she found a table in a corner where they might be unobserved for a few moments. The noise level in the cafeteria provided its own privacy. It would be impossible for anyone to overhear a conversation.

The courthouse cafeteria was not known for its food, but it was the social center of the building. More juicy gossip was exchanged in this place than anywhere else in the county. Lawyers, bailiffs, judges, clerks, porters, policemen—they all frequented this place, and they all were privy to the important events of the day. The courthouse was the heart of the system; the cafeteria was where everyone came to feel the pulse of the community.

Ellen took a napkin from the dispenser and brushed some crumbs off of the chairs. She slipped out of her suit jacket and piled it on top of their briefcases. McPherson soon arrived with two cups of steaming coffee.

While Ellen stirred the thick, black liquid, McPherson fumbled with a little packet of cream. Finally she could wait no longer.

"All right, boss, what's this all about?"

"Aren't you a suspicious little devil?" McPherson returned. "Can't an old man buy a pretty lawyer a cup of coffee?"

"Flattery will get you everywhere," Ellen responded. "But this isn't a social visit, and you know it." She leaned forward, folding her arms in front of her. "Look, Mac, I can read you like a book. There's something on your mind. Let's have it."

McPherson poured the sugar crystals from a tiny paper packet, watching them land on the surface of the hot liquid where they quickly disappeared. He coughed nervously.

"Ellen," he said, looking up, "you are making a mistake."

"What do you mean?" she asked.

"This Carol Rogers thing," he answered. "You're making a mistake taking on that case."

"How did you find out about that?" Ellen was incredulous. She hadn't decided to take the case until the night before, and had told no one about her decision.

"The news was all over the courthouse before you ever left Wentworth's office," McPherson replied. "That kind of news travels fast. You know that. I was told by at least three people in a ten-minute stretch. I was going to call you later, but I just happened to see you as I was passing by the Clerk's office."

"Why am I making a mistake?" she asked.

"Don't be naive, Ellen," McPherson replied. "You're bound to see the conflict. Good grief, woman, you represented the man she murdered in cold blood! Can't you see that?"

"Look, Mac, I've thought this through. I have searched the code and I can't find any technical conflict. I'll admit the idea gave me pause at first, just as it apparently raises questions with you. But if you stop and think about it, where's the conflict? We can't change the facts, and wouldn't even try. The only thing any lawyer can do for that woman is to try to make it as easy as possible, and I am as qualified to do that as anyone."

"I don't know about *technical* conflicts," McPherson responded. "You may be right. I haven't researched it. But I'll tell you this, in the public's eye there is an enormous *apparent* conflict, and you don't need to get involved in anything that looks bad, whether it really is bad or not. You know full well that a lawyer has got to avoid even the appearance of conflict. Frankly, Ellen, you are going to look like a damn fool to the bar and to the public. No one is going to understand any technical niceties—no one is going to give a damn about that kind of argument. All they're going to see is that you have flip-flopped from one side to another."

"I don't care what the public thinks," Ellen said. "What's important is how *I* feel about this. Let's face it, if either one of us cared what the public thought, we never would have defended Frank Jordan in the first place. Or have you forgotten about all of those phone calls and nasty letters? We can't let the public make our decisions, you know that better than I do."

Actually she cared very much about what the public thought. She was deeply concerned about public reaction to her representation of Carol Rogers. But she had resigned herself to accept criticism. McPherson didn't say anything. He just stirred his coffee.

"Mac," she said finally, "are you concerned about how this makes *you* look? Is that what's troubling you? We were in the Jordan thing together. I don't care about the public, but I care very deeply about you."

"No, I don't think that's a problem, Ellen," he said, rubbing his chin. "That never occurred to me. It's not me, Ellen, it's you. You're just getting started. Your reputation is still being made. And something like this is potential dynamite. It can affect your practice for years to come." He leaned forward and lowered his voice. "Let me tell you something, Ellen. If you really don't care what the public thinks, you had better start. That 'public' you are talking about is where your clients will come from for the next thirty years. What they think is crucial. Don't you see?"

"You know I don't mean it that way," Ellen replied. "Of course I care about my reputation. I care very much. But in the final analysis I have to follow my own heart and my own gut, even if it isn't the popular thing to do. If you didn't teach me anything else, Mac, you taught me that. A lawyer doesn't always have the luxury of doing what is popular."

They were quiet for a moment. Ellen sipped her coffee, which was now cold.

"In addition to everything else, you can't possibly win the damn case," McPherson observed dryly.

"That's never been a valid criteria either, and you know it," Ellen responded. "Besides, it depends on what you call a win. In this case we haven't defined that elusive goal yet, but we will. And whatever our objective turns out to be, you can bet we will work like hell to achieve it. That's another thing you taught me."

McPherson smiled. "It sounds like I've created a monster."

"If you've created a monster, then it's because you're a monster yourself. That's the irony of all this. I left your office to try to do things my own way, and here I am, less than a week later, doing my best to remember all that you've taught me. I guess I admire you more than I thought."

"Well, Ellen," he said, "I suppose at this point all I can do is wish you luck. Give it your best. I know you will."

"I will, Mac. I'll make you proud," she said as they both rose to leave the cafeteria. "Believe me, you would do the same thing. You would have felt the same way about Carol Rogers if she had come to you, Mac. She's not a killer. She's a decent woman who got caught up in a cyclone of emotion that she couldn't control. She didn't make this situation, she was its victim. Now she needs help, and she has come to me. That's quite an honor when you think about it. It's probably the most important decision she's ever made. She has come to me, and I'm going to do my best to help her. Who knows? There's no telling what we might accomplish. One thing's for sure. That woman doesn't deserve to go to jail."

"That's a good speech, but you'd better save it for the jury. You don't want to peak too early," McPherson said, taking Ellen's hand and giving it a squeeze.

Ellen smiled. She needed McPherson's moral support. She hadn't realized it, but she needed it. She needed to know that he was available if she needed help. She walked back out into the bright sunlight, feeling remarkably good about what she'd gotten herself into.

But at that same moment, several blocks away, Dr. Norman Green wasn't in nearly as good spirits.

‖23‖

"What did you say her name was?" Norman Green said.

"Jeffreys, Carol Jeffreys," Lois Bradbury replied. The name meant absolutely nothing to Dr. Green, but an intrusion on his tight schedule meant quite a lot.

He looked down at his watch. It was almost eleven-thirty. His handsome, tanned face wrinkled into a frown. "This is a hell of a note," he muttered, staring at the door to his outer office as if he could see through it and identify the intruder. "Jeffreys," he said, searching his memory. "Jeffreys. Never heard of her." He leaned back in his swivel chair and rubbed his chin.

The chair was quality, as was everything else in the office. It was made of leather, with heavy brass nailheads, and sat behind an impressive hand-carved desk. A dark walnut crown molding encircled the room. The walls were papered in warm, earthy tones; comfortable club chairs surrounded a brass and glass table. Everything was as it should be, except for the couch. Norman Green, Jr., M.D., didn't want to acquire an image as a stereotypical psychiatrist. There was no couch.

Green hadn't been in practice very long, but he had always felt that it was important to look established from the very start. Fortunately, money had been no problem. The same doting mother who had paid his way through medical school had made it possible for him to start his private practice in relative comfort. Nothing was too good for "her son, the doctor."

Norman Green had been a good boy almost all of his life. He had done well in school and had carried on as the titular head of the household after the untimely death of his father, a successful jewelry store owner, on his fourteenth birthday. Thanks to his mother's good business sense and an even better insurance plan, they had managed nicely. Her two boys were Iris Green's pride and joy, but Norman was her favorite. He had inherited his father's name and his mother's ambition, and he took full advantage of both. He had also inherited his father's dislike of his mother.

Norman had sailed through prep school and college. Medical school came next, as did his mother's first disappointment. Norman opted out of the physical aspects of medicine, choosing instead to explore the vague mysteries of the human mind.

Iris Green didn't understand psychiatry. Psychiatrists weren't real doctors. They did weird things with words, and spent their days listening to the neurotic prattlings of split personalities. What Iris didn't understand, Iris didn't like. But in spite of her protestations, Norman had chosen psychiatry. Iris had swallowed her disappointment and showed up at graduation anyway, to see what her money had bought. At least people would still have to call him doctor. That title was all she really needed to hear.

Norman Green could have done anything—neurosurgery, orthopedics, anything. He was smart enough and skilled enough. The truth was, he turned down any opportunity that Iris wanted him to take. There was no way he was going to give her the satisfaction of having a neurosurgeon for a son, or an obstetrician, or anything else that she preferred. He just didn't like her enough to do that. Besides, being quick of mind and adept of tongue, he knew what he wanted to do. He chose to talk his way through life. At an early age he had discovered his true gift.

His practice had progressed smoothly, if not spectacularly. Early on he had seized an opportunity to examine criminals for a large defense firm. It had been steady, profitable work, the kind of thing that paid the rent while waiting for private patients to seek him out. Furthermore, it gave him public exposure and many opportunities to demonstrate his considerable forensic skill on the witness stand. He was invariably well prepared, and quick-witted enough to be almost impossible to trap on cross-examination. He had become the favorite of a number of very busy lawyers, including Martin McPherson.

The Frank Jordan case had been his finest hour. Not only had his side won, but the renowned First Assistant D.A., Tom Sanderson, had been unable to tear down his testimony on cross-examination. Theirs had been a personal battle of wits, a contest between two proud, highly skilled individuals, winner-take-all. Green's sense of satisfaction at the victory had substantially transcended any feeling of impropriety over having let a professional matter deteriorate into outright competition.

Green's dislike of his mother had not affected his relationship with the opposite sex. He was actively pursuing several possibilities, and had talked at length to one of them only minutes before the unexpected arrival of this Carol Jeffreys. That was what was on his mind; he had anticipated their lunch date with great pleasure. Now his plans would have to change unless he could find a way to get rid of this intruder.

"Is this woman a referral patient?" he asked Lois Bradbury. He certainly didn't want to incur the wrath of a fellow doctor. His professional peers were his main source of business outside of the legal profession.

"No," Lois answered. "She's a walk-in, or I guess a call-in would be more appropriate. She called about a half hour ago. She was very apologetic but said that she was an acquaintance of yours and that it was very important."

"She is definitely not an acquaintance. I've never heard of her. Dammit, one of these days I'm going to build a back door to this place. . . . Oh, well, I guess I might as well bite the bullet. Show her in. Then call Rita at her office and tell her I'm going to be late. Fifteen minutes, max. Tell her to order the wine and I'll be there before the cork pops."

"Very well, Doctor," Lois said, a wry smile on her face.

As she walked out into the reception area, Green turned toward the mirror on the wall next to his desk, rumpled his hair, and loosened his tie. He wanted to look busy and in a hurry. Then he turned toward the door and started to beckon his visitor inside. But he stopped suddenly in mid-motion. His jaw dropped open. The woman standing in his doorway was Carol Rogers.

"Lois," he said in a voice loud enough to be heard in the reception area, "maybe you'd better tell Rita that I'm going to be tied up with an emergency. Tell her I have to cancel and that I'll call her tonight."

Carol Rogers shut the door behind herself.

"May I sit down?" she asked.

"Why not?" Green said.

"Thank you, I will."

Green sat back down, leaned forward in his chair, rested his elbows on the brown-felt desk pad, and spread his fingers out in front of him, touching their tips together in a tapping rhythm, all the while studying his unexpected guest.

"Let's begin with your name," he said.

"Carol Rogers," Carol returned.

He breathed an audible sigh. "That's not what I mean, and you know it."

"Jeffreys is my maiden name," Carol said.

"Why didn't you use your real name?"

"I was afraid you wouldn't see me if you knew who I was."

"Why not?" Green asked. "Why wouldn't I see you? What in the world would I have against you?"

Carol had developed an intense dislike for Norman Green during the trial. She had regarded him as the enemy. It never occurred to her that the feeling might not be mutual. She hesitated for a moment before answering.

"Well," she said, "we were on opposite sides at the trial." She was beginning to sound tentative, and she knew it.

"Mrs. Rogers, I wasn't on anybody's side at that trial. I wasn't a defendant or a prosecutor. I'm not a lawyer. I didn't represent anybody. I'm a doctor. I had a patient on trial. I testified about his condition. That's all." He spoke forcefully. "Did you come here to fuss at me? To complain about my testimony? To make me defend myself? If you did, you are going to leave here a very disappointed woman."

Carol shifted uneasily. This meeting was going downhill fast. She might as well speak her piece before he asked her to leave.

"I'll admit that during the trial I disliked you," Carol said.

"No, that's not true. I hated you. I might as well admit it. I detested you. I thought you were the one that was crazy, not Frank Jordan. I couldn't imagine how you could say anything that might even remotely result in his being set free. 'Fuss' and 'complain' are too mild. I wanted to shake some sense into you, to scream at you, to hit you, to literally beat you. You disgusted me completely!" Carol's words rushed out. They had been trapped too long.

"You don't mince words, do you?" Dr. Green said.

"If I had come here two or three days ago, I would probably be screaming at you. Today? Well, I'm not so sure. I still don't have it all together, but at least some of the anger has subsided. Now what I want is for you to try to help me understand all of this."

"All of what?"

"All this business about insanity and mental capacity. Mental illness. How it pertains to guilt and innocence," Carol answered. "I'm confused. I want to know everything you know."

Norman Green paused. He still didn't know exactly what to make of this meeting, or of this woman. But at this point he was in too deep to draw back.

"I can't talk about Frank Jordan's case," he replied. "His condition is a matter of physician-client privilege, except for what I said in court. You've heard that already."

"I could almost repeat it back to you, verbatim. I'll never forget it," Carol said. "But it's not his case I'm talking about, it's mine."

"What do you mean?" Green asked, walking around to the front of the desk. He took a cigarette case off the desk, opened it, and extended it toward Carol.

"No, thank you," she responded. He closed the case and put it back.

"I've been charged with murder," she said. "You know that, of course. It's been all over the papers. I'm guilty—you know that, too. I did it. There is no way to avoid that. Unfortunately I picked a rather public location." Carol laughed nervously. "My only defense, such as it is, is temporary insanity. At least that's what I'm told. Temporary insanity. When I was first hit with that idea, the very thought was abhorrent to me. I would have nothing of it, or so I thought. I'm still having a hard time dealing with it, as you might expect, but I'm willing to listen, willing to learn. Let's face it, I don't know what it's all about."

"Your disgust with my testimony in the Jordan case might also be because of the same ignorance," Green interjected. "Have you thought about that?"

"Yes, I have. And I know that's not true. Not at all. I'm still not convinced that Frank Jordan didn't know what he was doing. But I realize now that my anger was misdirected. It wasn't your testimony I was mad about, it was the possibility that Jordan might go free if you were right. I suppose you thought you were right. I couldn't deny that, not really. Who knows? The poor guy *might* have been crazy. No normal person would ever do what he did. But what if he was crazy? The real problem is that the courts really don't know how to handle crazy people. If they're crazy, they ought to be locked up. But they aren't, at least not for long."

She stopped. She had been rambling and she knew it. This wasn't at all what she'd planned. Norman Green said nothing, just stared at her.

"Anyway, I'm having a hard time living with the idea that I may have to rely on the very same defense. I don't feel right about it. But I'll do whatever I have to do in order to stay out of prison, and that may be my only chance."

"I'd have been surprised to hear you say anything else, Mrs. Rogers," Green said.

"That's why I'm here. You are the only psychiatrist I know that works in this area. In fact, you're the only psychiatrist I know anything about at all. You're it. You're all I have, and I need you to help me. I want you to explain this whole thing to me. I want to understand what's going on. I want to feel better about myself. I want you to make it okay for me to do what I have to do. Is that asking too much?"

"I think I could help you," Green said, leaning back into the comfort of his chair, "but I'm not sure I want to."

"That's not all I want," Carol continued. "I want you to testify on my behalf. I want you to keep me out of prison, just like you did Frank Jordan."

Norman Green stifled a smile. His heart began to beat faster; he struggled to keep his voice from rising. "There are plenty of other psychiatrists in the city, Mrs. Rogers," he said. "Good ones. You shouldn't have any trouble finding one you would feel comfortable with."

Carol leaned forward in her chair and returned his intense gaze.

"I don't care about being comfortable anymore, Dr. Green. If I cared about that, I wouldn't even be considering this defense. But this thing has gone beyond that. Way beyond. I want a gutter fighter, someone who'll go all out for me, someone who is smarter than the people who are trying to put me away. Frankly, Dr. Green, I want someone who isn't hung up about such details as right and wrong, someone who'll fight like the devil just for me. I've seen you do that. As disgusting as it may have been to me at the time, and as much as it hurts me to say it now, that kind of person is what I need. As far as I'm concerned, you're it."

‖24‖

Norman Green had started salivating at the first mention of becoming Carol Rogers's psychiatrist. The very thought of jumping right back into the most highly publicized case in the history of this city excited him enormously. But he didn't want to tip his hand too quickly, either. Should he reel this line in too fast, he might lose the huge fish that had suddenly appeared. Besides, excitement wasn't all he felt. Real discomfort gnawed at him, too. He wanted to be sure, absolutely sure, both personally and professionally.

The last time he had seen Carol Rogers was in the courtroom, on the very day that she had taken the life of his patient. He knew full well that she had let her anger at Frank Jordan spill over into a feeling of contempt for him as Jordan's psychiatrist. He had anticipated such a reaction; any other would have been abnormal. He had not been at all surprised at her hostility on those occasions when their eyes had met in the courtroom or in the halls. But her presence in his office a week after the end of that trial was completely unexpected.

"You're putting the cart before the horse," he said, recovering from his surprise. "You know that, I am sure."

"No, I don't," she said. "What do you mean?"

"You didn't find this office by looking under *W* in the Yellow

Pages," he responded acerbically. "I'm not a witness. I'm a doctor. I don't sell testimony, I treat patients. If one of those patients is referred by a lawyer, and happens to have a condition that affects his involvement in a legal matter, and if I am convinced that it is necessary, then I testify. I'm not for hire. I don't hire out just to help people on trial, or to hurt them either."

"What has to happen to make a doctor turn into a witness?" Carol asked. "What made it happen in Frank Jordan's case?"

"Mrs. Rogers, you aren't going to understand this and probably aren't going to like it. But you need to know something. Frank Jordan was no different from any other patient I have ever seen. His case was no better, and no worse. It was no more serious, and no more distasteful. You see, I don't make value judgments about what my patients have done. When I do, I become the judge and the jury, and the whole system gets screwed up. My job is not to make legal or moral decisions. My job is to try to figure out whether my patient was capable of making those decisions for himself."

"So it just didn't matter to you that he brutally murdered and raped an innocent child, is that it?" Carol hadn't expected to dredge up her negative feelings so quickly.

"Mrs. Rogers," Green replied forcefully, "I want you to listen to me very carefully, and try not to pass judgment on what I'm about to say, at least until I have finished. Okay?"

Carol nodded her agreement and bit her lip. She was still having some difficulty maintaining control over her emotions. They had been near the surface for a long time.

"In one sense that is true. I am a man. I hope someday to become a father. I am a civilized person who abhors violence. Of course I care what happened to your child. I care about what Frank Jordan did. I care very deeply; it matters a great deal. But in a strictly professional sense, once I agreed to establish a doctor-patient relationship with him, then I could no longer afford the luxury of caring. Of course I could have refused to establish the relationship, and maybe that would have been the best thing to do. But once I did, then I had to set aside my personal feelings and try to find out everything I could about Frank Jordan's mental state. So, in that sense, it really didn't matter. Do you understand the difference?"

"No," she said instinctively. Then she changed her mind.

"Well, maybe. I think I understand intellectually, but I still don't understand emotionally. And I certainly don't like it emotionally. If it had been your child, you would have felt differently."

"No I wouldn't," he said. "I'd have felt exactly the same. I'd still have felt disgust and hatred, only more so. But under those circumstances I'd never have been capable of divorcing myself from those feelings long enough to serve in a professional capacity. I wouldn't have taken the case at all."

"I understand," Carol said, her quiet voice masking her anger. "Since it was my daughter, not yours, you could just set your indignation aside and pick up a few bucks, is that it?"

Green looked down at the floor for a moment. He had no interest in engaging in a battle of wits with a person who had been to hell and back in the last few months, and was still showing the devastating effects of the trip.

"Mrs. Rogers, you're twisting my words around to suit yourself. I am glad to talk with you, and will try to explain this to you if I can, but not if you're going to seize every opportunity to insult me. I don't deserve it, and I have no intention of taking it."

"I'm sorry. It's just that I have such a hard time accepting the distinction between actions and feelings that you're talking about. It seems like just so much rationalization, a way for you to do your job and make a fee, without feeling guilty about it."

"That would be true except for one thing," he responded. "Insanity, or more properly diminished capacity, is a real thing. It exists, and it cannot be ignored. And in spite of the nature of the crime, it makes a real difference with regard to the moral guilt or innocence of the criminal."

"I haven't heard that phrase before," Carol said. "Diminished capacity?"

"That's the proper medical term," Green said. "It's pretty descriptive, when you get right down to it."

"What do you mean?"

"Well, in a normal person, to the extent that there is any such thing, there exists a certain capacity for each human emotion. But the capacity is never the same for all emotions. There is a natural difference. Some people might get quite angry over something that wouldn't even ruffle your feathers, or mine either. On the other hand, we might become upset and cry over an event that barely bothers someone else. That doesn't make either one right or wrong, just different. And the capacity to experience an event without responding with anger can even vary in the same person. In your present state, I have no doubt that you are getting very upset over things that wouldn't have bothered you nearly so much a year ago, before all this happened. Am I right?"

Carol nodded.

"What that means is that your capacity to tolerate anger or distress has changed over the past year because of the things that have happened to you. Outside events have made you adjust. You had no control over that; it was involuntary. But the capacity to tolerate anger can also be changed voluntarily, when one wills such a change. We can refuse to deal with our emotions and hammer them down into our subconscious. They are still just as real, but don't find recognition or expression. Unfortunately, they build up like steam pressure, and surface one way or another, sometimes violently."

"Is that what happened in Frank Jordan's case?" Carol asked.

"That's an oversimplification, but that's basically right. His situation was far more complex than that. I'm only trying to illustrate a principle."

"Please go on," Carol said.

"Well, the emotional area is not the only one in which the matter of capacity is important," he said. "Tied in with that concept is a person's capacity to *control* what he is doing, and to make rational judgments about whether his actions are morally right or wrong. Again there are different levels within the range of normal, but there are also times when a person's capacity gets so out of whack that it is no longer anywhere near normal. When that happens, that person is sick, just the same as if he had physical symptoms that you could see with your eyes. That's where I come in. My first job is to treat the disease. If I am asked to do so, it is also my job to explain the effect of the disease on the patient's actions, as it relates to guilt and innocence."

"You just lost me," Carol said. "How does all that come together? What does it have to do with guilt or innocence of a crime? That's where my problem develops."

"Look at it this way. According to the law, we punish people who know better than to commit a crime, but who do it anyway.

That's the bottom line, the principle on which the whole system is based," Green replied. "This principle was not my idea, and I couldn't change it if I wanted to. But it's there, and it's the foundation on which all of the rest of this is built. You don't have to agree with it, but you have to understand it, or you can't understand the system as a whole, and the rest of this won't make any sense."

"Okay, I understand that," Carol said. "Like you say, I don't especially like it, but I understand it."

"Well, the insanity defense is based on the principle that if a person really doesn't know better, or really can't stop himself, then he shouldn't be punished, but should be dealt with as a sick person, and either be cured or isolated. But that's different from being punished."

"It sounds so simple when you say it," Carol said, "but there's nothing simple about it when you start applying those principles to real life, when real people have been hurt. That's when it gets tough. My biggest problem with Frank Jordan wasn't his mental state, it was the possibility that he might get out someday and do it again."

"I don't blame you for feeling that way," Green responded. "In a real sense the system has let you down. There ought to be something more realistic after the verdict, something that will protect the interests of society and at the same time cater to the problems of the sick person. But make no mistake, in spite of that difficulty, mental illness is real. Temporary insanity, diminished capacity, whatever you call it, it's very real. We would be making a terrible mistake if we threw the baby out with the bathwater and abandoned that concept completely. There is much more involved here than one case."

Carol looked at her watch, then stretched her arms out to loosen up her muscles. She was stiff from sitting so long in one position. It was getting close to one o'clock. She hadn't intended to stay as long as she had.

"Mrs. Rogers, I know that insanity is one of those magic words that evokes all kinds of wild images in people's minds," Green added. "Like nuts, coo-coo, and crazy. Those words paint an unfortunate, distorted picture. We aren't talking about people who belong in nuthouses, not necessarily. All of us are subject to periods of mental illness, just as we all suffer physical illness from time to time. The trick is to bring this whole area out of the voodoo age and begin to recognize it for what it is."

"Somehow it sounds so much more palatable when you talk about diminished capacity instead of insanity," she said.

Norman Green picked up on her cue. "Mrs. Rogers, it really is possible that you might have experienced a diminished capacity at the time you shot Frank Jordan. I don't know for sure, but I'd almost bet on it. If you did, that doesn't necessarily mean there is anything wrong with you now. It wouldn't mean that you were insane. Certainly not. It would only mean that at that moment you were incapable of choosing not to do something which your emotions were forcing you to do."

"Are you willing to find out?" Carol asked.

"I don't know," Green answered. "I'll need some time to think about it. It still strikes me as being a bit bizarre, for me to be treating you and testifying for you. By the way, who is your lawyer?"

"Ellen Hayes," Carol replied.

Norman Green let out a long, low whistle. "Have you thought this through?"

"I'm just like you," Carol said, "trying to do the best I can under difficult circumstances." They both smiled.

"Let me think about this, Mrs. Rogers," Green said. "Give me a day or so, then call me. But let me warn you about something. If I take you on, it will be strictly as a patient. You'll have to cooperate fully. You'll have to show up when you are supposed to, and do what I tell you to do. In the end, if I believe you were mentally sick at the time of Frank Jordan's death, I'll say so. If not, you are going to be stuck with the consequences, because I'll say that, too. I won't be used. You are going to have to be a patient first and foremost, and cooperate fully. Is that completely clear?"

Carol agreed. In her heart she believed that Dr. Green was going to take her case. She was right. In *his* heart the gnawing discomfort still chewed away, but he had found the challenge and the opportunity irresistible from the start. All of his waking hours from this point forward would be spent trying to figure out a way to make it work:

A few moments later, as she emerged into the bright sunlight, Carol experienced a great sense of relief. She had passed another major milestone. Now she headed back toward Ellen Hayes's office, on the off chance that Ellen might be there, to tell her the good news.

‖25‖

Ellen was in her office and had a few minutes to chat. Carol started talking, but only made it as far as her arrival at Norman Green's office before she was interrupted.

"*You what?*" Ellen asked, almost shouting, her eyes wide with shock.

"I went to see Norman Green," Carol repeated, her defenses rising immediately. "What's wrong with that?"

"What's wrong?" Ellen asked. She stood up and began to pace the floor, throwing her hands into the air.

"What's wrong?" she continued, still pacing. " 'What's wrong?' the woman says. 'Why are you upset?' the woman says. 'Never mind that I have ignored your instructions. Never mind that I didn't check with you as you asked me to. Never mind that I hired a professional pimp to testify for me,' the woman says. What's wrong? Good grief! I can't believe this!"

Ellen finally finished her tirade. She plopped down in her desk chair.

"Professional pimp?" Carol asked, incredulous over Ellen's response. "Am I hearing things? *You* used him. You did that yourself. Why in the world should I have wondered if it was okay for me to call him? What could be more natural than for me to go to the person you chose yourself?" Carol wrung her hands nervously. She was very near tears.

"For God's sake, Carol, I told you I would give you some names, didn't I? I told you I wanted to make the decisions in this case. I told you specifically to call me if you had any questions. I am absolutely certain that I told you I wanted to be comfortable with the doctor we chose before you ever made an appointment. What was the big rush? Why did you go off half cocked? There's no way I can represent you if you're going to ignore what I say. Don't you see that?"

"What's wrong with Dr. Green?" Carol asked, ignoring Ellen's questions. "I don't get it. I deserve an answer. Why in the world are you so upset? This doesn't make a bit of sense to me!"

Ellen took a moment to gather her thoughts, then spoke again.

"Hasn't it occurred to you to wonder why I was so quick to take your case? All my friends think I'm crazy. They think I've switched sides for the almighty dollar. Don't you think I'm sensitive to that kind of talk? Every lawyer and judge in town thinks I've stretched the Code of Professional Responsibility to the outer limits of credibility. For the rest of my life I'm going to be infamous. I'll be pointed at and whispered about as the woman who jumped sides, who defended the killer of her own client. But I took your case anyway, even though I knew I'd have to face all that garbage. Hasn't it even occurred to you just once to wonder why?"

Ellen's words were heavy with emotion. Up to this moment she had deluded herself into thinking that her colleagues would understand why she had taken this case and would support her decision, but in her heart she knew better. She had known better all along. She had known, without admitting it, that she was going to be the subject of gossip, much of it sarcastic and malicious, for the rest of her professional career.

Carol watched Ellen, not knowing exactly how to react or what to say next. Seconds lumbered past, seeming more like an eternity.

"I haven't been fair to you, Carol," Ellen said. "I should have told you all this from the beginning. The reason I left Mc-Pherson's office was because I couldn't stomach our defense of Frank Jordan. For openers, I thought it was wrong for us to take his mother's last dime, when the public defender would have done it for free. Then the more I dealt with Jordan himself, the more I realized what a worthless scum he was. I had no sympathy for him whatever. I gave it my best, but the harder I tried to understand him, the more I realized that he was a freak, a mutation, a violation of basic principles of nature. He was a man without feeling, without remorse, without any sensitivity whatever. He was utterly without any redeeming qualities as far as I was concerned."

Ellen shifted in her chair. She had slipped off her shoes and tucked her feet up under her. As she continued to speak, she stared down at her hands. For the first time, she was articulating some very painful facts.

"I tried my best to mask my feelings, but that became more and more difficult as time went on. But I had a job to do, and all I could think about was the agony that your daughter had gone through. I became almost irrational about it. I couldn't sleep at night. Mac and I argued about it during the day. It clouded my thinking and affected all of my decisions in that case."

"How were you able to cope?" Carol asked.

"I don't know," Ellen responded. "Looking back, I don't think I did a very good job. I now realize that every time I went to see Frank Jordan in jail, I was saying one thing and thinking another. I was a complete hypocrite. I would sit across the table from him and pay lip service to his defense, instructing him as to what to do and what to say, all the while thinking to myself that I hoped to hell he'd fry."

She stood and walked over to the window, staring mindlessly at the traffic below.

"When the trial started, it got worse. All of a sudden the whole thing became so real to me, so personal. Wendy was no longer just a name or a statistic. All of a sudden she was a real child. Her suffering was real. Her pain was real. All I could think about was how I would have felt if she'd been mine. I wanted to reach out to you, to put my arms around you, to tell you that I understood. I literally wanted to jump sides, right then and there, to come sit by you and help you avenge that horrible crime."

Carol was dumfounded. She groped for the right words. "I

could tell that you understood what I was going through," she finally said. "I think I told you that when I first came up here. I had a feeling deep down in my heart that you were more in tune with me than anyone else."

"I was," Ellen said. "I finally had to go to McPherson and tell him how I felt about the whole thing. I knew I was being the worst kind of hypocrite. Funny, I guess I came full circle. I hated Frank Jordan because of what he'd done, but in the last analysis I felt sorry for him. I couldn't sabotage his case by staying involved. That would have made things worse."

"How did McPherson react?" Carol asked.

"He went through the ceiling. He couldn't understand at all. I was very disappointed. The principle was the only important thing. He launched into a speech about how every man is entitled to the best defense available. I can hear him now."

Ellen paused for a moment, recalling the experience anew. Then she continued. "It was the beginning of the end for us. He accused me of becoming too emotionally involved. 'That's just like a woman,' he said. He actually had the nerve to accuse me of being too sensitive, as if that was a female characteristic."

"Isn't it, though?" Carol asked. "When you get right down to it, shouldn't you have been more sensitive to me just because you're a woman?"

"Yes, of course," Ellen replied. "But his perspective was distorted. He didn't acknowledge my femininity like you would. He threatened me with it, treated it like a weakness, and used it as a weapon to bludgeon me into submission. He may not have said so in so many words, but he made it clear that he had no use for a woman lawyer who was truly female. What he wanted was a woman lawyer who could forsake her identity and act like a male. We went round and round about that, believe me."

"Did he ever get the message?"

"Not really, but he calmed down a lot. We finally agreed that I would finish out the trial as his bag carrier, but that I would make none of the decisions and do nothing except deal with things that didn't really matter anyway. For the rest of the trial I was like a kid who had been kicked out of school but allowed to go through the graduation line and picked up a blank diploma so nobody would know. I guess when you think about it, he was looking out for me, really. He let me save face. I appreciated that. But he never understood how I felt. And he certainly never agreed with me."

"What about Dr. Green? How did you feel about him?" Carol asked. "Obviously it's not what I thought, to say the least."

"I never agreed with Green's selection in the first place," Ellen answered. "I really didn't know anything about him as a psychiatrist, but I knew that he had developed a reputation as a professional witness. He had been on the stand so often that he'd lost his credibility. His reputation was that of a man who would reach whatever conclusion his client needed if the price was right. I urged McPherson to hire someone more respected, but he insisted that we needed a doctor who wouldn't get beaten to death on the witness stand. He was right, of course. That was Green's strongest point. He took great delight in being attack-proof on cross-examination. So the decision was made. I'm still convinced that we could have found someone else if we'd worked at it. That's what I wanted to do in your case."

"But that doesn't explain your strong reaction when I mentioned his name," Carol said.

"I didn't really think Green would find anything about Frank Jordan that would help us," Ellen continued. "I thought the state had a lock on the case. I thought a conviction was a foregone conclusion. I really believed you could put any twelve human beings in the jury box, any twelve at all, and no matter who they were, they would end up hating Frank Jordan and wanting to pull the switch themselves. I thought that defending Frank Jordan was an exercise in futility."

"So did I," Carol said. "So did I."

"Unfortunately, we were both wrong," Ellen said. "And the first time I realized that was when Dr. Green took the witness stand. Oh, I had read his report, of course. It was just so much psychological bullshit, if you'll pardon the expression. But I had let my bitterness cloud my judgment. I didn't think most jurors would understand what he was saying. And if they did understand it, I didn't think they'd buy it. Not on a bet."

"But they did," Carol mused.

"They sure did," Ellen continued. "He was superb. He was believable, understandable, and credible. I watched the jury while he was testifying. They were hanging on his every word. I couldn't believe my eyes. It was apparent from that moment on that the prosecution was in deep trouble. Sanderson did his best, of course. I was cheering him on in my mind. But Green was as skilled as any witness I have ever seen. Sanderson's cross-examination only hammered his conclusions home. By the time Norman Green had finished, I hated his guts. I detested him. I felt he was personally responsible for the verdict. It just made me sick."

Ellen finally finished talking. She leaned back in her chair and closed her eyes.

"I haven't hired him," Carol said softly. "I've only talked with him. It's not too late. We don't have to use him."

"I want to think about it, Carol," Ellen said. "I needed to talk this through, and I've done that. Now I want to take time to think it through. I don't want to act in haste. Let's face it, Green *is* good. He's very good. In the Jordan trial he was magnificent. I've got to keep all of this in perspective. After all, my job is to keep you out of prison. I don't want to lose sight of that. Just let me think about it."

"I want you to understand that if I have to choose between you and Dr. Green, I'll choose you," Carol said. She leaned forward and rested her hand on Ellen's arm. "Let me make that clear. I want you to represent me. I don't want to lose you. You are more important than anything else. I'm committed to you, and I really believe you're committed to me. That's the most vital thing, as far as I'm concerned."

"I'm not going to put you in the position of having to choose," Ellen said. "That's not fair. Our roles are reversed, yours and mine. I'm the one who should be looking for a doctor who can help you, and you should be the one hating Norman Green."

"Believe me," Carol said, "I hated him more than you can imagine. But for some reason I had to go to see him. I almost felt driven. I couldn't resist the urge to find out what made him do what he did in the Jordan case. Then, after I talked with him, I found myself convinced that he was sincere. I think he knows what he's doing. I think he can help me. I think he can help me better than anyone else I know of."

"Then that should be good enough for me," Ellen said. "After all, you are the one with the most to lose. Just give me a few days to think."

Carol stood to leave. There was nothing else to say. The two of them walked out into the hall. In the distance they heard the whine of a motor as the elevator returned to the eighth floor.

"Carol," Ellen said, "no more surprises, okay?"

"Okay," Carol answered. "I promise. No more surprises."

Carol stepped into the elevator. The doors slid shut behind her. Ellen returned to her office. Both women felt completely drained, yet it was clear that a bond had formed between them.

‖26‖

Early the next morning, Ellen went to the District Attorney's office to see Carlton Douglas. As usual, she had to wait. She sat quietly in a chair directly across from the infamous Helen Hawthorne.

The large reception room was painted a nondescript green. Uncomfortable wooden chairs lined the walls. The place was a busy thoroughfare. Human traffic scurried by, heading in and out of the office at a dizzying pace. Ellen was keenly aware of the fact that Helen Hawthorne had not notified Carlton Douglas that she was here. It was the old woman's way of maintaining control. She would let the District Attorney's secretary know about this interloper when she got good and ready.

"You may go in now, Miss Hayes," Hawthorne finally announced. Ellen fumed inside. That was another of the woman's irritating habits, referring to female lawyers as "Miss" as if they couldn't possibly be married.

Ellen entered the private office area through the inner door. She had been here before, but always to confer with one of the assistants. It had never been her lot to meet with the big man himself, and she had no idea where to go. But she wasn't about to let that rude old bat know that she didn't know her way to

Carlton Douglas's office. She followed the hall as far as it went, and got lucky. His name was on the door.

The District Attorney's secretary greeted Ellen warmly and ushered her in. General Douglas stood as she entered. He was coatless, his sleeves were rolled up, his desk was a jumble of papers. It was obvious that he was busy.

Ellen extended her hand. "I'm Ellen Hayes, General Douglas."

Douglas shook her hand perfunctorily. "I know who you are, Ms. Hayes, and I know who your client is. I presume it's the Rogers case that brought you here. Sit down, please."

Douglas was more abrupt than Ellen had expected.

"You're right. I am here about the Rogers case," she said. "Before we get too far down the road I thought we ought to talk. I don't know what the state wants."

Ellen intended the remark as an invitation to plea bargaining. Though she had no particular expectation, it was always wise to know what kind of concession might be obtained in exchange for a guilty plea.

"What the state wants is a conviction on premeditated murder," Douglas replied immediately. "What the state wants is for Carol Rogers to go to prison for at least the minimum sentence on that charge. That's ten years. If you're ready to plead your client on that basis, tell me right now and we will go before the judge tomorrow."

Ellen didn't know what to say. She didn't know if he was serious or whether this was part of his strategy.

"I thought perhaps there might be some room for compromise," she suggested. It was a weak statement. Too weak. She regretted it immediately.

"What did you have in mind?" Douglas asked.

"I thought perhaps a suspended sentence—"

"Hell no," Douglas interrupted. "And don't waste your breath on a lesser degree either. The answer is the same. The only concession I'll make is to save your lady the embarrassment of a trial. If she wants to plead and take her lumps, that's okay. But there'll be nothing else. No deals."

"I hadn't expected you to be so harsh," Ellen said. Another wrong thing to say.

"Harsh?" Douglas snapped back. "Grow up, woman! Your

client packed a gun in a courtroom. She was ready to shoot anyone who got in her way. She was out to get Jordan at all costs. She made a complete mockery out of our system of justice. She took two hundred years of American judicial history and held it in total contempt. That's what she did. You want to bargain? Like hell! If I sold this case for anything less than premeditated murder, the people in this community would ride me out of town on a rail. Furthermore, I'd deserve it. No way, honey, no way. You took this on for some crazy reason, and you're stuck with it. You'll get no help from this office."

"I suppose it would be useless to suggest the possibility of a plea on manslaughter," Ellen said resignedly.

"Why should I reduce the charges?" the D.A. retorted. "We have an airtight case of premeditation. The damn woman not only had to put the gun in her purse, she had to worry about how to get it into the courtroom, how to get it past the guards. She had to be pretty cool to manage that one, believe me. Cool, cunning, and deliberate."

Carlton Douglas leaned on one elbow and pointed his finger at Ellen to emphasize his point.

"Honey, your client armed herself intentionally. She knew that if it became necessary, she would shoot to kill. When the opportunity came, she was ready. She was ready because she had planned ahead. She knew damn well what she was doing. So don't waste your time talking to me about reducing the charges. This was a classic case of premeditated murder."

Douglas slumped back in his swivel chair and glared at Ellen. She returned his gaze as best she could but said nothing.

"You know what your client's problem is?" the District Attorney asked, clasping his hands behind his head and forcing the old chair as far back as it would go.

"What's that?" Ellen responded lamely.

"Your client thought she was going to be turned into some kind of a folk hero, that's what. She thought everyone would slap her on the back and tell her how wonderful she was, and how right she was to do what she did. That didn't happen, and now she's desperate. Now she wants to talk about justice and all of those wonderful concepts that she wasn't thinking about at all when she pulled the trigger. She's desperate, but it's too late."

Ellen stood up. Carlton Douglas pulled himself up out of his chair and faced her across his desk. His expression screamed out his contempt.

"You can tell your client that life doesn't work that way, Ms. Hayes," he said. "As far as I am concerned, desperate justice is no justice at all. Carol Rogers is just going to have to take her lumps like any other person who has committed a crime."

"Is that it?" Ellen asked, biting her lip.

"That's it," the District Attorney said, nodding toward the door.

A few moments later Ellen found herself once again hurrying past Helen Hawthorne, beating a hasty retreat after an unsuccessful encounter. Ellen knew intellectually that Hawthorne was totally unaware of the conversation she'd just endured behind General Douglas's closed door, but she felt transparent and self-conscious just the same. The old biddy had a way of looking right through people. Ellen didn't give her the satisfaction of returning her glance, but stared straight ahead and made her way through the bustling reception area, then out into the hallway.

‖27‖

In spite of its rocky beginning, the relationship between Ellen Hayes and Carol Rogers strengthened.

Ellen enjoyed the dubious luxury of extra time in her work day. Her practice was just beginning to get off the ground. She had taken a few small matters with her, but for the most part, the cases she'd been working on with Martin McPherson had stayed with him, leaving her to exist on small fees garnered from court-appointed representations and from occasional domestic matters until she established herself. Domestic cases did come to her from the start, however. Women naturally turn to other women for help in times of crisis, driven by the same feeling of compatibility and understanding that originally attracted Carol Rogers to Ellen. With the recent advent of a plentiful supply of female attorneys, beleaguered wives have at last found their champions, and women lawyers their client base.

Thus suffering from a diet of referral cases, hand-me-down clients, and emotionally debilitating divorces, it was no wonder that Ellen was able to find time for Carol. Indeed, the Carol Rogers's case was the brightest spot to date in her professional life.

The two women met frequently, at first at Ellen's office. Once the press got wind of their relationship and began patrolling Ellen's reception area in search of news, they shifted their meetings to other locations, in search of privacy.

Their primary objective at first was to keep up with the progress of Carol's case, but there really wasn't much progress to discuss. All pleas for mercy were routinely rejected by the state. Carol and Ellen developed a healthy respect for each other's talents. An easy friendship followed. But as far as the case was concerned, all of their talk only served to cement their bond and give them courage. There wasn't much to discuss about Carol's defense. It all depended on Norman Green. All of Carol Rogers's legal eggs were definitely in one basket. There was simply no other place to put them.

Ellen did finally decide to let Norman Green take Carol on as a patient. For his part, Green had wanted to do so from their first meeting; it was the kind of challenge he relished, and the likelihood of more public exposure was a great temptation. But the more he thought about it, the more wary he became of this engagement. He knew that both he and Ellen Hayes were going to be subjected to public scrutiny and criticism for their "turncoat" decision to defend Carol Rogers. As with any golden opportunity, this one had a price tag. He wanted to be absolutely certain that he was willing to pay it.

Before making a final decision, he met with Ellen Hayes and they talked for almost two hours. Neither could tell the other anything that might be helpful, but they shared their doubts and their enthusiasm. They both had misgivings, but these were largely based on the possibility of negative reactions by the public and by their colleagues. Neither could accept that alone as sufficient reason to refuse Carol's case. By the time their first meeting was over, they were jointly committed to victory on her behalf. They were also committed to working well with each other.

Ellen managed to set aside her former hostility and came to regard Norman Green as competent, enthusiastic, and honestly dedicated to discovering the truth about Carol's state of mind at the time she shot Frank Jordan. She found him to be much more pleasant and much less abrasive than she had thought. His enthusiasm for the task was contagious.

Shortly after the initial meeting, Norman Green and Carol Rogers scheduled a series of appointments on a regular weekly basis. As the clock wound down toward the mid-summer trial date, Green's search for the true state of Carol Rogers's mind finally got underway.

His sessions with Carol were different from his experiences with other patients, at least in content if not in form. Carol had an excellent attitude; she wanted to be helped. She arrived on time and responded well to the doctor's questions. She found him to be an effective listener. His patience was admirable; he never intruded on her silence, and seemed to have a knack for allowing her to follow each trail of inquiry to its appropriate conclusion.

Week after week they sat across from each other in Green's comfortable leather chairs, talking back and forth, searching and probing for the key that would unlock the mysteries of Carol's state of mind on the day the jury returned its verdict in the Jordan trial. Carol recognized the overwhelming importance of the task from the first. She was willing to spend as much time and energy as necessary. The two of them developed a genuine respect for each other. Carol found herself looking forward to their sessions.

But the uniqueness of Carol as a patient didn't just involve punctuality and demeanor. It was also related to the nature of her personality and the state of her mental health. After relatively few sessions, the most significant fact that emerged was that she was a healthy person, comparatively speaking. Clearly, if there was any mental aberration involved in this case, it had been temporary. An apparently happy, normal woman had been confronted with a series of extreme shocks involving both personal loss and profound grief, and had experienced a severe but temporary reaction. Thus the inquiry soon settled on a determination of the impact of those events, and her mental state, for that brief period of time during which she had become a killer.

This was a radical departure from the other criminal cases Green had handled. The common denominator of abnormality was missing in Carol's case. His previous criminal patients had been men and women with serious, debilitating mental problems arising from such things as broken homes, emotional deprivation, alcoholic or abusive parents, traumatic sexual encounters, and the like. None of these mind-affecting experiences had ever existed in Carol's case.

It became apparent early on that it was going to be very difficult to convince a jury that Carol was so very mentally ill for such a short period of time. The aberration in her mental state contrasted sharply with her normal childhood, and with the absence of any of the classic "producers" of mental illness that the jury might expect to see. Green was convinced that Carol wasn't able to stop herself from taking Frank Jordan's life, but he despaired of being able to explain to a jury exactly why that was true.

He'd agreed to prepare a report for Ellen's benefit and delivered it to her in person as soon as it was ready.

"What's the bottom line?" Ellen said as she took the folder from him. "I hope it's what I think it is."

"Well, to use an old saying, I have good news and bad news," Green responded. "You can figure out the good news, I'll wager. Carol had definitely lost the ability to control her actions when she shot Frank Jordan. She didn't have the ability to choose the morally right course. I feel strongly about that, and I will certainly say so. As for the bad news, well, it's a lot more complex than the good."

"Let me have it," Ellen said.

"While I'm entirely convinced that Carol had a diminished capacity at the time of the shooting," Green answered, "I'm not at all sure that I can make a jury believe it."

"Why not?"

"Medically, I'm on solid ground," he responded. "I can use all the right terms and follow all the right steps from a clinical point of view. I can make a record that will stand firm on appeal. But you and I both know that it takes a lot more than technical medical jargon to convince a jury. That's where we're in trouble."

"Don't beat around the bush, Norman," Ellen said. "Get to the point. I'm a big girl. I wasn't expecting miracles."

"For one thing, we don't really have anything here you can sink your teeth in. There's no previous incident, no violent attack, no severe post-partum reaction—nothing that a jury can accept as predisposing her mental lapse. We have the 'trigger' event, of course. The jury will understand that, and will be in complete sympathy. But her background is normal. While that's great for her, it's bad for our case. She's going to look like the kind of person you would never expect to react like this. We really need some kind of skeleton in her closet to pin this on, perhaps a prior experience with violent eruptions, something the jurors will understand."

"Anything else?" Ellen asked.

"Yes, there is, unfortunately," he responded. "The worst part is that although she definitely lost control of her ability to keep herself from reacting violently against Jordan, she never lost touch with what she was doing. She never lost her sense of right and wrong. She knew that what she was doing was wrong, even while she was doing it. She was simply powerless to stop herself."

"She knew what she was doing all along but couldn't stop herself. The D.A. will jump all over that," Ellen exclaimed. "But what about the gun? Did she say anything about the gun?"

Ellen had specifically asked Green to probe into this area. Carol had repeatedly told Ellen that she had no recollection of putting the gun in her purse, something she was adamant about. Ellen had been incredulous when she first heard that, and she still was. This was going to be a real problem.

"She told me the same thing she told you, Ellen," Green answered. "And she's stuck with it. I don't have any way of knowing whether she's telling the truth or not, but she sure has herself convinced that it's true."

"She remembers shooting Jordan but draws a complete blank about the gun. It doesn't make much sense, does it?" Ellen shook her head. "I sure don't relish trying to sell that to the jury."

"What choice do you have?"

"None whatsoever. I have to accept it as true. Believe me, she and I have argued over that issue. That's the only time I've really gotten mad at her, except when she confessed to me that she'd been to see you!" Ellen blushed. She hadn't told Green about her initial reaction to his involvement in this case. "Anyway, I did everything I could, short of accusing her of hiding something. But there comes a time when you either have to accept what your client tells you, or bow out. We reached that point and I backed off. I don't feel good about it, but I backed off. I'm afraid I know how the jury will react, though."

"Is there anything more I can do to help?" Green asked.

"The only thing you can do is to plug away at her about the gun and see if you can dig up anything. We really need to come up with a good reason for having that thing in her purse. I don't think I can push it any harder, so it's up to you. You're the only one who can find out anything, Norman. You really need to do that. The trial is six weeks away."

"I'm convinced that there's something hidden somewhere that will help us," Green said. "I don't know why she's holding something back, but my job is to create the atmosphere where she can let it all hang out, not to make demands that put her on the defensive and make her more determined to keep her secret."

"Well, one thing is for certain," Ellen mused. "If we don't figure this one out by the time we get in court, we're going to be in deep, deep trouble."

‖THREE‖

The Third
Monday
in August

‖28‖

"All rise!"

The bailiff called everyone to attention at exactly nine o'clock. The heat was already oppressive outside; in the short walk from Ellen's office to the courtroom, Carol had begun to perspire. The fabric of her blouse stuck to her shoulder blades as she stood and faced the bench while Judge Randall Wentworth entered the crowded courtroom and ascended to his proper place. He stood erect and solemnly waited for the bailiff to finish.

"Oyez, oyez, this honorable Criminal Court, Division One, is now open, pursuant to adjournment. All persons having business before this court . . ." The bailiff completed the traditional words. Everyone sat back down.

If the reality of her plight had not yet sunk in for Carol, it did so now as she listened to the words that followed.

"Call the docket, Mr. bailiff," the judge instructed.

"Case number 83503, State versus Carol Jeffreys Rogers," the bailiff stated. "Charge: murder. Defense: insanity."

Carol shivered at the sound of her name. This was it. This was for real.

The courtroom was crowded, the air-conditioning system severely strained. It was uncomfortably muggy. Some spectators waved fans back and forth, reminiscent of the summertime scene in a country courtroom.

For Carol and Bill Rogers it was to be a day of tedium, a day spent sitting quietly, nervously waiting, doing nothing, while Ellen Hayes and Carlton Douglas examined prospective jurors at length.

Surprisingly, the matter of pre-trial publicity was not belabored to any great degree. Frequently in cases with this much notoriety, pre-trial publicity is a major consideration. This particular case was a classic candidate for a change of venue. Never before in the history of this community had a crime been so publicly committed. The plight of Carol Rogers had been spread all over the local tabloids. Her face had appeared in thousands of homes. Local stations had run and re-run the tape of that horrible moment when she pulled the trigger, forcing Judge Wentworth to finally ban its showing some three weeks prior to trial. But no change of venue was granted, because none was requested. Ellen Hayes had decided early on that it would be virtually impossible to find twelve citizens who had not been exposed to the flood of media coverage about this case, so she decided to try to turn this issue to her advantage rather than to fight it. She met the question head-on.

"You won't have to decide whether Carol Rogers killed Frank Jordan," Ellen told the prospective jurors, "because I am telling you now that she did. But your responsibility is going to be to look carefully at Mrs. Rogers's life, at her role as a mother, at her love and devotion for her daughter. You are going to have to climb inside her heart and feel her pain. You are going to have to visit the recesses of her mind and think her thoughts on that fateful day. You, and only you, are going to have to decide if you think that this poor woman was capable of controlling her actions at that fatal moment when she pulled the trigger. If she wasn't, then it will be your responsibility to say so by your verdict, and to find her not guilty. Do you think you could do that?"

One by one the prospective jurors solemnly answered yes. Ellen didn't expect any of them to say no, and none did. As with many of the questions asked during jury selection, the real purpose was to educate the jurors as to the defense that was being offered on Carol's behalf.

Ellen had decided to take a chance. She was convinced that the prospective jurors would already know that Carol had "done it." But she also believed that they would be basically sympathetic toward her. Thus her questions were designed to provide them with moral justification for a "not guilty" verdict. She knew that if she could make the jury feel good about setting her client free, if she could make them feel that it was the morally right thing to do, then she would have a chance to win in spite of the legal fact of guilt.

When it was his turn to ask the prospective jurors questions, Carlton Douglas dealt first with the matter of sympathy. Many a case has been decided by a jury on the basis of their personal feelings for one side or another, in spite of the best efforts of the judge to explain that sympathy is not a valid consideration. Douglas knew that, and examined each prospective juror in detail in an effort to overcome this one major weakness in the prosecution's case.

Judge Wentworth rode hard on both lawyers, however. He tolerated no delays, and made them move along with dispatch. Thus in spite of the tedious nature of the selection process, by the end of the first day a jury of twelve and two alternates was sworn in, given their preliminary instructions by the judge, and sent to a local hotel for the evening. After the jury had been excused, Judge Wentworth thanked both sides for their diligence, then announced that the trial would resume promptly at nine A.M. the next day. Court was adjourned at five-thirty in the evening.

In spite of the hour, the day was just beginning for Ellen, and for her clients as well. After a brief meal, which no one really tasted, they all adjourned to the Rogers' home to continue their preparations for the next day.

Carol and Ellen sprawled out on the plush sofa in the living room. Both were whipped, unable to move, burdened down with physical and mental fatigue. Joe Holman was there; so was Jeffrey Rogers. Bill Rogers retired to the kitchen to mix a round of martinis. The cool, biting liquid would be a welcome beginning to the process of winding down from the day's tension.

Joe Holman sat in an easy chair across from the sofa. From that vantage point he could see the beautiful family portrait that hung on the wall behind Carol and Ellen. Wendy and Carol had looked very much alike when that picture was taken only a year ago, both vivacious, vibrant, full of life. Now Wendy was gone, and Carol looked so much older. He couldn't help but notice that the events of the last year had taken their toll.

Carol accepted a cold glass from Bill, wrapping a napkin around it to keep the condensation from dripping off. Bill served everyone else, then sat down on the arm of the sofa next to his wife. She leaned her head against his side as he slipped his free arm around her shoulder and gave her a brief hug. Bill's support over the past few months had been a great source of strength to her.

If Bill had been upset by Carol's visits to Ellen Hayes and Norman Green in his absence, he had not shown it. He had quickly grasped how important this was to her. Obviously she wanted to make her own decisions as much as possible; it had almost become a matter of pride to her. He had sensed that and had tried to be helpful by being patient and attentive.

He had also become her sounding board. Each decision that had to be made, each problem that had arisen, had been talked over and discussed until Carol finally felt comfortable. Bill wisely left the ultimate decisions up to her. He had been quick to interject his opinions and offer suggestions, but once a decision had been made he studiously refrained from criticism and second-guessing. Together they had worked their way through an imperfect situation, where all decisions were matters of judgment, and clearly definable "rights" and "wrongs" were rare, indeed. Now they were approaching the end of their long, hard journey. Whatever the outcome, they both took comfort from the fact that they had made that journey together.

"The main thing I want you guys to do is to get some rest," Ellen said to Carol and Bill. "You need to be fresh and alert tomorrow. Bill, I'm putting you in charge of seeing to it that Carol gets some sleep."

"That'll be his toughest assignment of this whole case," Carol said, giving her husband's hand an affectionate squeeze. "There's no way I can sleep tonight."

"What will happen first in the morning?" Joe Holman asked. "What can we expect tomorrow?"

"The first thing will be opening statements," Ellen answered. "Douglas will go first, then we'll have our say. Judge Wentworth has limited us to forty-five minutes each. That should take us to the morning break. After that the state will put on its case. I don't know how long that will take, but it shouldn't be long. I don't expect that they'll have more than two or three witnesses. With any luck at all, we should get started on our proof in the mid-afternoon."

"Will I go first?" Carol asked.

"I think so," Ellen said. "I had thought about saving you for last, but I think I'll go ahead and put you on first, to try and wipe out some of the damage done by the state's case."

"Please, for God's sake, put me on as soon as you can, and get me off as quickly as you can," Carol said. "I'm already scared, and it's going to get worse. I just know it. I hope I can remember my name, much less the facts. If I thought I had to spend one extra minute dreading what's coming, I'd just cash in my chips and crawl off and die."

"How do you feel about the jury?" Bill asked.

"I suppose I feel okay," Ellen answered. "You never know. I guess they're about as good as we might have expected. In a case like this I worry about people telling the truth. A whole lot of those folks just wanted to get on the jury. This is a big-deal case to them. I had the distinct impression that some of them would have said whatever was necessary to get a seat in the box. But by and large I'm satisfied. Ask me again in three or four days. Then I'll really be able to give an opinion."

"Sure," Bill said with a wry smile. "But by then we won't need your opinion."

"I could see that some of them were sympathetic to Carol," Joe Holman suggested.

"I felt that, too, Joe," said Ellen. "Trouble is, I also thought I saw a great deal of sympathy for Bess Jordan. She made quite a picture over there in that black mourning dress."

"Why shouldn't people feel sorry for her?" Carol asked. "She's lost a child, too. Lots of women will be inclined to sympathize with her, and men, too. Especially those who have children who didn't turn out just right, but who love them anyway. If I wasn't fighting for my life, I'd feel sorry for her myself. In fact, deep in my heart I guess I do. Let's face it. All the sympathy isn't on our side."

They were all quiet for a few minutes. Bill went back to the kitchen to make more martinis. Joe chatted with the women, first about one thing and then about another, doing his best to take their minds off of the next day's activities and to help them relax. It was a futile effort. Jeffrey, in a chair off to one side, followed the conversation intently.

Carol and Bill had worked hard to make life as normal as possible for Jeffrey during the past few weeks. He had been an innocent victim in this whole series of events, and a tragic victim at that. In addition to his own guilt over his sister's death, he had been worried sick about what might happen to his mother. His home life had been completely disrupted. He had become a dubious celebrity, forced to endure the stares and guarded whispers of insensitive classmates at school. But worst of all, he had been burdened by a gnawing uncertainty over his mother's fate, an uncertainty that affected him more deeply than his parents could possibly realize.

In their attempt to make life normal for him, Carol and Bill had excluded him from any ongoing involvement in the development of the case, at least up until now, and he had never asked to be included. At this point, however, his curiosity was at a peak as he listened with rapt attention to the conversation going on around him.

After a while, talk got back around to the business at hand.

"What's our weakest point?" Joe Holman asked Ellen. "What do we have to worry about most?"

Ellen was glad Joe had asked that question. She wanted to bring up the gun one more time, in hopes that Carol would remember something that might be helpful, perhaps even reveal whatever it was she was hiding. Ellen still believed that Carol was holding something back. She couldn't be sure, and had tried hard to suppress that feeling, not letting it interfere with their relationship. In her heart, however, she still believed that there was something Carol was keeping to herself.

"The gun, Joe. That's our Achilles' heel," Ellen said. "If we could just come up with an explanation for the gun, one that would put it in Carol's purse for some reason other than to use it against Frank Jordan, we'd be in much better shape."

"That wouldn't make much difference as far as guilt or innocence is concerned, would it?" Joe asked.

"No, but it might make a big difference on the matter of degree," Ellen responded. "The state is insisting that Carol's act was premeditated and deliberate. They say that Carol had to know in advance what she was going to do, otherwise she wouldn't have had the gun in her purse in the first place. We need to give the jury some other reason for the gun. Then if the jury doesn't buy temporary insanity, we can fall back and try to avoid premeditated murder. After that, our next battle would be over a suspended sentence. As a practical matter, it would be infinitely easier to get a suspended sentence on a manslaughter conviction."

"I know you've tried to explain that to us, but frankly, I have never really understood the difference," Jeff said.

"It's an oversimplification, Jeff, but it's a matter of determining whether Carol decided in advance that she was going to shoot Jordan. If she thought about it in advance, even if only to consider it as a possibility, then that would be what the law calls premeditation and deliberation, and she would be guilty of murder. But if she just got caught up in the emotion of the moment, and shot him without considering it ahead of time, then she would be guilty of manslaughter. That's what makes the gun so important. If we have no believable explanation for the gun being in her purse, the jury might believe that Carol put it there on purpose, intending to use it just as she did."

"And if they reach that conclusion, they'll most likely find her guilty of premeditated murder instead of manslaughter," Jeff concluded.

"Of course our main defense is temporary insanity," Ellen continued. "We're pushing that hard, and we feel pretty good about it. But if that fails, then we want to fight like tigers for manslaughter. It could make the difference between prison and home. It's just that simple."

Ellen stared at Carol, hoping for a response. She had put it as bluntly as she could, on purpose, but still Carol said nothing. Ellen felt a rising sense of frustration. I just know there's something more, she thought, but look at her. No reaction at all!

Had Ellen been looking in the right place, however, she would have seen all she needed to see.

In a short while the group broke up. Ellen left. Jeffrey slipped off into the kitchen, while Joe, Bill and Carol sat together for a moment. Joe offered a prayer. As with most of Joe's efforts, it was simple yet effective. Most of all, his prayer was exactly what Carol was feeling in her own heart.

"Dear Lord," Joe began, "we ask for your presence here tonight. Be with this family in their time of great need. We ask you to forgive Carol for what she has done. We know that you are the giver of all life, and we know that none of us has the right to take life away. Forgive her, Lord, and give her the courage to face the days ahead. We ask for no miracles, just for mercy, that this woman not be taken from her family, but that she be allowed to live her life with them, where she is needed, where she belongs. Forgive her of her trespasses, Lord, and bring her strength and comfort. We all need your help tonight. We cannot go on without it." He paused for a moment. "Amen," he said finally. There was nothing else to say.

Carol cried softly. Bill held back tears. Words were not necessary for these dear friends. Joe hugged them both one last time, then left.

Carol and Bill walked up the stairs to their bedroom. Bill put his arm around his wife's shoulders; she settled her cheek against his chest. Watching from the kitchen, Jeffrey sensed that they needed to be alone. He switched off the kitchen light and lingered in the darkness for a moment, then went upstairs himself, slipping past his parents' room without being noticed.

Once in his room, he quietly closed his door and crossed the carpeted floor to his closet. He pulled his desk chair over, climbed up on it, and reached for something on the back of the uppermost shelf, groping for a moment before finding what he was looking for.

It was a small scrapbook.

He put the chair back in its place and flopped across his bed, switched on his reading lamp, and began to flip through the pages of the scrapbook. All of the pictures included Wendy. There she was, at every stage of her life, with every member of the family, at every important occasion. He had put this book together over the past few weeks without his parents' knowledge, spending hours poring over old photographs that had been gathering dust on a closet shelf for years. It had given him something to do; it had been a way for him to deal with his grief. Whenever he was feeling blue, he would sit down with this book and look at the pictures, dredging up old memories and releasing trapped feelings. It always helped. But tonight he wasn't stopping to study any of the pictures. He was in a hurry. He was looking for something else.

Finally he found it. Pressed between two of the pages was a crumpled note he had rescued from the trash several months earlier. He hadn't understood its meaning then, but he had recognized the writing and had felt a strong desire to keep it. So he had tucked it away in the grief-laden scrapbook, among the painful memories. Now he was finally beginning to understand. All of a sudden he thought he knew why it had been written, and when. He wasn't certain, but he knew that it might be very important, and that somebody else needed to know about it.

He unfolded the note and pressed it flat. As he began to read it, tears rolled down his cheeks.

29

Carlton Douglas stood behind the small lectern, clutching the sides of the smooth wooden surface and leaning forward like a preacher about to make an important point. Yellow sheets of paper were spread out in front of him; a small brass lamp was attached to the top of the angled podium, lighting up the papers. Douglas glanced down at his scribbled notes as he waited for the state's third witness to take the stand. He looked nervously at his watch. It was ten-thirty, Tuesday morning. Things were moving along with dispatch.

Court had opened that morning precisely at nine o'clock, thanks to the coordinated efforts of Judge Wentworth and one of the local television stations. In thousands of homes in this viewing area, normal programming was being passed up in favor of this extraordinary event.

As expected, every available seat had been occupied since long before court convened. The involved, the interested, and the merely curious had begun lining up in the halls outside of the big double doors more than two hours before the appointed time. Security had been tight. Everyone entering the room had been thoroughly searched. All who left for any reason were searched again upon reentering.

At the prosecution table, Bess Jordan was seated next to the chair just vacated by Carlton Douglas. She was dressed all in black, wearing neither jewelry nor ornamentation, carrying only a small plain handbag. She presented a dignified picture of grief and despondency. At the table reserved for the defense, Carol Rogers was not nearly so somberly dressed, but her countenance and demeanor reflected all too clearly the agony of the past few months.

These two women, the "stars" of this grisly drama, were a study in contrasts. One was prematurely gray, uncommonly plain, beaten down by life's burdens, locked into a marginal existence by the accident of birth and the misfortunes of life. The other had obviously been born into better circumstances, and had apparently possessed both the means and the desire to take good care of herself. And yet there was a tragic common denominator. Both had suffered the ultimate loss that a mother can endure, under circumstances that resulted in their grief and misfortune becoming public property. Such grief is hard enough to bear in private; it is infinitely more difficult to cope with it under the constant pressure of public scrutiny.

Bess Jordan's part in the trial was already over at this point. It had been relatively short. She had been the first witness for the state, testifying succinctly but dramatically about what she had seen on that fateful afternoon. Her presentation had been masterfully choreographed by Carlton Douglas. The simplicity of her appearance had complemented the straightforwardness of her testimony, creating a dramatic effect that evoked maximum sympathy for this downtrodden woman. The impact on the jury had been obvious.

The second witness for the state had been the medical examiner. His responsibility had been to establish the "corpus delecti." Everyone in the courtroom knew that Frank Jordan had breathed his last breath no more than a hundred yards away on the floor of an identical room, but this technical presentation was necessary in order to make certain that there were no loopholes in the state's case.

Through a series of slides dramatically projected onto a large screen, the medical examiner had followed the path of each of the three bullets as they ripped through Jordan's flesh, drawing

out his blood, choking off his lifelines. The pictures were gory
but completely fascinating. By the time the medical doctor finished, the jurors not only knew that Jordan had been shot to
death, but they had relived that moment and played out its
devastating effects on their own bodies while following along
with the narrative.

There had been no cross-examination of the state's first two
witnesses.

Now, as Carlton Douglas stood and waited, the bailiff ushered
in a slight, pasty-faced man wearing thick glasses and an inex-
pensive suit that hung uncomfortably from his shoulders. The
witness took his seat in the box, tugged nervously at the heavy
knot in his knitted tie, then quickly stood again while the oath
was administered. He glanced furtively around the unfamiliar
room. The courtroom looked different in real life; he had only
seen it on television before.

Douglas glanced at his notes one last time. Then he faced the
witness and began his examination.

DOUGLAS: State your full name, please.

TALLEY: My name is Oscar W. Talley, Jr.

DOUGLAS: By whom are you employed, Mr. Tal-
          ley?

TALLEY: I work for Channel Six Television, In-
          corporated, here in the city.

DOUGLAS: What is your position, Mr. Talley?

TALLEY: I am an engineer. I work in the control
          room, and sometimes in the station's
          remote unit.

DOUGLAS: How long have you being doing that
          kind of work?

TALLEY: I have worked for the station for seven
          years, all of the time as an engineer.

DOUGLAS: Did you have to have any special train-
          ing for that particular job?

TALLEY: Yes, sir, I received a certificate of completion from Mid-State Community College. I went through a two-year program in electronic communication.

DOUGLAS: Exactly what do you do for Channel Six as an engineer? What does that job require?

TALLEY: My present responsibility is to operate the control board at the studio and in the remote truck. That means I tell the camera operators what to shoot. Then I watch the monitors to see what each camera is getting, and select the one to go on the air or on the tape. I feed that picture to the transmitter or the tape machine, sometimes both. In a sense I'm the director of the segment I'm involved in, unless there is another person with me who has that specific title and job.

DOUGLAS: You mentioned tape. What do you mean by tape?

TALLEY: Frequently television shows are recorded on three-quarter-inch videotape for later broadcast. Sometimes we tape live broadcasts at the same time that they're going out on the air, for one reason or another. In addition to my other duties, when I'm in the remote truck I operate the tape feed.

DOUGLAS: Does the videotape pick up the exact same picture as the live picture that's being broadcast?

TALLEY: Yes, exactly the same. Unless someone edits the tape by cutting sections out and splicing the pieces together, then what's played on a tape is exactly the same as what was picked up live by the cameras on the scene.

Oscar Talley's answers were precise and direct. Although most of what he was saying was common knowledge, Carlton Douglas was laying the proper legal foundation for admission into evidence of the videotape of Frank Jordan's death. His questions might have seemed tedious to the uninitiated, but they were a textbook demonstration of establishing legal admissibility.

DOUGLAS: Now, Mr. Talley, were you working for Channel Six Television on the day when the jury returned its verdict in the Frank Jordan murder case?

TALLEY: Yes, sir, I was.

DOUGLAS: What was your assignment on that day?

TALLEY: I was the engineer and the director for the live feed of the court session, the one where the jury was supposed to return its verdict. The picture was to be sent to all the local stations who wanted it, by special agreement. It was also to be taped, for use on the news programs later on.

DOUGLAS: Where were you stationed?

TALLEY: I was in our remote truck, which was parked behind the courthouse.

DOUGLAS: On that evening, did you, in fact, tape the proceedings in the courtroom exactly as they were being fed live to the stations?

TALLEY: Yes, sir, I did.

DOUGLAS: Do you have that tape with you today?

TALLEY: Yes, sir, I do.

Mr. Talley proffered a large videotape cassette, which Douglas took from him and had tagged and marked by the court reporter as State's Exhibit number 14. Then he handed it back to Talley and continued his examination.

DOUGLAS: Now, Mr. Talley, have you examined this tape this very morning at my request? I am referring to the tape which we have just marked as Exhibit 14.

TALLEY: Yes, sir, I have. I watched every minute of it, not more than an hour ago.

DOUGLAS: Did you find that tape to be exactly the same as what you televised on that fateful evening?

TALLEY: Exactly.

DOUGLAS: Had it been edited, altered, or changed in any way whatsoever?

TALLEY: No, sir, it had not.

DOUGLAS: So the tape you have handed me, which we have marked as Exhibit 14, is, as far as you are concerned, an exact representation of what took place in court during and after the jury returned its verdict in Frank Jordan's case. Is that right?

TALLEY: Yes, sir.

Douglas was leading the witness. Technically that was something he wasn't supposed to do, and the judge would have stopped him if Ellen had objected. She thought better of doing so, however. There was really nothing to be gained. Such objections are best left alone unless they will really do some good. Douglas went on with his questions. While it might seem like nit-picking, he knew that he needed to fill in that last one-hour "gap."

DOUGLAS:	Has that tape been in your custody and control since you watched it an hour ago?
TALLEY:	Yes, sir, it has.
DOUGLAS:	Has anything been done to alter it in any way during that hour?
TALLEY:	No, sir, it has not.
DOUGLAS:	May it please the court, I move the admission of this tape into evidence as State's Exhibit 14, and ask that I be allowed to exhibit it to the jury.
COURT:	Let it be admitted. Mr. Bailiff, darken the room.

The equipment was in place. The videotape cassette was inserted into a machine, the curtains were closed, and the lights were turned off.

Carol didn't watch the monitors; she had no stomach for a replay of that tragic event. Instead she watched the faces of the jurors. All twelve stared straight ahead, their eyes fixed on the television set in front of them.

The jurors' expressions changed as the drama unfolded. Their eyes widened as history repeated itself and the shots rang out once again. Horror and disbelief were reflected in their faces as the body of Frank Jordan crumpled once more at the feet of his terrified mother. Watching them as they took it all in, one might have thought that they were viewing a movie they'd never seen instead of a familiar scenario with an ending that was a foregone conclusion. The impact of the presentation was as significant as if it had all been brand new. As the lights went back on, the jurors leaned back in their chairs and breathed a collective sigh of relief.

Douglas returned to the podium once again.

"May it please the court," he stated for the record, "that concludes the state's case."

Judge Wentworth recessed court for thirty minutes to allow time for removal of the monitors and the tape machine. The jurors filed out for a welcome break. Ellen and Carol made their way out into the large hall, acutely aware of the stares of those around them. "Instant Replay" had made Carol a celebrity once again.

After standing around in the hall for a moment, Ellen excused herself and headed for the ladies' lounge. As she approached the door, someone touched her lightly on her shoulder. It was Jeffrey Rogers.

"Ms. Hayes," he began, "may I speak with you for a moment?"

"Sure, Jeff, go ahead." She waited for his response.

"Privately, please," he said quietly.

Ellen immediately sensed that the young man was upset. She led him across the hall and into the Clerk's office, where they found a quiet corner.

"What is it, Jeff?" Ellen asked.

"I have something for you," he answered. "It's something I don't think you know about. It may be important. I found it in the trash in our kitchen on the morning of the Jordan verdict, the day everything happened to Mom. I recognized Mom's handwriting, so I saved it."

He handed Ellen a wrinkled note. As she read it, her heart began to pound.

> Dear Bill and Jeffrey,
>   I want you both to know that I love you very much, more than you will ever know, but I just can't let things go on like this. I hope you will understand, and that you will both forgive me for

The note ended abruptly, the last sentence unfinished.

Ellen read the note a second time. For a moment she was lost in thought, trying to decide how to proceed.

"Thank you, Jeff," she said finally, folding the note and slipping it into her purse. "You're exactly right—it is important. You go be with your folks. Don't say anything about this, not yet. I have something I need to do right away." She led him back out into the hall, then hurried to the courtroom. Carlton Douglas was still packing up papers and straightening things out on the prosecution table.

"General Douglas, I need to see the judge right away. I need for you to be there, too." As Ellen spoke, she walked briskly through the courtroom toward the back hallway that led to the judge's chambers, not waiting for Douglas's response. He followed without hesitation. Ellen had pricked his curiosity. The judge was equally curious when the two of them suddenly appeared in his office.

Ellen asked Judge Wentworth to adjourn court until after lunch. The judge was reluctant at first. Things had moved along rather well, and he wanted that pace to continue. It was eleven o'clock. He had expected to start again shortly and to continue for another hour or more. He hoped to finish the proof that day, or at least by mid-morning of the next day.

Judge Wentworth was not totally insensitive, however. It was obvious that Ellen had prepared her case thoroughly. She had not asked for any continuances or special favors. This was the first such request, and he sensed that it was a matter of real importance to her.

"Your Honor," she said, "I've discovered a piece of evidence that may be crucial. It was called to my attention just moments ago; I didn't know about it before. I must pursue it. It would be terribly unfair to my client not to do so. Unfortunately, I can't reveal what it is, or tell you what this is about, until I've verified it myself. I know that puts you in a difficult position, but it is important, Your Honor, I assure you of that. And I promise both of you that I am not wasting the court's time. Not at all. You have my word."

Judge Wentworth granted her request without hesitation, but warned her that there would be no repeat of this situation. She thanked him and quickly left his office, leaving both him and Carlton Douglas mystified.

Ellen rejoined her group and advised them that the judge was not going to resume court until one o'clock. She asked Joe Holman to take Bill and Jeffrey to lunch, and asked Carol to come with her. All she would say was that they needed to go over her testimony one more time. The two of them fought their way through the usual phalanx of photographers and reporters, and took an elevator to one of the upper floors of the courthouse. Ellen had a friend in the Tax Assessor's Office. She gambled that she'd be able to borrow one of their conference rooms for a few moments. She was right; the conference room was empty, and they were welcome to use it.

Carol sat down in one of the upholstered conference chairs. Ellen put her briefcase on the long oak table and took a seat across from her. Carol was somewhat puzzled at Ellen's silence but asked no questions. She looked around the room. It was neatly furnished with tasteful, modern business furniture. Quality prints adorned the walls; indirect lighting illuminated the table. It was a far cry from the conference room in the District Attorney's Office.

Ellen opened her purse and took out the note. She handed it to Carol without comment. The look of shock and surprise on Carol's face spoke volumes.

"Where did you get this?" Carol asked. The paper shook noticeably in her hand.

"Jeffrey gave it to me," Ellen answered. Her voice was deliberately calm, quiet and controlled. "Apparently he saw it in the trash on the morning you shot Jordan. He recognized your writing and saved it. I don't know exactly why he did, but thank God he did. For some reason he realized now just how important it might be, so he gave it to me."

Tears gathered in Carol's eyes as Ellen continued in the same carefully controlled voice.

"Look, Carol, I should be screaming my head off right now, demanding to know why you haven't told me about this. But we don't have time for such luxuries. What I need to know, right now, is whether this means what I think it does. Were you thinking about killing yourself?"

For a fleeting instant a look of surprise and relief flashed across Carol's face. But it left as quickly as it had come. "Yes," Carol said hesitantly. "I was thinking about killing myself." She stopped for a moment to stare at the familiar handwriting. "I wanted to commit suicide. I wanted to badly, but I really don't think I could have. Yet I felt so bad, so discouraged. It was the night before the verdict came in. The jury had been out for what seemed like an eternity, but nothing had happened. I was really down. I couldn't sleep. I don't remember how late it was, but it was the middle of the night, I remember that. Maybe even early morning. I got the gun down, and I started to write this note. I heard Bill coming. I panicked and tossed the note in the trash. I thought it had been thrown away . . ."

Carol stopped again, swallowed hard, and continued. "Anyway, I hid the gun in my purse. It was sitting on the kitchen counter. It was the only place I could find. I had to hurry to keep Bill from seeing it."

Ellen offered Carol a tissue. Carol took it and dabbed at her eyes. This was very difficult for her.

"Why didn't you tell me?" Ellen asked. She couldn't resist the question. There was no anger in her voice; it was really too late for that.

"I didn't want anyone to know what I had been thinking. I couldn't stand any more pressure. There was just no way I could tell anyone about it." Carol wiped at her eyes and sniffled again. "And besides, I didn't have the note, and I couldn't prove anything anyway. I was afraid no one would believe me."

"Carol," Ellen said softly, "I'm going to have to ask you about this when you get on the stand. You know that, don't you?"

"Yes, I know," Carol responded, pausing for a moment to look into her friend's eyes. "But before you do, there's something else you need to know."

"What's that?"

"Oh, Ellen," Carol said as tears welled up in her eyes once more, overflowing onto her cheeks. "That's not the whole truth. I'm so ashamed."

"Maybe you had better tell me the rest of it, too," Ellen said, taking Carol's hands.

"Suicide wasn't the only thing I was thinking about when I wrote that note," Carol said. "It wasn't even the main thing. I was also thinking about killing Frank Jordan."

Ellen stared back at Carol, a stunned expression on her face.

"I thought about killing him first, then myself. I didn't know when or how. I had no plan, but that was what I thought, just for a minute. Whether I really meant it or not I don't know, but I know I thought about it. There's nothing I can do to change that. I hated him more than I ever thought possible."

"Is that why you put the gun in your purse?" Ellen asked.

"No, no," Carol answered quickly. "I was hiding it from Bill. That's all true. I dismissed the idea of killing Frank Jordan almost immediately. The very thought scared me to death. I never thought about killing him again."

The two women sat in silence for a moment.

"I forgot all about the gun, I really did. I know that sounds unbelievable, even stupid, but it's true. I was so upset with myself. I was angry with myself for being so weak, for harboring so much hatred, for even thinking about suicide. I was mortified. I blocked the whole thing out of my mind. Then, when I saw the gun in my purse in the courtroom . . . well, you know what happened. All of my hatred returned. I lost control."

Carol felt relieved, totally drained of all energy, all emotion. Ellen quickly sorted through all of the possibilities in her mind, trying to guess what might happen. But only one course of action was open to her now; there was no other choice. Both of them knew that the day of reckoning had finally come.

"Ellen," Carol said softly as she touched her friend lightly on the arm, "I want to tell Bill myself. Okay?"

"Of course," Ellen answered. "I'll run downstairs and bring him up here. You can wait right here. Joe promised me he'd have Bill and Jeffrey back from lunch by twelve-thirty, just in case they were needed. They should be back by the time I get down there."

"I'm sorry," Carol said, "I really am. I didn't mean to make things any harder for you than they already were. I hope you understand that."

"Don't worry, Carol," Ellen said, giving her friend's hand a comforting squeeze. "I think I understand. The important thing is that we now have to convince the jury, to make them understand the agony you went through. I hope to God they understand it. I guess as much as anything, that's going to be up to you."

‖30‖

When court resumed, Carol Rogers was the first witness. Ellen guided her through the events of the past year. Carol maintained her composure for the most part, and expressed herself well. Ellen led her skillfully. Carlton Douglas wouldn't have dared object to the leading, and Ellen knew it. Carol was a tremendously sympathetic witness. The last thing Douglas wanted to do was to play the ogre and give the jury an opportunity to choose between himself and this poor woman. The choice would have been obvious.

Carol reminisced at length about Wendy, about her birth, and the stages of her progress from sitting to standing to walking, from babbling sounds to first words to full sentences. She told how those early sentences communicated a love for life and an abiding affection for her mother. She spoke with pride about her daughter's accomplishments at school, and described the small-scale tragedies and triumphs that typically make up a child's life.

At one point, Carlton Douglas quietly objected to this line of testimony, asking the judge to exclude it as being irrelevant to the question of whether or not Carol Rogers killed Frank Jordan.

"Your Honor," Ellen pleaded, "the issue of Carol Rogers's state of mind is crucial. Her attitude toward her daughter and the nature of their relationship will be important for the jury to consider when dealing with this whole issue of murder versus manslaughter. After all, Mrs. Rogers's state of mind is very much an issue; how can the jury deal with her state of mind without knowing how she felt about the daughter she had lost?"

"Please continue," Judge Wentworth said quietly. "Objection overruled."

As Carol went on, she painted with sincere, well-chosen words a picture which came to life in each juror's mind, a vivid portrait of an affectionate daughter and an adoring mother, enjoying each other and looking forward with anticipation to the years to come, secure in the bonds of love created by their past experiences.

The jury hung on her every word when Carol described the discovery that Wendy was missing, and the horror of the days that followed, culminating with what Carol described as the very lowest point in her life, the day when she was called upon to go to the morgue and identify the violated body of her only daughter. Then she told about her reaction to the arrest and trial of Frank Jordan, carrying her narrative up to the moment when the jury returned.

HAYES: Now, Mrs. Rogers, I want you to tell me what you felt when you heard the jury return a verdict of not guilty by reason of insanity.

ROGERS: In all honesty, I cannot describe it. It was a combination of several feelings. Most of all, there was outrage. Sheer, incredible outrage. It was totally incomprehensible to me that the jury had found him not guilty. I knew, or at least I believed, that this meant he was going to be set free, if not immediately, then very soon. That seemed so terribly unfair. All I could think about was my precious daughter and all that she had gone through. All I could see was that man's face. He seemed to be gloating at me, right there in the courtroom. He seemed to be mocking me, and everything I believed in, everything I stood for. He didn't even look human!

HAYES: Was that all that you felt?

ROGERS: No, there was another feeling, perhaps the strongest feeling of all. It was hatred. The most intense hatred I have ever known. I hated that man more than I thought humanly possible.

HAYES: What happened next?

ROGERS: I reached in my purse for a tissue. The package was empty. I shifted things around to see if I could find one, and that's when I saw it. I saw the gun—my husband's little handgun, the one we keep at home for protection.

HAYES: What happened then?

ROGERS: Something inside me snapped. I felt as though all of my outrage and hatred had exploded, and was raging out of control, filling my whole body. I quit thinking. I quit hearing. I quit feeling. I just reacted. It seemed as though my real self was outside of my body, like I was watching what was going on instead of living it. I was powerless to change anything. I saw myself pull out the gun, aim it at that face I hated so much, and start shooting. Then I went limp and collapsed.

HAYES: At the time you found that gun in your purse, did you intend to kill Frank Jordan?

ROGERS: No. I didn't intend anything. I couldn't intend anything at that moment. I was incapable of it. I was completely beyond having any feelings at all. I didn't feel anything, I just existed. I reacted to what was going on. I know it's hard to understand. I don't understand it myself. It was as if all of my stamina, all of my reserve, all of my resistance had been worn away. I was an emotional void. All thought and all feeling just stopped. It was as if my system had overloaded and caused me to blow some kind of fuse. For a moment I was in limbo. There was nothing. Absolutely nothing.

HAYES: Did you plan to kill Frank Jordan that day in court?

ROGERS: No, I didn't.

HAYES: Did you ever think about that possibility in advance?

This was the most difficult part for Carol. Her voice trembled as she started to answer. She paused and cleared away a lump that had risen in her throat. She had held herself together pretty well until now; at this point her defenses finally collapsed, and she wept.

Judge Wentworth graciously allowed her a few minutes to compose herself. After a short recess, she resumed her testimony and told the mesmerized jurors about her depression, her hatred of Frank Jordan, her thoughts of killing him and then committing suicide, and all of the events of the night preceding the Jordan verdict. Then, to close her testimony, Ellen handed Carol the note. Carol identified it and read it to the jury, telling them how she had changed her mind and forgotten about the gun until that fateful moment in court. There were no dry eyes in the jury box when Ellen Hayes tendered her client for cross-examination.

Carlton Douglas's questioning of Carol was a model of brevity and effectiveness. In his most respectful and patient voice, he proceeded directly to her weakest points and exposed them to the jury's view.

DOUGLAS: Mrs. Rogers, I have to ask you a few questions. I don't want to upset you any

further. I know you have already been
through a great deal, but I'm afraid I
have no alternative. If you need to stop
for any reason, or if you need to take a
break, or if you don't understand my
question, please tell me, okay?

ROGERS: All right.

DOUGLAS: Now, Mrs. Rogers, at the time you shot
Frank Jordan, you still knew who you
were, didn't you?

ROGERS: Mr. Douglas, I really don't understand
what you are asking me.

DOUGLAS: Well, you have told the jury a great deal
about what you didn't know, and feel,
and understand. But you didn't lose
consciousness or anything like that, did
you?

ROGERS: No.

DOUGLAS: So you were fully aware of who you
were the whole time, weren't you?

ROGERS: Yes, of course I was.

DOUGLAS: And you knew *where* you were the whole
time, too, didn't you?

ROGERS: Yes.

DOUGLAS: And you knew who Frank Jordan was
the entire time as well, didn't you, Mrs.
Rogers? You didn't lose touch with
reality to that extent, did you?

ROGERS: Yes, I knew who Frank Jordan was.

DOUGLAS: Mrs. Rogers, I take it that when you
aimed that pistol, you were fully aware
that you were aiming at Frank Jordan.
That's true, isn't it? You knew that you

> were shooting at Frank Jordan, the man
> who had killed your daughter, didn't
> you, Mrs. Rogers?

ROGERS: Yes, I did.

Carlton Douglas stepped away from the podium and lowered
his voice somewhat to emphasize the next question.

DOUGLAS: Mrs. Rogers, you have described in de-
> tail your hatred for Frank Jordan, and
> you have admitted under oath that you
> considered killing him less than twenty-
> four hours before you actually did so.
> Isn't it a fact, isn't it true, that at the
> time you pulled the trigger and shot
> Frank Jordan, you hated him so much
> that you actually wanted him to die?

Carol nodded.

ROGERS: But I didn't plan it, it just happened.
> You've got to believe me!

Courthouse scuttlebutt had it that Carlton Douglas was little
more than an effective administrator who survived on the skills
of his assistants, a notion that was forever dispelled by this cross-
examination. He controlled his witness in a masterful fashion,
phrasing his questions so that Carol had no options and was
forced to answer yes or no. In a flash, he backed her into a corner
and forced her to remind the jury that she had been shooting at
a person she hated, someone she wanted dead, someone she had
even planned to kill at one time. There wasn't a thing Ellen
Hayes could do to avoid it. The inconsistency between that
admission and her claim that she didn't bring the gun into court
on purpose was painfully apparent.

The examination continued.

DOUGLAS: Now, Mrs. Rogers, lest there be any
> doubt in the jurors' minds, that gun

which you used to kill Frank Jordan did belong to your husband, didn't it?

ROGERS: Yes, it did.

DOUGLAS: And before it found its way into your purse, it had been safely hidden away somewhere in your home, hadn't it?

ROGERS: Yes. It was in a small cabinet above the refrigerator in our kitchen.

DOUGLAS: You are the one who took it from the safe place in your home and put it in your purse, aren't you?

ROGERS: Yes.

DOUGLAS: And you are the only person in your household who knew it was there, in your purse, aren't you?

ROGERS: Yes.

DOUGLAS: You did that only moments after thinking about killing Frank Jordan, didn't you?

ROGERS: I've told you that already.

DOUGLAS: And you are the one who decided to carry that particular purse to court on the day that the jury was to return its verdict in the Jordan case, aren't you?

ROGERS: Yes. It's the purse I use most of the time.

DOUGLAS: You had other purses you could have brought, didn't you?

ROGERS: Yes, I did.

DOUGLAS: But you chose to bring the one with the gun in it, didn't you?

ROGERS: I had forgotten it was there! I swear
            that's true!

DOUGLAS: I have no more questions.

Carol couldn't keep the tears from coming. She knew exactly
what Douglas had been doing, but was totally helpless to stop
him. At the rear of the courtroom, Tom Sanderson rose from
his gallery seat and left. As he walked out into the spacious
hallway, he slammed one fist into the other. Then he hurried
back to his office.

On redirect, Ellen let Carol explain the note and all of her
feelings one more time, in hopes of neutralizing some of the
damage done by the District Attorney. Hearing the story told
by Carol had to help some, but Douglas had gained some precious
ground for the state.

Bill Rogers took the stand next. His testimony was offered
mainly for emotional impact and to support his wife as much as
he could. He did his best, but there was little meat to his presentation. The state did not cross-examine him at all.

Finally, it was time for Dr. Norman Green.

As brilliant as Dr. Green was in his testimony on behalf of
Frank Jordan, he was equally well prepared on behalf of Carol
Rogers. He was medically accurate and completely understand-
able at the same time.

He admitted his involvement in the Jordan case, and confessed
his misgivings about taking on Carol Rogers as a patient because
of that involvement. With credibility, he explained his thought
process in making that decision, describing his visits with her,
the tests and examinations he had conducted, and exactly what
they were all designed to accomplish. Finally, after she had
skillfully constructed the proper foundation, Ellen asked the doctor for his conclusions.

HAYES: Doctor Green, based upon your tests, your
            examinations, and all of the history you
            gathered, were you able to form an opin-
            ion with reasonable medical certainty about
            the state of Carol Rogers's mind at the
            time she killed Frank Jordan?

GREEN: Yes, I was.

HAYES: Doctor, would you please tell the jury
          what your opinion is of her mental state?

GREEN: In my opinion, Carol Rogers's capacity to
          control her actions at the time of the Frank
          Jordan shooting had diminished to the ex-
          tent that she had no control whatsoever.
          When the impulse struck, she had no abil-
          ity to resist. She might have still known
          right from wrong, but she was powerless
          to choose right or to reject wrong.

HAYES: Doctor Green, can you tell us why this
          happened? And perhaps when it hap-
          pened, too?

GREEN: I think so. In the first place, the events of
          the preceding months had weakened Mrs.
          Rogers in two vital areas. One was phys-
          ical. She was physically exhausted and
          very nearly unable to function at all. On
          top of this, she was emotionally exhausted
          and deeply depressed over the loss of her
          daughter. When she walked into the
          courtroom that day, she was completely
          void of physical stamina and had abso-
          lutely no emotional reserve. She was on
          the edge of a breakdown, hanging on by
          a thread.

Dr. Green paused at this point to let the impact of what he
had just said sink in. His flair for the dramatic was obvious.

HAYES: Go on, Doctor.

GREEN: Well, while she was in that condition, Mrs.
          Rogers received two severe shocks in rapid
          succession. The first was the verdict. While
          she intellectually understood the possi-
          bility of a not-guilty verdict, she never

accepted that possibility emotionally. She couldn't. Such a result was impossible as far as she was concerned. So that was shock number one. The second shock came when she opened her purse and saw the gun. She had forgotten all about it. When she saw it, she suddenly realized that vengeance was within her grasp. In her condition, the combination of the two shocks was devastating. She totally lost touch with reality. She described it as well as it could be described in her own testimony. She felt nothing, heard nothing, saw nothing. She just reacted, as one would do in self-defense. There was no way she could have helped herself.

HAYES: I have no more questions. You may cross-examine.

Again, Carlton Douglas was brief, direct, and to the point.

DOUGLAS: Dr. Green, you were in the courtroom when Mrs. Rogers testified, weren't you?

GREEN: Yes, I was.

DOUGLAS: Then you heard her testimony, did you not? You heard her say that she knew, at the time of the shooting, who she was, where she was, who Frank Jordan was, and what she was doing. You heard her say that she had actually thought about killing him less than twenty-four hours before she actually did it. You heard all of that, didn't you?

GREEN: There is a difference between being aware of feelings and being responsible for actions, General Douglas.

DOUGLAS: Answer the question, please. You did hear all of that, didn't you?

GREEN: Yes, I did. Of course I did.

DOUGLAS: You wouldn't suggest to this jury that
           her statements weren't true, would you?

GREEN: Of course not. But I still must insist
           that there is a difference between
           awareness and responsibility. She might
           have been fully aware, and if she says
           she was, then she was. She might have
           thought about killing him in advance,
           too. But that doesn't mean that she was
           thinking about it later, and it certainly
           doesn't mean that she was capable of
           stopping herself.

DOUGLAS: You heard her say that she hated Frank
           Jordan enough to wish him dead. You
           heard that, didn't you?

GREEN: Yes.

DOUGLAS: You wouldn't suggest to this jury that
           she had lost her capacity to hate, would
           you, Doctor?

GREEN: No, apparently not.

DOUGLAS: Thank you, Doctor. Oh, one more thing.
           I almost forgot. You are being paid to
           come here and testify, aren't you? You
           are being paid by Mr. and Mrs. Rogers,
           aren't you?

GREEN: Yes, I am.

DOUGLAS: You were also paid to testify in the Frank
           Jordan case, weren't you?

Ellen was on her feet in a flash. "I object," she cried out.
"I withdraw the question," Douglas responded quickly.
Damn, Ellen thought to herself as she sat back down. I can't
believe it. She shook her head in disgust. She had meant to bring
that issue up herself. It was so elementary! But she had forgotten.

Expert witnesses were always paid, and it is always best to admit that at the front end so that there would be no misunderstanding. But she had forgotten, and now Douglas had made her witness look like a hired gun. Ellen returned to the podium flushed with embarrassment. She redirected Green, trying her best to resurrect his testimony, but considerable damage had been done.

After Dr. Green concluded, Ellen announced that the defense had presented all of its proof. Carlton Douglas immediately advised the court that the state would offer no more witnesses. That was it. It was all over, with incredible speed. Only one day had been consumed by all of the testimony. One day. Somehow it seemed to Ellen that this was an unbelievably short time, considering what was at stake.

Judge Wentworth commended both lawyers for the efficiency of their presentations. He then asked if there was anything else that needed his attention before he excused the jury and adjourned court for the night. Ellen responded that she had a motion to make on a point of law. The jurors marched out; she returned to the podium.

"Your Honor," she began, "the defense moves the court to direct a verdict on the premeditated murder count. The proof is undisputed. Mrs. Rogers did not carry the gun into the courtroom with intent to use it. She says she didn't, and there is no proof to the contrary, so no other conclusion is possible. We feel that we are entitled to have that count of the indictment dismissed."

Ellen's effort was half-hearted. While planning her strategy, she had thought that this might be the most important part of the case, that she might actually win on this motion. But now she knew better. Things hadn't gone as well as she had anticipated, and now she had learned about the note, and about Carol's earlier thoughts. She did the best she could under the circumstances, but her lack of enthusiasm must have shown; Douglas waived any response. Given his obvious confidence and her own feeling of resignation, Judge Wentworth's reaction was the only pleasant surprise during this long, difficult day.

"Ms. Hayes, I'm going to take your motion under advisement. I'll rule on it in the morning. Frankly, I'm just not certain. I have made pretty good notes on all of the testimony, and I want to review those notes and do a little research this evening. I'll decide one way or another in the morning. Close court, Mr. Bailiff." Judge Wentworth rapped his gavel sharply and rose to leave.

"All rise," the bailiff instructed. "This court is adjourned until nine o'clock tomorrow morning."

Ellen gathered up her papers. She was worn out. Now she faced the prospect of worrying all night about what she was going to say to the jury in her final argument. When she had finally collected everything, she started out of the courtroom with Carol and Bill. None of them was smiling. It had been a tough day.

As they filed out of the chamber, Carol came face to face with Bess Jordan. It was an awkward encounter. Ellen held her breath; the two made eye contact for the briefest instant. Then, as quickly as they had come together, they parted, each going her separate way, back into her own world of pain and loneliness.

‖31‖

The next morning at nine-fif-teen, Ellen sat in the courtroom and looked at her watch. Court was supposed to have started at nine. Judge Wentworth had a reputation for starting on time. You could almost set your watch by him. Precisely at the appointed hour, the bailiff's gavel would strike the small wooden block and the day in court would begin. But that wasn't true today.

When Wentworth had first taken the bench, his penchant for promptness had caught many lawyers by surprise. Accustomed to the more relaxed atmosphere in the other criminal courts, many found themselves racing into court and rushing up to the counsel table under the baleful glare of an already-seated judge. Those who experienced this embarrassment rarely found themselves late in Judge Wentworth's court a second time. Thus it was a surprise to almost everyone that he hadn't yet appeared.

Ellen was already extremely nervous. She awaited the judge's decision on her motion with great expectation. And no matter how that went, she would have to make her closing argument afterwards. Apprehensive as she was, each succeeding minute of delay seemed like an eternity.

Finally, the doors in the panelling opened. The bailiff came out of one door and stepped up to the bench. Judge Wentworth came out of the other and stood at attention. Everyone in the courtroom stood up, even before the bailiff rapped the gavel.

"All rise!" the bailiff began. "This honorable Criminal Court is now open, pursuant to adjournment."

Carol Rogers listened to the familiar chant. A few short months ago she had never heard it; now she could recite it in her sleep. She knew when to stand, when to bow her head, and when to sit again. She had been programmed.

When the bailiff finished, everyone sat back down. Judge Wentworth opened one of the folders in front of him and glanced down at his notes. He turned to the bailiff.

"Keep the jury in the hall for a moment," he instructed the bailiff. "I have a preliminary matter to deal with."

Ellen's heart began to race. She didn't think Judge Wentworth would grant her motion, but there was always a chance, always hope. The judge turned toward her and began to speak.

"Ms. Hayes, I have considered your motion to dismiss very carefully. In fact, that's the reason I was late this morning. After arriving at a decision last night, I decided that I would go over all of my notes and think this thing through one last time this morning. That's what I have been doing. While the decision was difficult, I am as convinced this morning as I was last night that the appropriate thing to do is to deny your motion."

Carol's heart sank. She had expected that decision, but hearing the official word was nonetheless a disappointment.

"In all candor, I tend to believe your client's story about how the gun got in her purse, how she forgot about it, and then discovered it on the day of the Jordan verdict. But I'm very much afraid that I believe her only because I *want* to believe her so badly. I prefer believing her to the only other alternative, which would be to accept the fact that she made a complete mockery of our system of justice. Somehow I cannot rest easy with the latter thought."

He believes her, Ellen thought. Maybe that means the jury might believe her, too. She felt encouraged.

"But in the final analysis," the judge continued, "I don't have the right to make that decision. That responsibility belongs to the jury. If I felt so strongly about it that I already knew that I would set aside a verdict of guilty if the jury returned one, then my responsibility would be to dismiss that count here and now. But I don't feel that way, not at all. I have an opinion, which I've expressed very candidly, but it is only an opinion. It is not a belief that rises to the dignity of a moral conviction. For that reason, I must leave this issue in the hands and hearts of the jury. Therefore, Ms. Hayes, the motion to dismiss is denied. Bailiff, bring in the jury."

Ellen didn't know what to feel. The judge had believed Carol; that was a plus. On the other hand, he had all but told Ellen that she might as well forget about filing any post-trial motions if the jury convicted Carol of premeditated murder, since his feelings about the matter didn't rise to the level necessary for him to set aside the jury's verdict.

When the jurors had settled into their seats, Carlton Douglas stepped up to the podium. He stood very still and began to speak in a calm, even voice.

"May it please the court, and members of the jury, I find myself in a difficult position here today, just as I'm sure you do. I don't envy you, any more than I relish the task ahead for myself. Carol Rogers is a sympathetic person. One could not possibly help but feel compassion for her in light of all she has gone through. I'll not detail her agony, as I am sure my opponent will emphasize that quite well. She will emphasize that aspect of this case because she *must* do that if she is to win. You see, sympathy is her client's only defense. She has nothing else to talk about."

Douglas went straight to Ellen's strongest point right off the bat, in an effort to defuse it. When sympathy naturally tends to weigh in favor of the other side, a skilled lawyer can often produce a "sympathy backlash" by exposing the invalidity of that issue to public scrutiny right from the beginning. This is what he was attempting to do.

"I suggest to you, members of the jury, that Mrs. Rogers is not the only woman in this courtroom who deserves your sympathy. Bess Jordan didn't enjoy Carol Rogers's success as a mother. Her child may not have been an example for all of us to follow, but Frank Jordan was Bess Jordan's flesh and blood. He was the only issue of her body, and now he is dead. Both of these women deserve your sympathy, and yet neither should get any sympathy whatsoever from you during this trial. For under our system of justice, neither side is entitled to any special consideration because of sympathy. No, your job is to decide this case according to the facts, and not according to whether you feel sorry for Carol Rogers, or even more sorry for Bess Jordan."

Douglas moved from that opening into a smooth chronological accounting of the significant facts concerning the killing, touching upon Carol Rogers's mental condition at that time.

"Members of the jury, other than sympathy, the only defense raised on behalf of Carol Rogers is that of temporarily diminished capacity. More commonly this is known as temporary insanity. Judge Wentworth will define that term for you when he gives you the law at the conclusion of these arguments, and I'll not attempt to do that now."

Douglas left the podium and walked over to the jury box. He looked straight at the jurors as he spoke.

"I want you to think for a moment about what the defense is asking you to believe. They are asking you to believe that a woman with a normal childhood, a woman with no history of mental problems, a woman with a thirty-nine-year record of unbroken mental stability, a woman who is mentally fit and essentially normal today, actually forgot that she had a loaded pistol in her purse. And they are asking you to believe that this same woman was insane for a period of no more than five minutes, and was not accountable for her actions during just that brief period in her life, a period in which she admits doing something she wanted very badly to do and had even been planning to do: killing a man she hated with every fiber of her being. The absurdity of that suggestion should be obvious."

He left the jury box and walked over toward the defense table. He stood at the side of Ellen Hayes's chair to emphasize what he was about to say.

"Just in case the absurdity of this is not yet obvious to any of you, members of the jury, just in case you still have some questions, then I want to ask Ms. Hayes to answer them when she speaks to you. I want her to tell you whether or not her client ever lost her ability to tell right from wrong. I want her to tell you whether or not her client knew what she was doing the entire time she was aiming that gun at Frank Jordan and pulling the trigger. And finally, I want her to tell you whether or not her client hated Frank Jordan so much that she wanted him dead, and had actually contemplated his execution at her own hands less than twenty-four hours before she pulled the trigger. Answer those questions, Ms. Hayes. These jurors have a right to know!"

It was an old trick, but one that Douglas pulled off rather well. Ellen was essentially left with two choices. She could either answer the questions or she could ignore them, but either way, she would start out on the defensive.

Shortly thereafter, Carlton Douglas closed his presentation, making only the briefest reference to the emotional aspects of the prosecution's case. He would get the last crack at the jury after Ellen finished; he was undoubtedly waiting until his final argument to do that.

The judge turned toward Ellen and nodded. She gathered her notes, stood up, and made her way to the podium. All eyes were on her. The pressure was enormous, yet at the same time she wondered if there was really any reason to bother. Hadn't the jury heard it all by now? Hadn't they made up their minds? Was there really any reason for them to listen to the biased arguments of two professionals? And yet her argument was the only thing standing between her client and a lifetime wasted in prison. That alone made it important enough to try her best.

She began by taking the bull by the horns, responding to the questions posed by Carlton Douglas in a most effective way.

"Members of the jury, General Douglas has asked that I respond to three questions. Well, I'm not going to try to answer them. You already know the answers, and so does General Douglas. You already know that Carol Rogers hated Frank Jordan. You know that, because you know that if you had been in the same circumstances, you would have hated him yourselves. You already know that Carol Rogers once thought about killing Frank Jordan and that she knew that it was the wrong thing to do. You know that because both she and her doctor admitted it. And for the very same reason, you already know that she was aware of what she was doing when she did it. You already know the answers, so I'm going to begin by telling you what General Douglas was trying to accomplish when he asked those questions."

It was an effective opening. Ellen told the jury that Douglas wanted to divert their attention away from the real issue. She explained that in spite of the confusing side issues, the fact remained that Carol Rogers did not possess the power to stop herself; therefore, as a matter of law, she could not be held responsible. The state apparently wanted them to ignore that, thus the smokescreen of irrelevant questions.

Ellen then described Carol's background, her relationship with her daughter, and the agony she felt over that child's death. She described Carol's feelings as the events unfolded, and related these to the slow buildup of pressure which Dr. Green had described as ultimately leading to her loss of control. She avoided the term "temporary insanity" and tried instead to explain the concept of emotional capacity and diminished capacity in the same understandable manner that Dr. Green had first explained them to Carol.

Ellen wanted the jury to understand and appreciate the fact that Carol was, indeed, an essentially normal person who had reacted to an abnormal series of events with a sudden loss of capacity. She emphasized the fact that Carol's reaction was a natural, inevitable reaction under the circumstances, which led to a natural, unavoidable, unfortunate conclusion.

That brought her to the final emotional appeal. It was at this point that she felt the most inadequate. As it turned out, she used that feeling of inadequacy to her advantage.

"Members of the jury, as you have probably gathered during this brief trial, I have very strong feelings about this case. I want you to share those feelings. I want that badly, possibly more than I have ever wanted anything before. And yet I don't know how to make you feel what I feel. I don't know where to begin.

"Perhaps if I were more experienced, like General Douglas, perhaps if I had been involved in this kind of case more often, I would know exactly what to say and when to say it. Certainly General Douglas has that ability, but, unfortunately, I don't. Yet I am all that Carol Rogers has. I am the only person who will speak on her behalf, the only one who can. I beg you to be patient with me and to forgive me if I say the wrong thing. I assure you that my only purpose is for you to know Carol Rogers as I know her, and to feel her pain and agony as I have over the past few months. For if you really knew her, and if you really felt her pain, then you would understand what made her do what she did."

Ellen stepped away from the podium, away from the safety of her notes, and stood in front of the jury, alone and vulnerable.

"Members of the jury, I am also a mother. Last night I tucked my only child in bed. I kissed his little blond head, and brushed the curls back from his brow. I sang a soft lullaby and whispered 'I love you.' He was sound asleep, and he didn't hear me, but those were the truest words I will ever say. I love him more than life itself."

Ellen paused for effect, then continued.

"I don't know how I would feel if someone killed him, if someone ended his life in a painful, brutal, degrading, violent way. But I can imagine. I don't know how I would react if that same person was to be brought to trial, and then through some quirk of injustice be set free, but I can imagine. Given a sudden, unexpected opportunity to gain revenge, to right the enormous wrong that I felt had been done, I don't know whether I would be able to maintain control of my emotions or not, but I can imagine. I don't know. I just don't know what I would do. But I do know that it is entirely possible that a mother who loves her child as much as I do, as much as Carol Rogers did, could lose the ability to control herself under those horrible circumstances.

"I also know that the condition which Dr. Green described can exist if a woman is pushed far enough, and tortured long enough. And I know in my heart that Carol Rogers was pushed as far and tortured as much as any human being could possibly endure. You know what happened. She finally broke. For a brief instant, she lost control. But she isn't a killer, and she doesn't deserve to go to prison. She is nothing more than a woman who loved her child, and whose heart was torn apart by the violent, senseless act of a depraved man. She is a woman who reacted to that overwhelming loss with sudden violence, violence which was contrary to her nature and her beliefs, violence which was neither planned nor premeditated, violence which erupted from deep within her soul because of the terrible circumstances into which she was cast by the hand of fate.

"Members of the jury, Carol Rogers needs to be at home with her family. She needs to be a part of their lives. She needs to go on with her life, to go on being a productive member of society. I beg you to give her that chance."

There was much more that she could have said, much more that she wanted to say, but Ellen was emotionally spent, and unable to go on. She walked slowly back to the defense table and sat down. Whatever the outcome, she had given it her best.

Carlton Douglas rose to complete the argument for the state. Ellen barely listened. There was no reason to do so; she couldn't respond anyway. She had anticipated this moment for so long. It had come, she had given her all, and it had gone. Now she had nothing left. She slumped down in her chair as her adversary concluded.

"Members of the jury, in spite of what you might feel for Carol Rogers, and I am certain all of you feel a great deal of sympathy, in spite of that, you have a duty, a responsibility to the American people and to the American system of justice.

"If you fail to convict Carol Rogers, then you will be saying to everyone in America that it is all right for them to take the law into their own hands, as long as they can show that they were hurt badly enough. You will be saying to criminals and to ordinary citizens alike that America is ready to return to the era of vigilante committees and lynch mobs. And you will be saying to all people that the American courtroom is no longer sacred, and that the American system of justice is no longer secure.

"Yes, there is more at stake here, ladies and gentlemen, than one woman. There is an important principle involved. Make no mistake about it, if this kind of self-imposed justice is allowed to exist without punishment, the next victim may be the judge, the lawyer, or even the jurors who dare return a verdict that is unsatisfactory to one of the parties. No one will be immune from the dangerous aftershocks if you refuse to make an example of this woman, unfortunate as she may be. She made a mockery of the system we all rely on, and chose instead to make herself judge, jury, and executioner of Frank Jordan. You cannot, you *must* not, let that happen. You *must* do your duty and return a verdict of guilty!"

With those words, Douglas slammed his fist down on the podium. Then he quit. It was all over, except for the decision.

Ellen sat quietly and watched the jurors as Judge Wentworth began to explain the complex details of the law. He told them, among other things, that they alone had to determine if Carol Rogers's capacity to choose the morally and legally right course of action was so badly diminished at the moment she killed Frank Jordan that she should not be held responsible for her acts.

"If you find that her capacity was diminished to that extent," he went on, "then your verdict must be not guilty by reason of temporary insanity."

God, I hope that's what they do, Ellen thought.

Thirty minutes later, the jurors retired to deliberate. There was nothing left except to wait.

As Carol Rogers stood up to leave, she glanced over toward the prosecution table. Bess Jordan remained seated beside Carlton Douglas. Carol stared at the sad, tired face of Frank Jordan's mother. Bess looked up, as if suddenly aware that she was being watched. Their eyes met. Again there were no words. Neither woman changed expression, neither acknowledged the other's presence in any way. It was as if the two of them could look right through each other without being aware that the other existed. And yet they were very much aware of each other. Very much, indeed.

‖ 32 ‖

Ellen paced up and down the hallway, occasionally stopping to make idle conversation with Bill Rogers or Joe Holman. Jeffrey Rogers sat next to his mother on one of the hard wooden benches that lined the hall. The five of them had spent the better part of the last four hours alternating between aimless walks that led nowhere and equally boring periods of sitting in silence.

Had they known that the jury would take this long, they would have gone to Ellen's office or somewhere else where they might have found comfort and privacy. Unfortunately, there is no way to predict how long a jury will deliberate, and they wanted to be immediately accessible if anything happened. So they did the only thing they could do. They hung around and waited, and worried, and then waited some more.

For litigants, as for their friends and families, the time spent waiting for the jury is a time of apprehension, dread, excitement, and boredom. No matter which side you are on, you can always hope for the best and believe that it's coming. But as time drags on, you don't know whether to be depressed or elated. Does this mean that they're having a hard time deciding? And if they are, does that bode well for your side, or is that a bad omen? These questions have no answers. Seconds stretch into minutes, minutes into hours.

For the lawyers, the time spent waiting for the jury is a time for soul searching. Why did I say what I did? Why didn't I do it another way? Why didn't I bring up just one more point? Would it have made a difference if I had? The possibilities are endless, of course. Second-guessing is the easiest part of a lawsuit.

But for the person accused of a crime, the wait is a special kind of hell. It is a numbing, stultifying wrinkle in time, a period when one hangs suspended between freedom and imprisonment, facing the unknown, fearing the worst.

For four hours Carol Rogers had been suffering alone, lost in her own thoughts, impervious to the confusion around her, oblivious to the attention focused on her every move. She replied politely when spoken to by well-meaning friends, but paid no attention to what they said. She had no interest in the useless exercise of second-guessing. She was beyond such thoughts. They were irrelevant. The only legitimate consideration was the jury's decision, and the only course of action open to her was to withdraw into her private world and wait.

The moment Ellen saw the bailiff coming down the hall, striding purposefully toward their group, she knew that the wait was almost over. She stood transfixed and watched him as he approached. Bill Rogers, sensing her tension, stopped in mid-sentence and turned around.

"Ms. Hayes," the bailiff said, "the jury is ready to return. Judge Wentworth wants all parties back in court right away."

"Thank you," Ellen said. "We'll be right there." She motioned Carol over and broke the news to her.

"Well, this is it. We need to get back inside."

Carol, Ellen, and Bill walked down the hall, followed by Joe Holman and Jeffrey Rogers. As they entered the courtroom, Bill and Carol embraced briefly, then separated. Carol went to her seat at the defense table; Bill joined the rest of their group in the first row of the gallery.

If the time spent waiting for a jury is a stultifying experience, then the moments that immediately precede the reading of the verdict are even worse. Everyone knows that a decision has been reached, but no one knows what it is, and there's no way to find out. It is a special kind of torture. Hearts beat at an unbelievable rate, pulses race out of control, breathing becomes rapid, and sometimes difficult.

There is no way to make things happen any faster. Somewhere, in someone's hand, there is a little slip of paper that bears the answer everyone has been searching for, the verdict that everyone has been fighting for. Inscribed on that paper is victory or defeat, agony or ecstasy, separation or reunion. It will be made public in due time, after the proper procedures have been followed, but no sooner.

Ellen and Carol sat at the defense table awaiting the entry of the judge. Ellen took Carol's hand. They both looked straight ahead, ignoring the stares of the gallery and the omnipresent glare of the television lights.

Judge Wentworth finally entered. Everyone stood up automatically, and the judge motioned for them to sit down.

"I am advised that the jury is ready to report," the judge began. "Do either of you have any preliminary matters that must be dealt with before we call them in?"

"No, Your Honor," Ellen replied.

"Nothing for the state," Douglas echoed.

"Very well," the judge said. "Bailiff, bring the jury in, please."

Once again it would have been difficult to predict the verdict by looking at the twelve jurors. They presented no consensus based on body language, facial expression, or eye contact with either side. The only obvious thing was that every single one had experienced some degree of distress in arriving at this difficult decision. All of them appeared upset. There were red eyes and puffy faces, ties askew and hair disheveled. It was obvious that they had struggled long and hard with the questions presented to them.

"Members of the jury," Judge Wentworth said, once they all were seated, "I understand that you have reached a verdict. Which one of you is serving as foreman?"

"I am, Your Honor," answered an attractive, brown-haired woman in the middle of the first row. She stood up, holding the slip of paper in her hand.

"Have you reached a verdict?" the judge asked.

"We have, Your Honor," the foreman replied.

"What is that verdict?" the judge asked.

The foreman looked down at the paper. "We, the jury, find the defendant, Carol Jeffreys Rogers, guilty of manslaughter."

A steady murmur swept the courtroom. Ellen stared blankly ahead. She really didn't know what to feel. They had lost, but it could have been worse. Far worse.

Carol buried her head in her arms and began to sob softly. For her, the distinction between premeditated murder and manslaughter wasn't important. All that mattered to her was that she was now one step closer to the hell of separation from her son and her husband. She had lost. She was crushed.

Judge Wentworth rapped his gavel three times in rapid succession, sending a staccato of shocks through the room. By the time the echo of the last blow died down, order was restored. He then addressed the jury.

"Madam foreman, the court submitted to you the issue of the mental condition of Mrs. Rogers at the time of the killing of Frank Jordan. I realize that your answer to that issue is implicit in the verdict you have rendered. However, I want to leave no room for error. Therefore, I want to ask you a question which I want answered for the record. Did you as a jury deal with the question of Mrs. Rogers's capacity to choose right over wrong at the time of Jordan's death?"

"Yes, we did, Your Honor," the foreman replied.

"What was your decision on that issue?"

"Your Honor," the foreman continued, "we didn't think that Mrs. Rogers was temporarily insane."

Judge Wentworth leaned back in his chair, satisfied with that response.

Ellen Hayes was incredulous. She was appalled by the incredible irony of it all. The earlier jury believed that Frank Jordan couldn't help himself when he committed a brutal crime, yet this jury was insisting that Carol Rogers was perfectly sane when she reacted violently to that brutality.

"Members of the jury," the judge went on, "I want to address all twelve of you. Is there anyone on this jury who does not feel that this verdict accurately represents his or her separate verdict?"

No one said anything. No hands were raised. Several jurors shook their heads. Judge Wentworth then wheeled around to face the defense table.

"Ms. Hayes, do you want the jurors individually polled?"

"No, Your Honor," Ellen replied.

The judge asked General Douglas the same question. His answer was the same.

"Very well. Will the defendant please stand?"

Carol and Ellen stood together. Carol's eyes were watery and her face was puffy and red, but she stood tall and faced the judge with all of the courage and resolve she could muster.

"Mrs. Rogers," the judge stated solemnly, "the verdict of this jury now becomes the judgment of this court. I pronounce you guilty of the crime of manslaughter. I will postpone your sentencing until one week from today, to give the probation department an opportunity to file a pre-sentencing report."

"Your Honor," Ellen said, "I plan to file a motion for a new trial and a motion for a suspended sentence—"

The judge interrupted her. "Ms. Hayes, I assumed that you would do so. All motions must be filed at least two days before the sentencing hearing. I will deal with the question of suspension at the same time that I pronounce sentence, one week from today. Any other motions should also be filed by then, but a decision on them will be reserved for a later date. Bond will be continued until that hearing. Anything further?"

"No, Your Honor," Ellen said quietly. Again, Carlton Douglas's answer was the same as Ellen's.

"Very well. Members of the jury, you may be excused. Please report to the jury assembly room when you leave here. Bailiff, adjourn court!"

Judge Wentworth quickly exited; the jurors filed out. As soon as the judge had left, Bill Rogers rushed up to Carol and they fell into each other's arms. Jeffrey fought his way through the crowd and ran up to hug his mother. Ellen gathered up her papers and prepared to leave.

Across the courtroom, Bess Jordan sat in stony-faced silence, staring intently at the scene taking place at the defense table. Her face was void of all emotion as she watched the dejected Rogers family file out of the courtroom in the company of their friends.

‖33‖

Later that evening, Carol and Bill went to Ellen's office for a postmortem. It was time to plan their next step. Although all three were still upset, Ellen was the most visibly distressed, and the most vocal.

"I really owe you an apology," she said. "I really do. I should never have taken this thing on in the first place. I just blew it. That's all I can say. I just blew it."

Bill and Carol tried to comfort her, but to no avail. Ellen felt responsible for what had happened, and the burden of that responsibility was more than she could bear.

"I should have followed my instinct from the beginning. I let Carlton Douglas walk all over me. He tried every trick in the book, and damn if most of them didn't work. Everywhere I turned, he out-foxed me. I just didn't have enough experience for this kind of case. It was too big. I shouldn't have tried it."

"Ellen, don't do this to yourself," Carol said, putting an arm around the distraught lawyer's shoulder. "You did everything you could. There wasn't anything else to do. We just lost, that's all. The jury didn't find our way. If you had won every skirmish, they still might have done the same thing. It isn't going to do you any good to try to punish yourself by worrying about what you might have done differently. It isn't going to accomplish anything."

Carol meant it. She and Bill were disappointed, but it never occurred to them to blame Ellen.

"There really isn't anything we can do about it now," Bill interjected. "We need to pull ourselves together and focus our energy on next week's hearing. That's the most important thing right now."

"Of course you're right," Ellen responded. "I just can't help feeling that I let you down. It probably didn't make any real difference, but some of the dumb things I did made me feel so bad that I just wanted to crawl under the table. And to think, everyone told me Carlton Douglas couldn't try a lawsuit. I feel like I've been duped."

"Well, at least you convinced the jury that it wasn't premeditated," Carol offered. "We can be grateful for that."

"Yes, I know—" Ellen began, but was interrupted by a knock on her office door. She glanced at her watch. It was eight-thirty. She looked over at Carol and Bill, a quizzical expression on her face. "Who could that be?" she said. "I'm not expecting anyone." She opened the door.

"May I come in?" Tom Sanderson asked.

"Of course," Ellen answered, a look of surprise on her face.

Sanderson greeted Carol and Bill Rogers warmly. They hadn't seen him since the Jordan trial. Sanderson had developed a kinship of soul with the Rogers family during the weeks of preparation for that case, but they had all been so involved in other things since then that their paths hadn't crossed. He had avoided the courtroom during Carol's trial because he just couldn't take it; seeing Carlton Douglas go after Carol like that had made his blood boil.

Unknown to Carol and Bill, Tom had refused Carlton Douglas's request that he testify for the state, insisting that it wasn't necessary since the prosecution had such an airtight case. His refusal had widened the gap between Douglas and himself.

Ellen pulled up a chair and offered Tom a seat.

"Ellen," Tom said, "I want you to know that I think you did a magnificent job. I kept up with the trial on a day-to-day basis and I also overheard much of what Douglas had to say during breaks. You really had him running, believe me. He would come storming into the office, fussing and fuming and cursing your name. It was beautiful. I've never seen him so upset."

"Thanks, Tom," Ellen responded, grateful for his praise. "I'm not feeling very good about it right now. I was shucked like an ear of corn at every turn."

"You weren't, I can assure you. You should be very proud," Tom assured her. "The D.A. thought he had an absolute lock on premeditated murder. He wasn't the least bit worried about temporary insanity. He really thought it was in the bag. Believe me, if it hadn't looked like a sure winner, he never would've taken the case on himself. In case you haven't noticed, he is super-sensitive to public opinion. Right now, since he didn't get premeditated murder, he feels like he's been burned. At this very minute he's stomping around his office, barking out orders, acting like a little dictator. He'll be up all night!"

Ellen's spirits lifted with his words.

"Anyway," Tom continued, "one week isn't a lot of time. We need to get to work on a plan for the suspended-sentence hearing."

"We?" Ellen and Carol asked in unison, glancing at each other.

"Yes, we. At least in a manner of speaking," Tom answered. "That's what I came over here for, to offer my help. If you think you can use me, I want to help you. I don't want to see Carol in prison any more than anyone else. You did a great job keeping the conviction down to manslaughter. That's got to help your chances on your motion. I want to do whatever I can to help you get a suspended sentence, if you feel like you can use me."

"What can you do?" Carol asked. "Better yet, what are you *willing* to do?"

"Well," he answered, "for one thing I can advise Ellen on how to handle the motion. I've been in Wentworth's court on dozens of such motions. I've always represented the state, of course, but from that perspective I've been able to see what he likes and dislikes, as well as what works and what doesn't. I think I can keep Ellen from wasting time on things that aren't important, and help her focus on the things that will impress Wentworth the most."

"That's got to help," Ellen interjected, "it sure won't hurt. As far as I'm concerned, your input would be welcome. But it's really up to Carol. I'm working for her."

"Are you kidding?" Carol responded. "I need all the help I can get."

"Won't Douglas go through the ceiling when he finds out?" Bill asked.

"He won't find out, at least not for a while," Tom responded. "Anyway, that's a chance I'm willing to take."

"Then that settles it. Welcome aboard, Tom," Ellen said, extending her hand.

Unlike some lawyers who might have felt that their ego was on the line, Ellen was not at all threatened by his offer of assistance. This case was no ego trip; she had passed through that stage long ago. She didn't care who had the ideas and who got the credit, as long as they all did their best. Like Carol and Bill, all she wanted was to win.

"I don't know how to thank you, Tom," Carol said.

"There's no need for that, Carol, at least not yet. It may be a bit early for optimism, too. We have a rough job ahead of us. We are all going to have to work together to get this done. The deck is stacked against us. It's going to be tough, but it's not impossible. We can worry about gratitude when it's over."

He turned to Ellen. "There's one more thing, Ellen. If you'll let me, I want to testify on Carol's behalf. I want an opportunity to tell the court what an injustice it would be if she were sent to prison."

Ellen was stunned. "Tom, that could cost you your job," she said.

"I've thought about that," Tom answered. "I've thought about it long and hard. My days are numbered anyway, and Carol's fate is too important. You forget, we worked together for months. I was involved from the beginning. I felt like a part of the family. When Wendy's body was found, I felt the loss personally. I hated Jordan almost as much as Carol did. I know what kind of person he was, and what kind of person Carol is. I just can't sit by and do nothing."

All four were silent for a moment. Carol extended her arms toward Tom.

"I can't thank you enough," she said as they embraced. Tom's presence gave her a feeling of renewed hope.

"Tom," Ellen asked, "do you think it would do us any good ___ ro go and talk to Douglas? Do you think he would be open to any kind of a compromise? I'm a little scared of him, to tell you the truth. When I went to see him about plea bargaining, he was so belligerent that I'm wary. But if you think it will do any good, I'll be glad to give it a try."

"Don't waste your time," Tom responded. "It's hopeless."

"I'm sorry to hear that," Ellen said. "I would've hoped that since he'd extracted his pound of flesh, he might ease up some."

"No such luck," Tom sighed. "In fact, just the opposite. He's already told his staff that he'll oppose any attempt at probation. He's so adamant about it that he's almost irrational. That's what made me come over here. I couldn't sit around and listen to him rant and rave without getting angry. He's turning this thing into a personal vendetta. That just isn't right. It made me mad. That's part of the reason I want to help."

"Can he *keep* us from getting a suspended sentence?" Bill asked. "I mean, what is the practical effect if the state opposes probation? Will that make any difference with the judge?"

"That's the bad part," Tom answered. "There is kind of an unspoken law that applies here. It has nothing to do with rules, or cases, or precedents. Not really. It's just that in all of my experience, I've never heard of Wentworth granting probation when the state actively opposed it. It's something he never does. I'm afraid it's a matter of principle. We are fighting an uphill battle against tradition, believe me."

Carol and Ellen looked at each other. Their depression returned all too quickly.

‖34‖

The week flew by. It was filled with frantic activity. Carol and Bill had several meetings with officials of the Probation Department, giving them information and filling out an endless stream of forms. Ellen, Carol, and Tom Sanderson met several times to evaluate the various possibilities open to them. They decided to involve Norman Green in the probation hearing; this necessitated even more meetings. Fortunately, Green was more than willing to cooperate.

All of the sessions involving Tom had to be held at night. He still hadn't "gone public" with his participation and didn't want to have to field questions about his absence from the office. He wanted to help Carol for personal reasons, but was careful to avoid any suggestion that he might be passing inside information along to Ellen Hayes. Indeed, he was not doing so. His only involvement was to help Ellen plan strategy, based on his own experience in Judge Wentworth's court. Still, he was treading on dangerous ground and he knew it.

Limited though his contribution was, it was nonetheless valuable. He was able to pass along vital insights. For one thing, he warned Ellen that Judge Wentworth would not want to hear any testimony from live witnesses, but would do so if she in- and that she should insist. He urged her to keep the involvement of Bill and Jeffrey Rogers to a minimum. The judge didn't need to be told that they loved Carol, and that they needed her at home. He knew that already. Ellen searched in vain for a middle ground that would satisfy the judge's penchant for brevity, the desire of Bill and Jeffrey to express their feelings, and the emotional need of Carol to have them support her effort to remain free. By the eve of the hearing, no solution had been reached.

Tom also suggested that Ellen instruct her witnesses to get directly to the point, say what they needed to say, and then quit. There was no time for background information or belabored explanations. She should put them on the stand, lead them right to the heart of the matter, go over it once, then stop, more like a good cross-examination than a lengthy direct.

As she entered the courtroom on that final morning, Ellen was still searching for that delicate balance between simplicity and thoroughness. She wanted to engender sympathy and understanding without overdoing it, a tough assignment which greatly increased her nervousness. Her emotions were at a fevered pitch as the bailiff opened court.

Moments later, as Judge Wentworth began pronouncing sentence, the jam-packed courtroom was completely quiet.

"Ms. Hayes, General Douglas, this court has before it the Probation Department's pre-sentencing report on Carol Jeffreys Rogers. The court has read it and re-read it. It says exactly what one might expect it to say; it presents to the court a thirty-nine-year-old woman with no history of criminal involvement and no history of anti-social behavior. There is no criminal record, no history of domestic instability, and nothing to suggest any mental problems. Indeed, this report paints a picture of a typical American housewife, one who has raised two children, who has practiced domestic skills with some excellence, and who has created an atmosphere that's resulted in a happy home. That's no small accomplishment. In sum, this is a woman who is an ideal candidate for special consideration from this court."

Judge Wentworth closed that file and shifted it to one side. Ellen looked at Carol; delight was written all over their faces. The judge reached for another file, opened it, and began to speak again.

"Unfortunately, that report does not tell the whole s

have also read and re-read the transcript of the testimony in State versus Carol Jeffreys Rogers. It presents to this court a woman who entered a court of law, one of the last bastions of stability and order in the world today, carrying a loaded weapon. That single act is as offensive to our system of justice as any act can possibly be. That single act demonstrates an utter and complete disregard for the sanctity of the courtroom and for the safety of the people who had assembled in that chamber on that day for the purpose of resolving their disputes and administering justice in a civilized way."

He closed the second file and shifted it to one side, leaned forward, and clasped his hands together. Now Carlton Douglas was feeling more optimistic. He turned toward Bess Jordan and smiled. She did not react, but continued to listen intently to the proceedings with the same dispassionate expression that had characterized her demeanor from the start. The judge continued.

"This, then, is the dilemma facing the court. On the one hand there are the positive qualities and characteristics of the defendant, on the other hand the outrageous and heinous nature of the crime itself.

"No one here needs to be reminded of how important it is that the kind of conduct exhibited by Mrs. Rogers on that day not be condoned. At the same time, it is equally important that this court be sensitive to the nature of the people involved in this and any other matter, and the impact of its decisions on them and those who care about them. Frankly, I have never in my life had more appreciation for the symbol which represents my chosen profession—blind justice. That noble woman, standing tall and holding her sacred scales, weighs with care the relative merits of controversies, searching for the most equitable decision. More than ever I understand how much it must pain her to have to make a decision in some cases. She does so blindfolded, without having to see the faces of the people affected by her decisions. I don't have that luxury. The faces of the people involved in this case keep haunting me, pulling me in one direction or another. Nonetheless it is my duty to decide. It is a duty which I cannot and will not attempt to avoid. I must decide, and I have done so."

While it didn't occur to Ellen Hayes or Carlton Douglas at the time, both would later realize how unusual it was for Judge

Wentworth to lapse into the first-person pronoun. Like many judges, he usually referred to himself as "the court," reflecting a tacit understanding that the office itself transcends personal considerations. His use of the first person gave insight into the enormous difficulty he'd experienced in deciding this matter. When he got down to the actual decision, however, he became more formal.

"This court has previously pronounced judgment in this matter. That judgment, which was the verdict of the jury, was that Carol Jeffreys Rogers was guilty of the crime of manslaughter. For the crime of manslaughter, this court sentences Carol Jeffreys Rogers to serve not more than five years in the state penitentiary."

Carol was stunned. Far from being angry or upset, she was suddenly drained of all feelings, rendered numb, void of emotion.

The sentence was the minimum for manslaughter. She had known for at least a week that such a sentence, or perhaps one far worse, was a real possibility. But there are some things that the human mind cannot accept emotionally. For Carol, the idea of imprisonment was one such thing. She had clung tenaciously to every slim thread of hope. Now those words, those final, terrible, permanent words rumbled through the darkest corners of her mind, crushing out all joy, destroying her will.

". . . *Carol Jeffreys Rogers to serve not more than five years in the state penitentiary*."

Hearing her name in this context, hearing this awesome, unreal pronouncement was something Carol could never have prepared herself for, no matter how much time she'd been given.

". . . *five years in the state penitentiary*."

They were words that civilized people shouldn't have to hear—obscene, offensive words, foreign to her ears.

". . . *the state penitentiary*."

Horrendous images of emaciated, gaunt, hollow-eyed prisoners crowded into her mind, mocking her, laughing at her, beckoning to her, calling her to join them in their hell.

". . . *penitentiary*."

Anger finally welled within her, filling the emptiness in her soul. Suddenly she felt like screaming. She pressed her hands against her ears, closing off all sounds, as if she could avoid reality by the simple act of refusing to allow these words to enter her mind. But it was too late.

Carol sobbed softly, caught between a need to let her emotions flow and a desire to appear strong. She wanted to hold herself together for Bill's and Jeffrey's sake, if for no other reason.

Sitting next to her, Ellen Hayes closed her eyes. She was transfixed, her mind preoccupied with the pain that she knew her friend must be feeling at this moment. Suddenly she realized that the judge had said something to her and she had missed it. Fortunately, he repeated it.

"Ms. Hayes, is there anything else from the defense at this time?"

Ellen's mind returned to the real world. She stood up, hastily grabbed a legal pad, and hurried to the podium, beginning to answer the judge before she arrived.

"Your Honor, we have filed with the court a written motion to suspend the sentence. We would like to be heard in support of that motion."

Ellen's voice wavered and cracked. At one point she paused briefly and choked off a sob that had crept upward in her throat and very nearly escaped. She cared so much for Carol and hurt so deeply for her at this moment that she was having considerable difficulty concentrating. More than anything else she wanted to stop the proceedings, to call time out, to make everyone else wait while she rushed to her friend's side, put her arms around her, and offered comfort. But she had no choice. She had to go on.

"Ms. Hayes, this court has already read and considered your motion carefully, as you can probably imagine," Judge Wentworth said. "This court has no doubt that the jury felt compassion for Mrs. Rogers. That is the only logical explanation for their decision to convict her of the lesser offense of manslaughter, rather than the more serious charge of premeditated murder which could have been justified under the proof. Thus, in the court's view, Mrs. Rogers has already experienced benevolence from the jury itself.

"Those same benevolent considerations prompted this court, against its better judgment, to mete out only the minimum sentence for manslaughter. Thus Mrs. Rogers has twice benefited from a serious and sympathetic consideration of her personal circumstances. This court would not suggest that her case hasn't merited such consideration. Indeed, she's deserved all of the understanding and compassion she's received. But the implication, as far as your motion is concerned, should be obvious."

In a nice way, the judge was trying to tell Ellen that she was wasting her time, and his as well. The message was received. Ellen was discouraged. Nonetheless, remembering Tom Sanderson's admonition, she marched onward with her plan.

"May it please the court," Ellen responded, "I am not unmindful of the generosity of both the court and the jury. Mrs. Rogers is grateful, I can assure you. Nevertheless, we would like to present proof in support of our motion."

"Very well," Judge Wentworth said, leaning back in his leather chair, assuming an expression of resigned indifference. "You may proceed."

This was it. Bottom of the ninth, two out, last batter. Ellen's last chance for victory; Carol's last hope for freedom. Discouraged though she was, Ellen took a deep breath and plunged ahead, giving it her best shot. She closed her eyes for an instant, said a silent prayer, then called her first witness.

‖35‖

Ellen put Bill Rogers on the stand first. He made a very simple, emotional plea, begging the court not to take his wife away from him and their son. It was brief and to the point. Then she tendered him to the court and the state for cross-examination. Neither General Douglas nor Judge Wentworth asked anything. He was excused. His appearance was dramatically effective.

Jeffrey Rogers took the stand next. She tendered him for cross-examination without asking him any questions, explaining to the court that she didn't want him subjected to the emotional trauma of testifying. It was a brilliant move. Jeffrey's red face and puffy eyes spoke eloquently of his love for his mother and his need to have her at home. Mere words would have added nothing to the impact. Again neither the court nor the prosecution had any questions. There was nothing whatsoever to be gained by interrogating someone so vulnerable, so obviously deserving of sympathy. Jeffrey was excused without ever saying a word.

Dr. Green was called to the stand next. He dealt with Carol's present condition rather than her state of mind when she killed Frank Jordan. He did his usual thorough and effective job, blending medical accuracy with lay terminology.

He testified that Carol was essentially normal, having no residual problems as a result of her one bout with mental illness. When it was time for the prosecution to question him, Carlton Douglas aimed his brief cross-examination squarely at the most important issue: whether or not Carol Rogers might ever become violent again.

DOUGLAS: Dr. Green, you didn't treat Carol Rogers before she shot and killed Frank Jordan, did you?

GREEN: No, I didn't.

DOUGLAS: And yet, according to your testimony at the first trial, and according to your testimony today, you feel you have worked with Carol Rogers long enough, and probed deeply enough, that you are able to draw a conclusion with reasonable medical certainty about her condition, her state of mind, shortly before that tragic event. That is correct, isn't it?

GREEN: Yes, it is.

DOUGLAS: Good. Then I want to ask you a specific question about her state of mind right before that killing took place. Let's talk about the one week immediately preceding that event. I want you to focus in on that period. Can you do that?

GREEN: Yes, I'll be glad to try.

DOUGLAS: Now, tell me, Doctor, do you believe, based on what you know now, that you would have been able to predict Carol Rogers's violent behavior if you had actually examined her during the week prior to that event taking place?

Dr. Green paused for a moment. Carlton Douglas had created a dilemma. If he said yes, then he would be contradic~~~

own prior testimony, since he had earlier claimed that there was nothing wrong with Carol's mental capacity during the moment right before she lost control. If he said no, Douglas would make him admit that he also couldn't make such a prediction now, nor could he do so regarding the future. If he avoided the question entirely, claiming that he didn't have enough information to answer, that would weaken or totally destroy his original diagnosis, which would be the worst of all. Having little time to weigh the pros and cons, Green chose to take his lumps.

> GREEN: No, I could not have predicted it.
>
> DOUGLAS: And it is equally true, isn't it, that you have no way of predicting her conduct now, or in the future either. Isn't that true, Doctor?
>
> GREEN: I think it is safe to say that the irresistible forces which bore down on her then—
>
> DOUGLAS: Answer the question, yes or no.

Green looked pleadingly at the judge, but to no avail. Judge Wentworth instructed him to answer the question.

> GREEN: That's true, but—
>
> DOUGLAS: And it is also true, isn't it, Doctor, that you have no idea what kind of forces will bear down on this woman in the future, or just how irresistible they might be? That's true, isn't it?
>
> GREEN: Of course I don't know. How could I?
>
> DOUGLAS: Thank you, Doctor. No more questions.

It wasn't a big point in the grand scheme of things, but Douglas had drawn attention to it effectively and dramatically. No one really believed that Carol would ever be subjected to those kinds again, yet Green's admission that he couldn't make such a prediction cast a pall over Ellen's efforts. She asked some questions on redirect in an attempt to resurrect his testimony, but the psychological damage was done.

In the face of this setback, Ellen sought to regain the advantage by pulling her own surprise.

"May it please the court, my next witness is Tom Sanderson."

Ellen made this announcement with a certain flourish. As Tom Sanderson strode through the jammed courtroom, the judge registered mild surprise but said nothing. The look of shock on Carlton Douglas's face was apparent to everyone.

In reality, Sanderson's testimony was anticlimactic. He didn't say anything that everyone didn't already know, but its true impact derived from his mere presence on behalf of the defense.

He told about his involvement with the Rogers family during a difficult period in that family's life. He described in grisly detail the investigation and discovery of Wendy Rogers's body, and his trip to the morgue with Carol and Bill. He spoke of Carol's courage and resolve during the long months of preparation, and of her strength during the trial. He said nothing negative about Frank Jordan, and yet he described the despicable nature of the crime with sufficient clarity to present a dramatic contrast between Jordan and the Rogers family.

Sanderson's appearance was well planned and well presented, effectively eradicating any advantage the state might have gained from Douglas's cross-examination of Norman Green. When Sanderson's direct examination was concluded, Douglas asked no questions. It was painfully clear, however, that he would have a number of questions for Sanderson later.

The last witness for the defense was Carol Rogers.

Carol's appearance took an unexpected and unplanned twist. After being sworn in, Ellen asked her to state her name for the record. She did so in a soft, quiet voice and then began to cry, not a dramatic outburst, just a soft, natural cry, as though she could express herself no other way.

Carol's spontaneous display of restrained emotion was so heartrending, and so totally honest, that Ellen followed a sudden impulse and asked no more questions, but simply tendered Carol for cross-examination. Then she sat down, leaving Carol alone in the witness box. Carlton Douglas, caught off guard, had no questions. Carol was excused and allowed to return to her place.

at the counsel table. All in all, it was as effective a plea for mercy as anyone could remember seeing.

Ellen then announced to the court that she had no more proof. Judge Wentworth addressed Carlton Douglas.

"What position does the state take in this matter, General Douglas?" he asked.

There had been no public indication of a position from the District Attorney's office, but thanks to Tom Sanderson, Ellen knew what was coming when Douglas rose to speak. He was intentionally brief. The room was filled with sympathy for Carol Rogers. He knew that he could produce a dangerous backlash if he said too much.

"Your Honor, the state, on behalf of the citizens of this community, respectfully opposes probation in this case."

As Douglas sat back down, a murmur swept through the courtroom.

"Very well, General Douglas," the judge responded.

Judge Wentworth looked down at the papers that were spread out on the bench in front of him. He reached over and picked up a thin folder, fumbled with it briefly, then bowed his head and massaged his temples as if to rub away the tensions of the moment. It was obvious that he did not relish this task. Almost as an afterthought, he made a perfunctory inquiry to be certain that everyone was finished before he pronounced his judgment.

"Does anyone else have anything to say about this matter before the court renders its decision?" he asked. His eyes swept the courtroom, then returned to his papers. He didn't expect a response; certainly not the one he got.

"I do, Your Honor!"

Judge Wentworth lifted his head quickly, glancing around the room. All eyes were turned in the direction of the prosecution table. The huge chamber was instantly filled with excited chatter. The judge pounded his gavel and restored order.

"Who spoke?" he asked. "Who was that?"

"It was me," Bess Jordan said, rising stiffly from her chair. "I would like to say something, please!"

‖36‖

Carlton Douglas jumped to his feet. "Your Honor," he said, almost yelling at Judge Wentworth in his excitement, "I would like a moment to confer with Mrs. Jordan. Perhaps a short recess?"

"I don't see the need for a recess, General Douglas," answered the judge. "This has been a long hearing, and we are very near the end of this matter. Go ahead and take a minute. Talk to Mrs. Jordan. We'll wait."

The noise level in the courtroom increased once again. Judge Wentworth leaned back in his chair. He didn't gavel for order this time, choosing instead to leave things as they were until Douglas finished his discussion with Bess Jordan. The cavernous room soon filled with a steady, unbroken rumble—just enough noise to keep anyone from hearing the conversation at the prosecution table.

It was obvious, however, that the discussion was heated. Carlton Douglas appeared flustered. Bess Jordan's stoic expression gave way to a look of anger mixed with determination. The omnipresent television cameras zeroed in on the two of them, eavesdropping mercilessly as their conference continued. Finally Douglas rose to speak, a resigned look on his face.

Judge Wentworth gaveled for order. The jammed courtroom became quiet immediately. No one wanted to miss this.

"Do you have a statement to make, General Douglas?" Judge Wentworth asked, as if he didn't know.

"Yes, Your Honor," Carlton Douglas responded. He walked over to the podium before he continued. "Your Honor, Mrs. Jordan wishes to address the court. Whether or not she may do so is a question which concerns the court, and not the state. However, Mrs. Jordan is the prosecuting witness in this matter. Therefore it is inevitable that what she says will reflect upon the state's position in this case. For that reason, I want the court to know that if she testifies, she does so as a private citizen and not as the prosecutor in this case, nor as a representative of the state. The state's official position has been, and still is, one of complete and unqualified opposition to probation. We want it clearly understood that Mrs. Jordan's comments do not represent any change in that position."

With that statement, a flustered and unnerved Carlton Douglas absolved his employer and his conscience of all responsibility for whatever Bess Jordan was about to do.

"Thank you, General Douglas. Your position is now a part of the record. As for Mrs. Jordan's request, while this procedure is highly unusual, this court is determined to give everyone a full opportunity to be heard, and to find the most equitable resolution of this matter. Thus the court would like to hear what she has to say. Please come around and take the witness stand, Mrs. Jordan."

Bess Jordan slowly rose to her feet, took her purse from her lap and placed it on the table in front of her, brushed the wrinkles from the front of her black dress, then started walking toward the front of the courtroom.

All eyes followed her careful, deliberate movement. Both television cameras recorded her walk, sending the image of this forlorn, dignified, simple woman out into the community. Thousands of eyes were transfixed as she climbed the small steps and took her place in the witness box. She stood in front of the witness chair as the bailiff held out a large black Bible. She placed her left hand on its leathery surface and raised her right hand heavenward as the bailiff administered the oath.

"Do you solemnly swear or affirm that the testimony you are

about to give will be the truth, the whole truth, and nothing but the truth, so help you God?"

"I do," Bess Jordan replied in her quiet, clear voice.

"Be seated, please," the bailiff instructed. Bess sat upright, her head erect, her hands clasped together in her lap. She stared straight ahead, not knowing exactly what she was supposed to do next. Judge Wentworth sensed her uncertainty.

"Mrs. Jordan," the judge said in a gentle voice, "you have told this court that you want to make a statement. General Douglas has indicated that he doesn't want to put you on the stand as the state's witness, and I can understand that. Obviously Ms. Hayes cannot ask you questions, nor can I, since neither of us really knows what you want to say. So, I guess the best thing for you to do is to just say what's on your mind. Pull that microphone a little closer so that you can be heard. When you finish, if Ms. Hayes has any questions, or if I have any, then we'll ask them."

Bess reached out and pulled on the gooseneck mounting that supported the microphone. It made a rasping sound as she pulled; she let go of it suddenly. The bailiff reached over and adjusted it for her. Finally, when everything was ready, she began to speak.

"Judge Wentworth, I hope I'm not doing the wrong thing. Mr. Douglas seems to be unhappy about this, and I guess I don't blame him. But I feel that it's important for me to say what I think. If this is not the right thing to do, well, I'm just sorry."

"Mrs. Jordan," Judge Wentworth said, "you need not worry about what General Douglas thinks. This court has given you permission to speak. It is appropriate for you to do so, and you may say whatever you wish."

Carlton Douglas bristled.

"Thank you, Judge," Mrs. Jordan said, pausing to clear her throat. She took a deep breath, obviously nervous.

"Judge, I loved my son. He—" She choked back a sob, and continued in a wavering voice. "He was my only child, he was all that I lived for. I know things didn't work out very well for him. I did the best I could, but I just couldn't handle him. He just got wild. But he was a good boy down deep, Judge, he really was—" Again her voice broke.

"May I have a Kleenex?" she asked. "I left my purse over there."

The bailiff handed her a tissue.

"Anyway," she continued, "I was so upset over what he did, I just couldn't believe it. In my heart I knew it was true, though. I felt so sorry for that little girl. I suppose I should have felt sorry for her mother, too, and the rest of the family as well. I just didn't think about them. But I did think about the poor little girl. I thought about her a lot. And yet in spite of it all, I never quit loving my son. I still love him to this very day."

She shifted in the hard wooden chair, dabbing at her eyes with the tissue.

"Well, when Frank went on trial, I felt sure that he would be convicted. I really did. I tried not to think about it, because I couldn't face it. But I knew that he was going to be convicted. I prayed and prayed about it. Mostly I prayed that he would not be sentenced to death. I didn't even think about him being set free, because I knew that wasn't going to happen.

"We didn't talk about it much, Frank and me. He never would talk about anything serious—he said he didn't want to upset me. And I didn't really understand this business about him being insane. He wasn't insane, not as far as I was concerned. He was just a poor boy who had been through some tough times. He was badly confused, that's all. Well, when the jury returned its verdict, I couldn't believe it. I didn't understand it. All I heard was the words 'not guilty,' and I jumped for joy. And then . . . then . . ."

She paused for a moment.

"Well, when I saw my son lying there with blood pouring out of his head, I just died with him, right then and there. That's all. I just died. I couldn't believe that this was happening right in front of me. I looked over at Mrs. Rogers. All of a sudden I felt this terrible hatred. I hated her more than I could ever imagine hating another human being. I wanted to climb over the table and claw her eyes out. I wanted to beat her and scratch her, to make her hurt the way I was hurting!"

She punctuated her testimony with grasping gestures, her eyes widened in anger. Carol Rogers shifted uncomfortably in her seat. Then Bess began again in a calmer voice.

"Judge, I have had a lot of time to think about all of this since that day. In fact, I have thought of nothing else. And I have come to understand some things that weren't clear to me then.

I've come to understand that it wasn't necessary for me to make Carol Rogers hurt. She has already been hurt as much as I was. That's what made her do what she did. I could easily have killed her then, and I wanted to do so. Because I felt that way, because I could have killed her, I think I understand why she did what she did. I don't agree with what she did. I still miss my son. I miss him every day. What she did was wrong, and I hate her for it to this day—I'll always hate her. But I understand her. Do you see the difference, Judge?"

"Yes, I think I do," Judge Wentworth said quietly, surprised by the unexpected question.

"Anyway, there is one thing I know for sure. I have been punished terribly for the mistakes I made with Frank. I have suffered the worst punishment I can imagine. And Mrs. Rogers has been punished just as much as I have. And there is something else I know, too. We can go on punishing each other forever if we want to, but that's not going to bring back either of our children. It's not going to make either of us feel one bit better. Nothing in this world will ever do that."

Tears were rolling down Carol Rogers's cheeks as she watched Bess Jordan struggle with her emotions.

"I guess what I'm saying, Your Honor, is that there really isn't much point in doing anything else to Mrs. Rogers. It won't help me, and it won't bring back my son. And you can't hurt her any more than she's already been hurt. As far as I'm concerned, this thing has gone far enough. It's time to bring all of this heartache to an end, once and for all. It's time for both of us to get on with life, to do the best we can. I guess that's all I wanted to say."

For several moments after Bess stopped talking, no one stirred in that old courtroom. You could have heard a pin drop, so profound was the silence. There wasn't a person there who hadn't been deeply touched by the words of Bess Jordan. Not one.

‖37‖

Agusty breeze rippled Carol Rogers's skirt and fanned her hair as she walked out of the courthouse door into the bright midday sunlight. She held one hand up to shade her eyes and clutched at her skirt. Then she laughed as she watched Ellen Hayes chase a piece of paper which had been blown out of her hand by the sudden wind.

Ellen cornered the elusive document just a few yards away, retrieved it, then rejoined Carol and her husband and son. The four of them walked down the granite steps of the courthouse, toward the street. The wind finally subsided as the group reached the bottom of the steps. They paused for a moment.

"You understand what you are supposed to do now, don't you?" Ellen asked Carol.

"I think so, Ellen," Carol answered. "Anyway, I'm sure my probation officer will probably repeat all of it over again when we get together Thursday morning. And you can bet I'll remember that appointment, that's for sure!"

"If you have any questions, just give me a call," Ellen said. Then she looked back up the steps. Someone had called her name. It was Tom Sanderson.

"Ellen," Tom called out as he hurried down the steps toward them, "I'm glad I caught you. I wanted to congratulate you!"

"Congratulate me?" Ellen asked. "Wow, I should be congratulating you! You were superb! Without your help, I don't know what would have happened."

"I've got a great idea," he said to Ellen, his voice full of enthusiasm. "Why don't we pat each other on the back over dinner tonight? How 'bout it?"

"Well." Ellen turned to Carol and Bill in mock surprise. "Oh why not?" she laughed.

"Great!" Tom exclaimed. "We've got lots to talk about. Like the fact that I'm about to be unemployed. Looks like I'm going to need a place to hang my hat!"

"Oh, Tom, no!" Carol said.

"I'm afraid so," he answered. "Douglas didn't mince any words. He wants me out. Believe me, I can't leave there fast enough. Say, Ellen, don't you think Sanderson and Hayes has a certain ring to it?"

"Hayes and Sanderson," Ellen retorted. They both chuckled.

"I knew that would get a rise out of you!" Tom said. "Anyway, I'll pick you up at seven-thirty, okay?"

"Sure, great!" Ellen answered. Then she hesitated. "No, make that eight-thirty," she added. "I want to be around the house this evening long enough to tuck in a certain curly-headed little boy."

"Why don't you two join us?" Tom asked Carol and Bill.

"Thanks, but I think we're going to enjoy staying home tonight and relaxing for the first time in a long time," Bill answered.

"Besides, I have a certain curly-headed boy who I want to be around to tuck in, too," Carol said, reaching up to rumple Jeffrey's hair.

"If you're gonna tuck me in, you'd better plan to be up late," Jeffrey quipped. They all laughed again. Laughter came with ease now, a welcome relief from the enormous tension they had just experienced.

Beneath the bronze relief of Blind Justice at the top of the steps, another lone figure emerged from the courthouse door, almost unnoticed. The same breeze that had brought laughter to Carol Rogers caught a strand of Bess Jordan's gray hair and pulled it across her face. Bess reached up and tucked the strand behind one ear. She looked at the familiar group at the foot of the steps and could almost hear the sound of happy voices as sh watched Tom and Ellen wave good-bye to Carol, Bill, and Jeffrey. She watched Carol walk across the broad boulevard, escorted by the two men in her life. She followed along with her eyes as Carol slipped her arm around her son's waist.

The slightest hint of a smile tugged upward at the corners of Bess Jordan's lips. It was the first smile in many months. But like an uncomfortable guest, it didn't stay long. Sadness quickly reclaimed her features as she started down the granite steps, all alone.

‖Epilogue‖

Six months after the final decision had been handed down by Judge Wentworth, Carol and Bill Rogers separated. Although initially elated over the outcome of that case, as time went by both came to realize that their relationship would never be the same as it had been before the bizarre series of events which began with the abduction and death of their daughter. Their separation was without acrimony; it was simply a recognition of the significance and permanence of the changes that had taken place in their lives.

With the court's permission, Carol Rogers moved to another city to begin life anew. She enrolled in a local community college and began a course of study leading to a degree in early-childhood education. Jeffrey went with her, and has adjusted well to his new situation. No-fault divorce papers have been filed. The case is pending.

Ellen Hayes continued to engage in the practice of law by herself, with considerable success, developing a reputation as a very good criminal defense attorney. At this writing she is expanding her office to accommodate increased business.

Tom Sanderson is associated with the prestigious firm of Bennett and Silverstein, which he joined shortly after his departure from the District Attorney's Office. He practices civil law exclusively. Ellen Hayes and Tom Sanderson saw each other socially for a brief period, but no longer do so.

Bess Jordan still lives alone. She is presently employed as a sales clerk in a large department store. She hopes to retire and take her social security in the near future. She has no plans beyond that.